W9-BFD-909

Millie Harrison

LOVE AND TREASON

LOVE AND TREASON

—BY—

DAVID OSBORN

NAL BOOKS

NEW AMERICAN LIBRARY

TIMES MIRROR

NEW YORK AND SCARBOROUGH, ONTARIO

For information address The New American Library, Inc.

Published simultaneously in Canada by
The New American Library Of Canada Limited

 NAL BOOKS TRADEMARK REG. U.S. PAT. OFF. AND FOREIGN COUNTRIES
REGISTERED TRADEMARK—MARCA REGISTRADA
HECHO EN CRAWFORDSVILLE, INDIANA, U.S.A.

SIGNET, SIGNET CLASSICS, MENTOR, PLUME, MERIDIAN AND
NAL BOOKS are published *in the United States* by
The New American Library, Inc.,
1633 Broadway, New York, New York 10019,
in Canada by The New American Library of Canada Limited,
81 Mack Avenue, Scarborough, Ontario M1L 1M8

Library of Congress Cataloging in Publication Data

Osborn, David, 1923-
   Love and treason.

   I. Title.
PS3565.S37L6 1982   813'.54   82-12415
ISBN 0-453-00421-0

Designed by Leonard Telesca

First Printing, September, 1982

1 2 3 4 5 6 7 8 9

PRINTED IN THE UNITED STATES OF AMERICA

PUBLISHER'S NOTE

LOVE AND TREASON

To LSN

Prologue

"Mrs. Volker, when you married did you consider keeping your own name to safeguard your personal identity?"

Alexis looked down from the speaker's platform. The woman who'd asked the question was at a table close by. She was in her midthirties with short hair and a narrow uncompromising face, and Alexis wondered whom she reminded her of. It was someone from long ago. Beyond the woman, the sea of faces that filled the hotel ballroom blurred and seemed like flat pebbles under shallow water.

"I'm sorry," she replied, "I thought I had made my position clear in my talk. I gave up television because my own special need was to play a traditional role in marriage. In part, that meant sharing my husband's name."

The sharp response was insistent. "You mean you were willing to surrender your personal identity completely?"

Alexis said patiently, "I never believed being a wife and mother was surrendering anything. I always saw it, for me, as finally becoming someone whom deep down I had always wanted to be." She looked for another raised hand. "Anybody else?"

It was the twenty-fifth anniversary luncheon of WIN, Women In the News, a national organization honoring those women its membership felt had brought distinction to their sex. Alexis had just finished a thirty-minute talk on the career-marriage dilemma faced by many modern women. Her appearance there had been Harold's idea. She had no desire to talk of the past. Not of her years as a United Broadcasting Company correspondent and television's first national-network anchorwoman. Nor of her early career as an investigative reporter in Detroit. And most certainly not of her childhood. She'd put all that behind her when she married. But it seemed politically important to Harold. The husband of WIN's president was a senator with whom he was having trouble.

She'd worried about the speech for days—and nights, too. Everything had gone well, however. She'd come, lunched, refused the efforts of the WIN president to get her to have a relaxing drink, and had made her speech to warmly enthusiastic applause. Now, only a few more questions and it would be over.

Another woman was asking, "Would you mind telling us what your answer was to General Volker's famous marriage proposal, if the story is true?"

Alexis said, "The story is true and my answer was only one word, 'Wow!' "

There was laughter and applause.

It was four years ago. She'd just come off the evening news. The production assistant handed her a telephone. "General Volker."

Alexis took the receiver. On the air, she'd very nearly accused him of involvement in a Pentagon contract scandal.

His voice said, "Alexis Sobieski?"

"Yes?"

"I'm Harold Volker. I could and should sue you for what you said about me five minutes ago, but I think a more intelligent move would be to ask you to marry me. When could we meet?"

Four months later and after the most publicized wedding Washington D.C., had seen for years, their marriage was a fact.

Alexis saw a hand. "Yes, please."

"I had another question." It was the narrow-faced woman again. "In talking about your career, you never mentioned sex harassment. How much of it did you have to put up with?"

Oh, for God's sake, Alexis thought. How hyped-up could you get about liberation? And how boring? She tried to make her reply lighthearted. She had worked hard to keep her audience in that sort of mood and felt so far she had. "Harassment? None, really. Well, guys used to make passes from time to time, being guys. But I always wondered how I'd feel if they didn't."

There was more laughter. Another hand shot up, but the inquisitor wasn't finished. Her voice rose even before the laughter died. "In your experience, then, do many women in television use sex as a means of advancement?"

The ballroom hushed waiting. Alexis studied the woman. She wore a faintly insinuating smile. You mean did I?, Alexis thought. You bitch. And then, she remembered whom the woman reminded her of. One Christmas, years ago in Detroit, she'd been invited with other foster children to a more privileged home. She'd wanted to bring a present and had made a little rag doll, dressing it in material she ripped from the hem of her own dress and using her foster mother's makeup to give it a face. She would never forget the superior and condescending smile of the little girl it was for, nor the beautiful new store doll she clutched so arrogantly. Her questioner wasn't the privileged little girl grown up, but her manner was similar.

Alexis stared at her a moment longer, making her wait. She felt a surge of confidence and anger. This wasn't Christmas in Detroit and she wasn't a foster-home child any longer. TV journalism was one of the toughest, no-quarter businesses there was, and she'd made it all the way with no help from anyone. She wanted to smash the woman.

She said icily, "I take it what you'd really like to know is did I personally screw my way to the top. The answer to that is, I never found carnal leverage could dig up a major news story, write it for me, and finally read it off a teleprompter without seeming to."

There was dead silence. Then the ballroom erupted with supportive applause. The woman sat down, her smile gone. Five minutes later, Alexis was leaving, hemmed in on both sides by friendly smiling faces and outstretched hands.

One camera of a TV unit covering her speech had gone to the lobby to watch her exit. There were a lot of people milling about, but Alexis saw only the camera and the young woman correspondent standing by it. She was brand-new, barely in her twenties, and talking very brightly to her mike as she came forward with her cameraman to ask a question. Something deep and nostalgic wrenched at Alexis's heart. Seeing was more painful by far than remembering. She wanted to stop for the girl, say hello and talk to her, and for a brief moment rejoin the world which for so many years had been her life and her only home. But she didn't. She pushed past her and kept going out onto the street where her car waited. When she fell in love with Harold Volker, she had determined never to compromise her commitment to marriage by clinging to the past. Television for her could no longer exist. Her preferred role was wife to the man who had since become United States Secretary of State and mother to the children they would someday have together.

She could think of nothing she would ever allow to interfere with that. Absolutely nothing.

One

Alexis didn't like the room very much. It was two flights up in an old house on tree-shaded Twenty-fourth Street and functional: beige carpeting, bookcases, a desk cantilevered between two tall windows flanked by thin cotton drapes, a small couch in slightly creased leather, and an upholstered armchair covered in some rough cream-colored material.

She saw it as a sterile place. If you had to reveal your innermost feelings to a psychiatrist, she thought, then what you really wanted around you was cozy and protective warmth.

Harold had suggested Dr. Wyndholt. He was young and attached to George Washington University Hospital a few blocks away. People said he was one of the best men in Washington. Several months ago, she'd begun to experience a strange nameless fear, a terror of something she couldn't identify. She'd reached a point where she couldn't go on, unable to sleep and half the time exhausted by stress. She'd started seeing Wyndholt several times a week. Recently, however, she'd found talking to him more and more of a struggle. She was beginning to hate his relentless questioning.

Seated in the armchair, hands in her lap, she avoided looking at him and was angry with herself because she did. Before she married Harold Volker, when she'd been Alexis Sobieski, a household name and face synonymous with the

UBC evening news, she'd often had to confront people who where maddeningly right and never wrong. She'd usually given them the look that had never failed with millions of viewers. She had composed the slender lines of her golden face into professional softness; she had brought appeal into her light amber eyes, the left one with its intriguing slight cast; she had put a faint, vaguely sexual smile on her wide mouth. In doing so, she had always conquered. The few times she'd tried it on Wyndholt, however, he clearly didn't give a damn. Bastard, she thought. She still had ten minutes to go with him and wished it were over.

The silence dragged. He broke it. "We were talking about the time you went to a sex club. Wasn't it pretty risky? Considering who your husband is? And who you are? What made you do it?"

"I don't know. We'd had a lot to drink and everyone seems to go once in their life. Anyway, it's a place where you wear a mask."

"You went with another couple?"

"Yes." Her tone was edged.

"And besides sex with your husband, you had sex with the other man?"

"Well, yes." She added defiantly, "We swapped, if you insist. I mean that's what that sort of place is all about, isn't it? You think you're going just to look and the next thing you know, you're involved."

"You didn't find it degrading?"

"If you take it out of context, of course. It's hardly something I'd ever want to do again. But at the time, I didn't think. Period. All that disco music and everyone naked and all the sex going on all around you, you lose sight of everything."

"What did your husband say about it?"

She shrugged. "It was something we shared."

"You didn't feel," he demanded, "you'd been promiscuous?"

"Promiscuous?"

"The way you said you felt during a lot of your youth."

"I never said promiscuous. I didn't use that word. I said I regretted some guys I went to bed with. In school and college, especially. Looking back, I think they were a mistake. But I liked sex and still do, so that's that. Whatever I regret, I'm stuck with."

Wyndholt looked at his notes. "You mentioned Harold's bisexuality. Do you ever see it as a threat?"

She glanced up sharply. How had they got so far off the track? She said, "I didn't say he was bisexual."

"Last week," he reminded, "you mentioned he'd once had a childhood experience with another boy. And you thought, during the war, an adult encounter."

Her irritation increased. She said, "Doctor, surely everyone has some homosexuality in them. So if Harold had sex with some guy years ago, it doesn't mean he's gay." She laughed angrily, "Harold? Good God, you must be kidding. He's so into women it's scary and our sex life is fabulous."

Wyndholt glanced at his notes again. "Do you ever miss the man you lived with before?"

"Adrian James and I didn't actually 'live' together," she said. "We had separate apartments. And yes, I do miss him sometimes. But just as a friend so that's hardly what's wrong with me."

"What is wrong, then?"

Alexis felt tears of frustration sting her eyes. She managed to control herself and not shout. "Dr. Wyndholt, if I knew, I wouldn't be here, would I?"

"Or beginning to have a drinking problem at thirty-four?" He held up a hand before she could protest. "I didn't say you were an alcoholic. I said *beginning* to have trouble. You did tell me people were talking, didn't you? There were hints by some of the columnists?"

She didn't answer. He leaned back in his chair and clasped his hands behind his head. "Let's get back to square one for a moment. You abandoned television, it being only an interim necessity which you conquered because that's the kind of woman you are. What you actually always wanted to do was to raise children. And take care of a home. To be that other kind of woman nobody dares mention nowadays—a housewife. Right?"

"Yes," she said.

"But you really aren't a housewife, are you? You don't cook, you don't take care of a house, you have no children. Didn't you sacrifice your brilliant career without getting what you wanted?"

Her eyes flashed. "Harold's not going to be Secretary of State forever. Washington's only temporary. We can't have children with Harold always away and when our home is half-office and crawling with security agents. We both agree on that. But we will. And I will have a home to take care of because Harold's been offered a chair at Princeton when he quits the government."

Dr. Wyndholt thought briefly of Volker himself: youthful-looking, outdoor-casual, brilliant, a German-born Jewish refugee with enough style and ability to become first a two-star General in the Air Force, then Secretary of State. It was easy to see why any woman would fall in love with him.

"All right," he said, "but did it ever occur to you that all your past lovers fit a mold and the mold is hardly staid suburbanism. You didn't marry a humble lawyer or engineer. You married a superstar with enough position for ten women."

"For God's sake," she argued. "You don't have to marry a dull, boring guy to have kids and a home, do you?"

He thought a moment. She hadn't seen his point yet or perhaps was deliberately avoiding it. It was pretty obvious. He said carefully, "No, no, you don't, but if the

8

Administration wins the next election, your husband could be Secretary of State for another six years, couldn't he?"

He got the reaction he expected. Something happened in her. He could see it in her eyes. The defiance disappeared. A brief but acute anxiety flared like a flame, then was instantly put out.

He looked at his watch and said, "When do I see you again?"

"Monday." She rose slowly and slung her bag over her shoulder. "And then not for a week." Her body language said he'd shaken her. Women of thirty-four who wanted children didn't usually want to wait any longer. At that age many were already desperate.

He studied his calendar. "That's right. You're going down to Brigham Bay."

It brought a faintly triumphant smile to her face. "I'm going to have six whole days of Harold all to myself. Just him and me."

"Good." He smiled back. "What about until then?"

"There's something on at the White House tomorrow. An East Room concert. Segovia, I think. There are some people for dinner at home tonight. I forget who. Harold has to go to Camp David on Saturday."

"Will he take you?"

She brightened visibly. "I hope so. I like it up there. And I like the President. Last time we played tennis, I beat him. Six-two, six-love." She laughed. "I think he's the only person I *can* beat."

She went to the door, slim and blonde in her light summer suit. The room was suddenly filled with her, with her perfume and chic and personality. She'd stopped being a confused, angry patient on the defensive.

When she'd gone, Wyndholt closed her folder. He felt a certain professional satisfaction. He was beginning to know something about an underprivileged Polish-American child raised in Detroit's soulless slums, a child whose only escape from the barren realities of a foster home had been in fantasies of a perfect family life in some idealized suburban street. He saw an awkward, intense young woman barely out of high school and shot too soon into the hard world of big-city reporting. A young woman who worked her way through college, haunting radio and TV stations with any free-lance news item she could sell. Or even give away. Until they recognized her.

And who'd held onto her child's dream throughout it all until she'd found a man she felt she loved enough and trusted enough to share it with.

Wyndholt pushed her folder away. He liked her and in a way he liked few patients. There was a deep loneliness there somewhere. What was it she hid from herself? Couldn't face and because she couldn't, suffered from insomnia and drank too much and justified sordid misadventures like sex clubs. He suspected she was in for a bad time and was going to need a real friend, someone who really cared and who wasn't her psychiatrist. He hoped she had one somewhere and if she didn't, he hoped fate would turn one up for her.

He pressed the button on his desk which would tell his nurse he was ready for his next patient.

Two

When Alexis got downstairs, the dark blue Lancia convertible Harold Volker had given her last year as a fourth-anniversary present was waiting at the curb. Sandy Muscioni was behind the wheel. The late afternoon sun was hot and Sandy had put the roof down. She was an athletic young woman of twenty-eight with short blond hair, a cheerful outdoor face, and a disposition to match. Behind her Ray-Ban sunglasses, her eyes were light blue and quickly intelligent. She was Alexis's personal bodyguard, but it was hard to believe she carried a .25 automatic usually strapped to the upper inside of one thigh. She'd been specially transferred from the Secret Service to the State Department Office of Security six months ago after Alexis received a series of telephone threats.

Alexis had objected. Danger far greater than mere threats had been her life during all her television years. She didn't want a shadow. The calls were surely only some crank. The Office of Security and her husband had thought otherwise. To her surprise, Sandy turned out to be not at all like her husband's agents, who Alexis thought took themselves much too seriously. Sandy was low pressure. She knew when she needed to be a bodyguard and when she didn't. Half the time she hardly seemed to be around and within a week they were friends. They had things in common; Sandy had also come from a deprived background.

"Do you want to drive?"

"No. Go ahead." Alexis slid into the passenger seat, wincing at the hot leather. Sandy started the motor and they drove across H Street and turned up Twenty-third.

"Where to?"

"Home." Alexis leaned her head back and closed her eyes. An hour of Wyndholt had exhausted her.

Sandy saw and said, "How was the witch doctor?" There was concern in her voice.

Alexis smiled. "My head's two sizes smaller."

"Do you want to play tennis, work it back to normal?"

"I'd love to, but I've got a stack of letters to sign and calls to make."

The Secretary of State's home was on R Street, bordering the old Oak Hill Cemetery at the very top of Georgetown. It was a large, colonial, yellow-brick house shaded by sycamore and oak trees and, unlike its neighbors, was set back from the street and approached by a gravel driveway which cut through a well-tended lawn. It didn't belong to Harold Volker. It belonged to Arnold Wilderstein, the New York banker and president of ACT, the American Credit and Trust Company. He had also lent them Brigham Bay, a small country home on the Potomac where it broadened into the Chesapeake. He seldom used the place, residing mostly in New York or at his country home in Maine. Wilderstein had reputedly spent a fortune fostering Volker's diplomatic career. So far, neither he nor any of his powerful establishment friends had ever asked for a specific return on the investment, but Volker sometimes speculated on it to Alexis.

"Someone's bound to some day," he once said. "Meanwhile, I guess they just like my political style."

They'd been married a year. It was early one spring evening and he'd come home from a grueling session before the Senate Committee on Foreign Relations. They'd made love, showered together, and for a while, before

12

dressing for a reception at the British Embassy, had sprawled on their bed. Volker had a drink in one hand and Alexis lay perpendicular to him, head on his thighs, knees up, enjoying the closeness to him, his clean masculine smell, and the lean hardness of his suntanned body.

"They like the way you handle the third world." She'd been unable to keep irony from her voice.

He laughed, stroked her hair. "You mean the way they think I handle it. Alexis, no Administration is ever going to stop the big boys from ripping off the world's helpless. Only Congress can do that and guess who lobbies Congress the hardest? I just try to soften the blows as much as I can without frightening the gods into destroying me. Out of sight, I'd be no good to anyone."

"Sometimes diplomacy stinks," she observed.

"I agree, my darling. It's politics all over again, only with a so-called polite name."

On M Street, Sandy slowed and turned up Twenty-ninth. As they climbed Oak Hill the houses became more luxurious, more spread out, the trees bigger and giving more shade. Just before the cemetery, they turned right onto R Street and then were there.

Sandy drove through the open wrought-iron gates with their massive, grinning lions' heads. The Lancia's tires crunched on the gravel driveway. They parked. There were no uniformed guards. Although Volker had three around-the-clock State Department security agents as bodyguards, they were most of the time invisible.

Alexis and Sandy got out and Sandy retrieved her .25 automatic from under her seat and slipped it back into the thigh holster beneath her skirt.

"Speaking of Dr. Wyndholt," Alexis said, "what would Freud say about you?"

Laughing, they went to the white limestone front steps. Sandy said, "Two of General Volker's agents are on house duty and you'll be in your office with Allison until the

General comes home. May I take off?" Her smile explained the request to Alexis. She had her own apartment downtown and she had found herself a lover. She jokingly called him Batman and they had an arrangement. Neither wanted to be seriously involved. When he happened to be free and it didn't interfere with her official duties, Sandy would sometimes ask Alexis for extra time off.

"Sure, take the car," Alexis said.

She watched Sandy drive away and felt faint nostalgic envy. Doing what she wanted, casual uncomplicated lover on the side. When you married, you gave up all that.

She went inside. The front hall was federal, the walls graced by expensive paintings. It was cool and silent. Everett greeted her. "Good afternoon, madam." He was the English butler Arnold Wilderstein had sent down from New York. She told him she'd like a double vodka and tonic, and ignored his stony lack of expression which was a sign of his disapproval. When he disappeared through a heavy oak door beneath the wide, curved double-stair to the second floor, she headed for the corridor leading to her husband's private offices and her own adjoining it.

Volker did as much work at home as at the State Department, perhaps more. He had held his appointment nearly two years now with little diplomatic experience except as a special envoy to China and had startled Washington and the world with a freewheeling kind of diplomacy which constantly outraged the professionals. Harold Volker believed in starting at the top, on his own and in not giving the "opposition" as he always termed the head of any other country, enemy or ally, a chance to reflect.

"Sit down, do some fast trading," he always said, "*then* let the groundwork experts in. Once you've made the deal, they won't dare mess around. Their jobs will be on the line."

The media loved it and called it "24-hour-blitz diplomacy." The public loved it, too. Coming on the heels of a decade of foreign humiliation and lost face, it gave them back their pride. Who cared if occasionally the success was off-balanced by subsequent Communist reaction. If someone else failed, that was their problem. Nobody had pushed Uncle Sam around.

Going by the door to his office, Alexis saw his secretary talking to Steve Riker, one of his security agents. Riker was in gym clothes and looked hot. She moved on quickly before he saw her. He'd been driving the night she and Harold had gone to the club she'd told Wyndholt about and on another night when she'd drunk far too much. Although his demeanor was always courteous, whenever she had to speak to him she felt stripped naked.

Her own office was across the corridor from the small luxury movie theater Wilderstein had installed for private viewing. Allison Palmer looked up from her typewriter in the outer room. She was a tall, patrician girl in her mid-twenties, the perfect Washington appointments secretary except she'd had a better start than many. Her father was Senate minority leader. For the first few months, she'd been deferential. Then, her awe of Alexis's television fame had given way to social snobbery. It was subtle, but Alexis found it wearing.

She smiled formally and went right on typing. Alexis offered a frozen smile in return and closed her door firmly behind her.

Her office was spacious and air-conditioned. She went to her desk, hung her shoulder bag over the back of her chair, and began to riffle through the letters Allison had left for her to sign. There were two framed photographs on the desk. One was her husband in the cockpit of an Air Force jet. The other was of a heavyset older man whose benign gray eyes looked out on a troubled world with sympathy and understanding.

In fifty years of broadcasting, twenty-five as news

anchorman for the United Broadcasting Company, Andrew Taylor had become a kind of national father figure. His photo was the only one Alexis kept from television days. It was two years since she'd seen Taylor or anyone else from television. Scores of other pictures of celebrities and colleagues were locked away—even the famous news photo of herself when, microphone in hand, she was held hostage by a crazed Detroit gunman.

She'd gone with her camera crew to cover a shootout in a downtown bar. While the gunman held a cocked .45 automatic to her throat, her crew kept their cameras running. They'd caught the SWAT sniper's shot that exploded the gunman's head. When she made her on-the-air report, she was still spattered with his brains, her hair in bloody tangles. But she made it with her head up, her voice strong and calm. She hadn't surrendered to terror until afterward.

Taylor had run tapes of the incident and had requested her transfer to Washington. He had found a daughter and, he thought, the right person to replace him when he eventually retired. Her leaving television had been a terrible blow.

Alexis finished signing letters and glanced at the guest list for tonight's dinner. It was an informal affair, only a dozen people, but among them were the Wildersteins, and that was a bore. Arnold Wilderstein would subtly remind them, as he always did, that they were living in his house. Nettie would display her crass ignorance of anything political.

One name was unfamiliar. She spoke into her intercom. "Allison, who is Alfredo Nasciemento?"

The return voice was crisp. "It's General Nasciemento. He's Portuguese. His visit here is unofficial. Secretary Volker asked me to invite him. I sat him next to Mrs. Wilderstein."

"Thank you." Alexis switched off. Her door opened. Everett materialized, carrying a tray with a bottle of

vodka, some splits of tonic, ice in a cooler, and a glass.
"Your vodka, madame." He set the tray down and disappeared as silently as he'd come. Alexis made a face at his departing back, fixed a drink, and went to her bookcase for a special loose-leafed and up-to-date State Department *Who's Who*. She tried to find Alfredo Nasciemento, but couldn't. He wasn't listed under either the Portuguese Army or under Portugal's Foreign Service Section. Perhaps he was some sort of special envoy, his title left over from colonial days in Mozambique or Angola.

She returned to her desk and sat thinking about it. She felt a strange sort of anxiety. She couldn't remember Harold ever mentioning the man and he'd never before asked someone to dinner without briefing her on who it was.

Presently, she forced it out of her mind. She was giving something very minor an importance it didn't deserve. Wyndholt had warned her against doing that. She firmly got out her personal telephone book and began to make her calls. She had half-dialed the first one when she became aware of a presence—not seen, just felt. Someone was standing silently in front of her desk.

She put back the receiver and looked up. It was her husband.

Three

For an instant, she was only aware of his eyes, more blue than ever because of his deep tan, and his unruly brown hair which hardly showed any gray at all and as usual was badly in need of cutting. Then she saw he was wearing khaki jeans, a tennis shirt, and running shoes.

"Hi. Where have you been?"

"The White House."

"Like that?"

"What's wrong? It's the all-American uniform, isn't it? The only thing missing is a tractor hat." He quickly produced one from his hip pocket. It said "Marines" across the front.

She came from behind her desk and put her arms around him, happy he was in a good mood. "You're absolutely mad."

"No. Just teasing you. I got home early and Riker's been giving me a Judo lesson."

She felt vaguely relieved, yet simultaneously annoyed with herself for being so conventional. Perhaps he really should go to the State Department dressed that way and shake them up even more than he already had.

She laughed and pushed his hair back from his collar. It was impossible to believe he was in his fifties. He looked forty. "What's happening in Libya?"

He frowned, kissed her lightly, broke from her embrace,

and slouched down on her couch. "Nothing. Twenty locked-up diplomats. One egomaniac bastard by the name of Khadhafi. *Plus ça change, plus c'est la même chose.*"

The moment she'd asked the question, she'd wished she hadn't. When first married, they talked about every nuance of his career. But these days, more and more, he seemed not to want to talk about any aspect of it, even though much of his work took place during private conferences during and after dinner parties. Wyndholt had advised her he was probably overtired, especially where the nerve-wracking situation of the hostages was concerned. He'd said to avoid asking too many questions. She came and sat next to him and backed away from the subject. "He's got to let them go someday. I guess when the blockade really starts to have any effect. Harold, who's Alfredo Nasciemento?"

He glanced at her, but didn't answer immediately. He began to pour himself a drink.

She said quickly, "I'm sorry. I know you're beat, but I have to ask. After all, he's coming to dinner, isn't he?"

He shrugged. "Of course. He's a Portuguese General."

"Yes, but which one? I mean is he important?"

"He's an aide to Figueira and Figueira's Army Chief-of-Staff."

It was abrupt, a warning to drop it. Somehow she couldn't. "Are we entertaining him," she persisted, "for some particular reason? What should I talk to him about?"

He rose, drained his drink. His answer was casual, thrown away. "They've got a lot of trouble over there. Elections coming up, Communists threatening. I thought I'd get briefed from the horse's mouth, so to speak." He started for the door, stopped at a Wyeth painting she'd recently acquired. "Where did you get that?"

"The auction I went to. In Philadelphia."

"I like it."

He walked out of the office. She watched him go, feeling

19

chagrined, slightly hurt, and also annoyed with herself for being defensive. Asking questions about a dinner guest was hardly dragging his job into their personal life. Was there something about Nasciemento he didn't want her to know? And why get briefed on Portugal by a mere aide-de-camp?

She poured another drink, nursed it while she made her phone calls, finished it, and poured another. She arranged her calendar for the next day, said good night to Allison and left. It was six o'clock.

She found her husband in the bedroom, stretched out on the bed reading the *Heidelberg Review*. It was a scholarly journal published by the Bavarian University and a last link to his youth as a German. It came every month and he always studied it religiously, reading every dry academic article between its somber covers. He had an abiding passion for history and his hero was the Frankish king, Charlemagne, whom he considered the greatest European ever.

He didn't look up. She went and sat silently at her dressing table. It was much too early to get ready for dinner. She knew she was a little tight and shouldn't drink any more. She sipped the vodka and said, awkwardly, "I've upset you, somehow. I'm sorry."

"Don't worry about it."

That was all. Obviously he didn't want to talk. She began to take off her makeup. He suddenly laid aside the *Review,* studied her, then got up and came over. He put his hands on her shoulders. "Alexis, I'm sorry. That wasn't fair of me. About Nasciemento. But I have to deal with idiots all day, every day. Real idiots. There are times when the thought of another one is just too much." He laughed. "Maybe I'm being unfair to him, too. I've never met him. Maybe he's brilliant."

He pulled her to her feet and ran his hands beneath her hair and clasped them behind her neck. "We have an hour

20

and a half before we have to be on parade. That's not much so I'll race you to the shower." He pulled her close to be kissed. "Okay?"

"Yes." She felt herself let go inside. Everything was all right. It was all in her mind. Wyndholt had said that often. She built anxieties and atmospheres that just weren't there. Only imagined. She opened her mouth softly to his. "Oh, yes."

She won the race by cheating. She unbuttoned her blouse and unfastened her skirt while he was kissing her.

Four

As he started up his car, the Portuguese calling himself Alfredo Nasciemento felt the evening had definitely been a most pleasant one.

The Secretary of State and his wife stood in the doorway of their home waiting for him to drive away. He waved, they waved back. He put the car in gear and eased down the gravel driveway. A moment later, the massive wrought-iron entrance gates were closed behind him by a security agent and he was on R Street. He turned down Twenty-eighth and descended through the relatively dark quiet of Georgetown toward busier M Street with its shops and late-night restaurants.

A most attractive couple, he thought. The Secretary was clearly a man of great drive and energy, his wife brilliant and beautiful, often very witty and always good fun. She was hardly the typical Washington hostess. It had worried him once or twice during the evening that she drank a little too much. But it worried him more that she was a woman whose business for years as a reporter had been to ferret out the truth about people. The truth was not something she should ever know about him. Not just because of the danger that would mean to himself, but also because of the terrible danger it could put her in. He wasn't sure yet, but he suspected there were forces at work to whom a single human life, no matter whose, meant absolutely nothing if seen as even a minor threat. He could only hope she was sufficiently in love with her husband not to become seriously interested in anything or anybody else.

He reached M Street and turned right toward the Key Bridge. He didn't have far to go—just across the Potomac to the Marriott Hotel. He'd decided for discretionary purposes not to stay at the Embassy. There was no point in calling attention to himself since theoretically he was still in Lisbon. He'd flown over on a false passport which gave his name as Alfredo Nasciemento and also endowed him with the title of General. Recognition of who he really was would have had to be visual, but the risk of that these days was considerable. He could think of several dissident Portuguese groups whose agents lurked about Washington, and his photo had surely been circulated among a number of Communist cadres, especially the Cubans who had a powerful espionage force in the United States.

He stopped for a light. There was traffic now. The Kennedy Center had let out. Restaurants were closing. People were driving home to suburbs, their silhouettes soft in the dashboard-lit interiors of their cars.

An extraordinary man, Volker, he reflected. From penniless refugee to where he was now, he hadn't made a wrong move. All the way, he had showed the uncanny political ability to have everything precisely as he wanted it. Who else, without seriously alienating either the center or the moderate Left, could have managed to be sponsored by a man who exemplified the conservative Right?

It was thus doubly gratifying that this evening's deception had worked. The Secretary had readily accepted his credentials as General Figueira's representative. He did represent General Figueira, true, but that was deceptive as well. He played a double game. Gaining the confidence of the Portuguese Chief-of-Staff had taken months of painstaking work. And risk. Figueira's own position was precarious. In the politically powerful Army, he suppressed his extreme Rightest loyalties in favor of a moderate majority and the expediency of his own economic needs. It would not pay to be caught betraying him.

His mission was simple: to use his position of trust with Figueira to discover why the Chief-of-Staff had recently been communicating unofficially with Volker. The two men were known to have held several meetings in Lisbon and in New York. Figueira had also recently aroused some unease in Portugal because of certain clandestine associations he was suspected of there.

Of course there would be little to be gained on this first trip to Washington. The purpose was for Volker to look him over. Confidences, if any, would come later.

His mind flew back over the evening again, the wonderful dinner, the excellent champagne, and the fine Chablis wine. The lobster souffle had been cooked by a master, surely, the Norwegian crepes also, and the apricot sherbert had been perfection. Finally, the coffee was real coffee, not the usual American colored dishwater. He would see Volker again several times. He looked forward to it. With a feeling of well-being he turned onto the Key Bridge. Crossing it, he took in the soft lights of the Kennedy Center and the Lincoln Memorial. Far down the mall, flood lights splashed off the Obelisk and, even farther on, from the dome of the Capitol.

He came off the bridge into the Rosslyn Circle and immediately turned into the Marriott's parking lot. He drove through it and along the Potomac side of the hotel with its shrubs and trees and additional parking. There was a guest garage at the rear. He parked, locked the car, and started back for the hotel. His room on the second floor was approachable from one of several side entrances, open all night.

He was within ten feet of the door when the two men materialized from the deep shadows of shrubbery. They were very ordinary looking. He thought for a moment they were guests. One had gray hair and was older. The other,

24

younger, was balding. They wore business suits. Then he saw they were also wearing gloves. He felt two things simultaneously, the sheer terror of what he knew was going to happen to him and the bitter chagrin of having been so careless.

They were professionals. That was obvious from the speed with which they acted and from their confidence. The barrel of the revolver jammed into his kidneys. There was hardly time to cry out from the pain before his left arm was seized and twisted up behind his back.

"Don't make a sound. Don't struggle." The voice was low, flat.

He tried to place it, couldn't. The accent seemed American.

A hand jammed between his legs, seized his genitals, pulled hard. Pain lanced his pelvis. Another hand seized the hair on the back of his neck, pushed his head. He pitched forward, helpless, through the open door of a parked car and into its back seat.

The heavy body of one of his captors crushed down next to him. Doors slammed. He sensed his other captor behind the car's wheel. The motor started.

"Turn this way."

He was pulled backward, his body twisted awkwardly so his neck and shoulders were on the seat, his head on his captor's lap.

"Open your mouth."

He obeyed. A sharp and intense pain. What was it? He couldn't understand. Blood oozed around his tongue. Then he realized. The revolver barrel had smashed through his teeth. It gouged the back of his throat, gagging.

He swallowed, blood rushed.

"Lie still, don't move."

The car pulled away.

He thought of the pain. He thought of his imminent death. He thought of the cyanide capsule he always kept in the false top of his fountain pen. There was no way to reach it.

He prayed his captor would pull the revolver's trigger and end his misery. He knew they wouldn't. His captors would have other far worse plans. Whoever was paying them would want an example made of him. A horrifying example to intimidate others who might try to do what he had been attempting.

He hoped it would be so bad he would faint right at the beginning.

That was the only thought his terror allowed him.

Five

Not everyone thought Harold Volker beyond reproach. There were some among the elite world of foreign policy analysts and other intelligentsia who considered him a disaster.

It was Monday morning. In the Langley office of Virgil Fein, the CIA's second assistant Deputy Director of Intelligence, a young woman was stating just such an opinion. Her intense and rather lovely dark eyes expressed outraged scorn, her laugh bordered on contemptuous. She let the dog-eared, four-page, Xeroxed memorandum she'd been reading fall to Fein's desk. "The son of a bitch," she said quietly. "I'll bet every damned word is true."

Helen Carson, still in her twenties, was a modern, white-collar mercenary and typical of a whole new breed of young executives who were changing the complexion of the intelligence community. She had graduated Phi Beta Kappa in History at Vassar and had gone on to Johns Hopkins in Baltimore for her masters in Political Science preparatory to entering Foreign Service. Instead of the State Department, however, she had ended up in the CIA, not by choice—she scorned the Company—but because a junior advisory job had offered immediate promotional opportunities more in line with her ambitions, which were considerable and often ruthless.

Virgil Fein stared bleakly at the memorandum. The

CIA received scores of such worthless reports put together at taxpayers' expense and consisting of oddball theories, transparent grudges, even hoaxes, supposedly backed up by evidence usually so contrived or flimsy as not even to be considered circumstantial. He'd seen this particular piece of nonsense before. He'd studied it and thought about it because it was his job to do so. And he had dismissed it. So had everyone else, including their Berlin station. Berlin had checked it down to every last detail and had pronounced it, in what Fein thought a classic understatement, as groundless and amusing speculation.

He shifted wearily in his chair. He suddenly felt much older than forty-five. His day had started normally. He'd got up in a good mood, had stoically borne with his wife's usual breakfast complaints about how hard it was to live on sixty thousand a year in a fashionable suburb. His commute to Langley was only fifteen minutes. When he arrived at his comfortable and sunny office, there was coffee waiting for him courtesy of his always cheerful secretary. There were no heavy meetings on his calendar; no disasters were reported on the news via his TV monitor. Even the world, represented by a large, interior-lit, relief globe mounted on its own table, remained tranquil.

In a few well-chosen words, Helen Carson had just wrecked all that. He couldn't believe she was taking the memorandum seriously. He looked up from it as she ran one slender and artistic hand through her wiry dark hair, silver wrist bangles clinking. Her lithe young body coiled forward from her chair as though she were about to spring. Her blouse fell loosely over her small firm breasts. And yet, simultaneously, she looked relaxed.

"At the risk of sounding racist," she said, smiling, "once a Kraut, always a Kraut. *Deutschland Uber Alles* and all that crap."

Virgil Fein tried a conciliatory tone. She drove him half-crazy when she got into one of these moods. And frightened him. Her increasing aggressiveness could easily become a danger to her job and since he was her immediate superior, an embarrassment to him.

"Helen, it's a joke. Nothing more. Why do you think I showed it to you? And even if it weren't," he added, "it doesn't prove a thing against General Volker himself. Not even circumstantially." He was aware that his tone was condescending. He'd started going to bed with her a month ago and was now having difficulty in seeing her professionally. Knowledge of her uninhibited and passionate sexuality kept getting in the way, as did an uncomfortable feeling she was beginning to dictate all the shots, not just how they made love, but in the office as well.

She didn't buy his plea. She picked up the offending memorandum again. It came from a U.S. Army Intelligence office in Munich, Germany, and was signed by a Captain Shenson. It had to do with one of his agents found executed in a Bavarian forest, his head split open by a heavy-caliber pistol bullet. Shenson believed it was KGB work. He also discussed the recent death of one Joanna Volker, a German spinster cousin of the Secretary of State and with whom General Volker frequently corresponded and occasionally visited. The memo vaguely hinted that the two deaths might be linked.

Helen Carson held it up pointedly. "You see this thing as a joke, Virgil?" Her tone was sarcastic awe.

He tried flattery. "Yes. And I thought you of all people would, too."

"Virgil, if I read this correctly," she said, "it suggests that General Volker's cousin was murdered."

"Not murdered. Drowned in the Necker River at Heidelberg. Suicide or a mugging, the police aren't sure which."

Her answering voice, lowered, had the quality of a

prosecutor closing in. She smiled. "It also suggests she had a lover who might be KGB."

Fein hung on doggedly. "Speculates, Helen. Not suggests. The whole damn thing is nothing but speculation."

She ignored him and turned pages looking for something. "A Professor Schaeffer, I believe. Yes. Here. A professor of History at the University of Heidelberg. It suspects that under a different name he might also have once been a school friend of Volker before Volker came to the States. It says this friend was a rabid Marxist."

Fein felt his patience waning. Dammit, he was the boss, after all. His voice rose slightly. "Berlin could find no evidence anywhere that Schaeffer is really someone named Melkin. Melkin died sometime during the war. Probably when the Russians poured into Berlin."

"You mean disappeared."

"All right. Disappeared."

"What about Schaeffer not having any records to prove he existed before the war began?"

"If you look again, you'll see they were all destroyed in the Allied fire raids on Dresden."

"How convenient! And what about this?" Helen Carson jabbed a slender finger at a line halfway down another page. "Where it says Volker had an affair with this Melkin back in their school days at the Munich gymnasium."

"Helen, it says 'rumored.' " He saw from her face he wasn't getting through. He made his tone conciliatory again. "Where do you expect me to go with it, Helen? Suggest something." He nodded at the memorandum.

She dropped it back on his desk again. "With this? No place. As you say, it's been checked out by experts. So let's get off it for a moment. I'd like to talk about Volker himself."

Fein guessed what was coming and groaned inwardly.

"What's our latest CIA explanation," she demanded,

"for all the Communist gains made since he's been Secretary?"

"Russian Imperialism, Helen. Look, forget it. The American people love Volker."

"So does Moscow."

"Oh, come on!"

"I mean it, Virgil. Take any fiasco, Indonesia, Venezuela—you name it. 'Twenty-four-hour blitz' diplomacy. A Volker sponsored right-wing coup 'stabilizing' democracy and alienating half the world while it does. And with the Reds always having a subsequent propaganda field day or deciding to follow up Volker's coup with one of their own."

He didn't answer. The best thing was to let her run down. She went on. "Okay for Wilderstein and his Wall Street cronies who clean up on Volker's little victories, short term. What about America and the rest of the world, long term. Another five years of General Harold Volker and we won't have a friend left. Or a world either, probably."

She stopped. There was a silence. Fein waved at the memo and tried hard to keep sarcastic incredulity from his voice. "And all that is connected with this somehow?"

She answered with lethal softness. "Can you afford to think it isn't?"

"Oh, Helen, please . . ."

"Virgil, I'm serious. Just suppose it were! Just suppose all the suspicion and innuendo in there were true!"

"And he was deliberately screwing us up abroad? General Volker?"

"Yes. Volker. Maybe he's not just an egomaniac with two left feet and an Arnold Wilderstein to keep happy. Maybe he's smarter than anybody gives him credit for. Even Wilderstein." She held up an arresting hand. "Hold it. I'm not saying he is. I'm saying just suppose. I'm saying just suppose one day it turned out he *was* and we'd been in a position to do something about it and we hadn't because you'd decided it was all just a joke. Okay?"

She glanced at her watch. "Jesus. I've got a report to write." She rose and collected her coffee cup to go back to her own office. "He's going over to Portugal this month sometime. We all know the mess that country is in. What happy little solution do you suppose he'll come up with there? And that's not Third World. Portugal is NATO and the southern gate to Uncle Sam's personal Atlantic Ocean."

At the door, she stopped. "A few years ago when Willy Brandt ran West Germany, they caught his top personal aide. Red-handed. KGB." She paused and added, "To say nothing of all those Englishmen. Wasn't one of them big in M.I.5?"

The door closed gently behind her and Fein contemplated the duality of women who with a few words could reduce a man to nagging anxiety while simultaneously remaining desirable.

The same thought lingered in the back of his mind the next morning. Staring out at the wooded Virginia countryside, he kept remembering her words, "Just suppose." They had run unpleasantly through his head all yesterday and last night also. He spun his chair back to his desk to glance again at the file he'd had sent over from the Pentagon after Helen had left him. He'd checked on the writer of the offending memorandum. Captain Shenson's career was indistinguished, his promotion to major would make a great deal of difference to his pension when he retired in three years. Twenty minutes ago when he'd talked to the captain over the telephone, he had detected something in the man's voice that had made him have long second-thoughts.

What he'd heard was fear and suddenly he'd seen a flaw in the captain's report. The captain clearly had never wanted to write it in the first place. That was natural. Who would want to be involved in anything possibly detrimental to an all-powerful Secretary of State who had the complete confidence of the President? At the same time, the Captain had clearly worried that if he did not make the report, whatever information it contained might someday surface in time to wreck his promotion. So he had carefully hedged and written something that could not possibly cause offense either way.

Virgil Fein had a sick feeling in the pit of his stomach. He swung back to look at his view, but didn't see it. He was also unaware that his secretary had come into his office. She was standing by his desk with a sheaf of papers and telling him he had an appointment with someone who was waiting in the reception room.

Helen Carson had mentioned Portugal as NATO and the southern gate to the Atlantic. He could see her expression now and hear her voice. "Just suppose . . ." In Portugal, a friendly centrist government would soon be challenged in national elections by a new Communist-Socialist coalition. It looked as though the centrists would easily win, but what if, for some unforseen reason, they did not? Unlike most Euro-Communists, the Portugese Comnists were rabidly pro-Moscow.

His secretary finally broke through.

"Sorry," he said. "Sure, send him in." He added, "After you do, get David Farr over at the FBI. See if he can have lunch today or tomorrow."

"He's with the Intelligence Division?"

"Correct. I think his extension is 374." He turned back to his desk and handed her the Shenson file. "And put this on hold."

"Yes, sir."

He began to try to remember why his visitor was coming to see him.

Six

The offending article was small, metallic, and surprisingly heavy. It was shaped like a triple-thick coat button and was about the same size. One side was punctuated with a pattern of tiny holes and slightly convex. It lay on the desk of the State Department's Director of Security, a gray-haired senior man who had come up through the ranks in a lifetime of service. He thoughtfully turned it over a few times between fingers thickened by backyard gardening before he articulated another question to the young woman who sat across from him.

"Did it strike you as odd to find it where you did?"

"In an unused electric plug? A little, sir. Yes." Sandy Muscioni shifted in her chair and smoothed down her denim skirt. She'd played a lot of tennis with Alexis over the weekend and her skin was bronzed, her hair bleached. "That's a pretty amateur hiding place."

The Director examined the bug again. "Interesting. I don't know that we have anything like this. What's the sending radius again?"

"About one hundred yards."

"Far enough for someone to pick it up in a parked car?"

"Yes, sir. It broadcasts clearly. Just to its limit. When we went too far, we lost contact quite abruptly. I'd say within feet."

"I'll turn it over to the FBI," he said. "See what their lab boys can make of it."

"Shouldn't Mrs. Volker be warned, sir?"

"Not yet. I'd rather install some sort of interrupter. Maybe we'll put this back just to throw someone off the scent."

Then he said, "Any thoughts on who might be responsible?"

Sandy was thoughtful. "Somebody who suspects General Volker may sometimes talk to his wife," she replied, "and thinks she's not likely to be as security conscious as he is. Especially since she sometimes drinks too much." She shrugged. "Starting with the least likely, it could be the media, sir." She smiled. "Or the FBI running a routine on everybody." Her smile faded. "A more likely guess would be the KGB doing a heavy scene. And it could also be some Portuguese faction. General Volker's arming up right now for their elections. He had a dinner party last Friday. Some Portuguese general came."

"Alfredo Nasciemento?"

"Yes, sir." Sandy was surprised, but didn't ask how he knew.

The Director examined the bug again. "Who do you think did the actual planting?"

Sandy thought. "As far as I know, nobody has come into the house this month. I mean no outside person, no TV repairman or plumber or anyone like that."

"Just staff. Servants, secretaries?"

"And us, sir."

The Director hadn't thought of his own people. "That makes it ugly," he said. "Do you really think there is any possibility there?"

In his mind he ran quickly over half the agents he had protecting General Volker. They were all outstanding and highly experienced people. Steve Riker and Sandy, the only two who were not veterans of long-term service, had

35

both come from the FBI with impeccable records, although Sandy had done an interim term with the Secret Service at the White House.

He heard Sandy answer. "No, sir. Not really." Her smile was wry. He liked her. You couldn't look at her without thinking of California surfing or backpacking the Sierras. It was hard to conceive how far she'd come in just ten years since she'd started off in perhaps the toughest outfit of all, the Los Angeles Police Department.

"How many servants?"

Sandy ran through their names and their clearance. "Frankly," she insisted, "unless they're genius actresses, I can't believe either of the maids is intelligent enough for this sort of thing. And Everett had NASA clearance when Wilderstein first hired him as well as everything we and the FBI put him through.

"The secretarial staff?" It was an academic question, but Sandy reminded him the two older women attached to Volker had come from the State Department's Security Command where they had been attached to Threat Assessment. Allison Palmer had been carefully screened, too, in spite of her family's social prominence.

The Director changed the subject. "How do you get along with Mrs. Volker?"

"I like her. I really do." Sandy laughed. "And I don't mean because of who she was, all that glamour stuff. She's not a snob. I always feel she's still just a working girl like me."

"How about the drinking?"

"I try to help her keep it down to a muffled roar."

"Any particular reason for it?"

"I don't know. She's always most vulnerable after she's seen her stupid shrink."

"Regrets she left broadcasting?"

"I don't think so. She really wants the home and mother scene. She's got a big thing about it."

36

"Does she ever discuss it with you?"

"No," Sandy answered. "She's pretty tight-mouthed about her personal affairs. Even with me. But I can tell."

"Perhaps that's just as well." The Director nodded at the bug. "In view of our little mystery here." He paused and added, "There's one more thing. The General Nasciemento you mentioned. Perhaps you ought to see this." He held out an interoffice report.

Sandy read it silently. When she handed it back, her face had lost all animation. "That's horrible," she said.

"You didn't hear either General or Mrs. Volker ever mentioned his real name?"

"No, sir. They just referred to him as General Nasciemento. I'm sure Mrs. Volker didn't know who he really was. She said she tried looking him up in the Department's *Who's Who*. She does that with every guest, but she couldn't find him. Does General Volker know about this, sir?"

"We told him this morning. He was pretty shaken. He doesn't want Mrs. Volker to know."

"What about the press?"

"They're cooperating. The police have imposed a blackout."

Sandy rose, getting ready to go. "Does anyone have any ideas on a motive, sir?"

"General Volker says he represented Figueira. My guess is he was either caught double-crossing or some political faction thought he might get too much for Figueira out of Volker. I doubt we'll ever know." He picked up the bug from his desk. "You may be right that he could have been responsible for this, but that's something else we'll probably never know." He glanced at a schedule on his desk. "You have the rest of the week off, I see."

"Yes, sir. Accumulated time and I'm not needed at Brigham Bay. I'll be playing tennis in Virginia."

"Sounds fun. What time do the Volkers leave?"

"Mrs. Volker said about three-thirty. She's coming to my apartment for a deli lunch before they go. I'm picking her up at the hairdresser first. Three of the guys will follow her and General Volker down to the country."

He glanced at the schedule again. "The Wildersteins?"

"They're driving down direct from the airport."

"When was their visit decided?"

"Last night apparently. They called up and asked themselves."

He pursed his lips. "How did that sit with Mrs. Volker? The last time we talked you told me she didn't care much for them."

Sandy was again surprised. He didn't miss a trick. She said, "Mrs. Volker was pretty upset. She'd expected to be alone with her husband."

"And the General?"

"I don't think he cares one way or another. He's taking down a briefcase of homework."

He saw her to the door. "Okay, Sandy. Good work. Keep it up."

"Thank you, sir."

In the Department's vast underground garage, she found Alexis's Lancia where she'd left it amidst a maze of other cars, private as well as official. She showed her ID to Security and drove up onto Twenty-first Street. She'd been with the Director for over forty-five minutes.

On Twenty-second Street, she stopped at a delicatessen where she'd ordered two fresh Maine lobsters put on ice for her that morning along with cole slaw, potato salad, and a chocolate mousse dessert they were famous for. She had them put a bottle of expensive chilled Italian Spumante in the bag with everything else. She'd be half-broke for a week, but she wanted Alexis to relax and enjoy herself. It would help take a little of the edge off the Wildersteins.

Going out, she suddenly remembered Batman. It was a

physical shock and her heart leapt. She'd forgotten to tell him about Alexis. He knew she had the week off and might have come to her apartment. It was one thing for Alexis to know she had a lover. It would be quite another for her to know who he really was. There was a wall pay phone. She put in a dime and dialed her own number. To her relief, he answered.

"It's me," she said. "Listen, I'm sorry, but I clean forgot. I've asked the boss to lunch."

"Here?"

"Yes."

"That figures. I was just about to step into the shower."

Something in Sandy froze instantly. The annoyance in his voice, his proprietary tone, were not part of their deal. Nobody owned her. Or ever would.

"I wouldn't advise that," she said. Her tone was like ice and without a trace of care. Care, for her, had ceased to exist in California years ago. She was twenty and desperately in love and the world a wonderful place. She'd come from a broken home and never believed in anyone before. Then the guy walked out and moved in with an older woman who had enough money to buy anything she wanted. No warning, no good-bye, no explanation. Sandy found them in bed in the woman's Malibu Beach home. They'd ignored her and had gone right on making love as though she didn't exist. Later, when Sandy had made scenes, the woman pulled strings to get her fired from her job. That's when she'd joined the police and she doubted she'd ever had any real emotion for anyone since. Certainly not for any man.

She heard him laugh awkwardly. He realized he'd overstepped himself. "Okay. Sorry. When do I see you again?"

She thought a moment. She was in control once more and her annoyance began to fade. Alexis was due to meet her husband at three. "What's your evening like?" she asked.

"I'm available."

"I get off duty at four. Call first, just in case." She hung up without waiting for an answer, picked up her shopping bag, and went out to the car. She got behind the wheel and for a moment leaned her head back, her eyes closed to the hot sun. Her heart was still beating heavily. It had been a close call. She couldn't believe she'd nearly made such a stupid mistake. She was getting soft. She'd have to pull herself together and be more attentive. The job was too important for her to mess up.

After a few moments, she started up the car and continued on to pick up Alexis at the hairdresser.

Seven

Brigham Bay took its name from its location, a quiet Maryland estuary. The house was on a high point and its views took in not just the Potomac and Chesapeake Bay, but also over two thousand acres of marsh and woodlands flanking both sides of the estuary itself and broken only by an occasional small tenant farm. Arnold Wilderstein's father had bought it for next to nothing during the Depression from a family who had owned it for six generations and had fallen on hard times. Arnold used it only for late-autumn duck shooting when he'd come down from New York or Boston with a half-dozen banking cronies.

The first year Harold Volker was Secretary of State, he made the property available to him. "A celebration and a belated wedding gift, both," he said. "I don't hunt anymore, and Nettie has her hands full with Maine and New York and the beach house at Southampton. I can't give it to you because I need it as a tax deduction and anyway you'd go broke keeping it up. Just regard it as your own. Use it, enjoy it."

The house, built in 1801, was small but charming. It had narrow white clapboarding, sagging green shutters, and old brick chimneys. There was a nearby mansarded cow barn half covered with ivy which had been converted into staff quarters. Over the hundred and eighty years of its life, the gardens around it had reached the rich maturity only time can create. The impenetrable box hedges whose rich scent permeated everywhere were as tall as a man's head. The mossy trunks of massive beech and maple trees were gnarled by decades of wind off Chesapeake Bay. The colorful perennials also had the appearance of always having been there. Perhaps it was the set look of their beds, the deep turf of their borders. In one small park where there was a weathered stone sundial, yew trees planted seventy-five years ago nearly met overhead. And the herringboned brick walk leading up to the heavy green front door with its white limestone threshold, brass knocker, and wrought-iron boot scraper, had seen most of its bricks replaced a half-dozen times, although here and there one of the originals still remained.

Alexis loved the place. There was sensuous secrecy about it that made her feel safe whenever she was there. At the same time, its continuing existence in her life gave her a deepening sense of frustration. To love and not to possess was hard. There was always the sad knowledge that one day it would revert to the Wildersteins who didn't care for it one way or the other.

Sometimes, when spending a few days there alone with only Missy and Sam Crandall, the old black caretakers, as company, she'd feel a coconspirator with the house itself. It was as though she had to help it defend itself against the future. At those times she hated Arnold Wilderstein, and his money and the house came to represent the constant dependence Harold allowed the homemaking side of their marriage to have on the banker. While she cried for Brigham Bay, at the same time she yearned for a home of her own.

She and Harold left the R Street house in her Lancia slightly after three-thirty. Security agents followed in another car with a secretary. The Wildersteins were coming from Boston in their private Lear jet. A limousine had probably already met them at the National Airport.

Harold drove. Alexis tilted her seat back and propped her sandaled feet against the glove compartment, enjoying the afterglow of lunch with Sandy. The meal and the wine had been wonderful, exactly what she'd needed before trying to cope with the Wildersteins.

Without closing her eyes, she could still see Sandy's apartment. She'd had one like it when she'd first started in broadcasting. Maybe every young bachelor woman did. Rush mats on the floor, the kind of furniture you bought cheap and repaired and covered yourself, a bleached wooden cocktail table, ottomans covered with bright rough cotton, posters on the wall—a Lautrec and a Mucha. There was a small bedroom with a queen-sized mattress on a plain wooden platform, rice paper lanterns, and a kitchen partitioned from the living room by tall shutters hinged together as a screen.

It was feminine and felt like home. They'd had vodka and tonic first. "I don't care if you are half on the wagon or not," Sandy had said. "It will help you unshrink." When Alexis finished hers, she said, "Are you ready for greater adventure?"

Alexis thought she meant another drink and declined.

"I didn't mean vodka. And if you ever tell on me, I'll practice my judo on you."

Alexis finally understood and laughed. "You mean you have some?"

"Not me. I'm John Law, more or less. But Batman smokes it like breathing and to bust him might be self-defeating." Sandy disappeared into her bedroom and came back with a joint. They lit up.

"I haven't done this since the good old days in Detroit," Alexis said. She told Sandy about her first television anchor solo. "It was when the boss got ill at the Chicago convention, remember? I had to go on in his place, and found myself interviewing everyone right up to and including the President. It was really hairy. By three in the morning I was jelly and one of the cameramen had some stuff. When we went off the air we lit up like it was amnesty day and got smashed out of our heads."

Kids, having fun. Halcyon days. Later, work became too serious with too much at stake. Nobody swarming the main ladder in Washington or New York drugged. Off guard for one instant and you ended up at the bottom again. Or out all together. But the stress was killing and they drank, most of them. Too much.

Remembering back again, Alexis's mind left Sandy and lunch. Familiar faces from her television years ghosted the Lancia's windshield, voices echoed, incidents replayed. They had turned off the Beltway onto Route 5 headed south toward Maryland's Potomac shore when Harold Volker snapped her out of it.

"Hey! Where are you?"

"Still having lunch."

"Was it that good?"

"It was terrific."

Alexis twisted in her seat and studied him. His wind-whipped hair showed hardly any gray at all and his arms, sleeves rolled up, were muscular and bronzed, his hands solid on the steering wheel. She took in his body. His stomach was flat, his thighs solid muscle. He had on a T-shirt and jeans and espadrilles.

"You're incredible," she said.

"What?"

"Never mind." She leaned over and kissed his cheek and said, "I love you and I'm looking forward to six whole days with you."

"I'm honestly sorry about Arnold and Company." Company was his favorite word for Nettie. Privately he never made any bones about his disdain for her. They'd stopped for a light. He rested a hand on Alexis's knee. "We'll barricade the bedroom door and I'll put a pillow over your mouth."

"Put a pillow over *my* mouth. What about your own?"

"A diplomat knows when to be silent."

She laughed, and jabbed at his ribs. He retaliated. She shrieked and jerking away from him found herself looking into the disapproving glare of an older couple who had pulled up next to them. The Security agents by Harold's side studiously had their eyes elsewhere. The light changed. Harold gunned the Lancia leaving rubber on the road and the two other cars barely moving. It was like her college days, Alexis thought. She moved close, put her head against his shoulder. Tonight, she decided, to hell with worrying about the Wildersteins in the guest room. If she or Harold made too much noise, too damn bad.

In a little while, the ugly semisuburbs of East Washington gave way to the soft countryside of the western shore. Shopping plazas yielded to scattered farms and they were completely out of the world they had left behind. Forty minutes later they rolled up the dusty country lane that led to Brigham Bay.

The barn appeared first, Sam waving from the garden where he was gathering vegetables for dinner. Missy would have been in the kitchen for hours now, she so loved to have people to cook for. Alexis felt a wave of happiness. But when the house came into view, her heart sank. A long, dark-blue Cadillac limousine was already before the door, a uniformed chauffeur busying himself with bags. The Lancia pulled up behind it. She got out and went down the brick walk to the green front door.

Nettie Wilderstein stood in it, her fluffy blue-gray hair a beacon, her powder-pale vacuous face set in a practiced but empty smile above her dowdily dressed and shapeless body.

"Welcome to Brigham Bay."

Words rose to Alexis's lips. "I'm the one who's supposed to say that to you, Nettie." But something froze in her and she didn't say it.

Instead she gave Nettie's dark-red lipsticked mouth her cheek, squeezed her heavily jeweled hand, thanked her, and dutifully followed her indoors.

Arnold Wilderstein was already at the sideboard mixing drinks.

"Hi, beautiful. Early cocktails time." He was tall, his silver hair balding, and going to flesh. He had on a pink shirt, dark Bermuda shorts with high socks, and golf moccasins. His round face was bland. He didn't look like the country's most powerful banking figure, a reputedly ruthless man who always got his own way.

"Hello, Arnold." She let him give her a vodka and took it out onto the terrace. She crossed the worn flagstones and sat on the old stone wall which separated them from the lawn that rolled down to the water where there was a boat house and a little sandy beach. Giant elms spread shade. It was very hot, the sun still well up over the woods at the head of the estuary. The late afternoon air was sultry and smelled of tidal marsh and brackish water. Cicadas whirred. All her good intentions not to be upset by the Wildersteins had vanished. She felt a stranger and a prisoner.

Harold came out with Nettie, trying to explain Portugal to her. "Portugal's a key country in NATO, Nettie. They've been democratic since the Army revolted in 1974 and kicked out a dictator. They have a parlimentary system of government with a president and a premier. It's the latter who is up for reelection. No, no, he's not a Communist." He laughed patiently. "He's a moderate, all the way. He's an ally, our friend. The Reds would like him out, themselves in, naturally. But they're not strong enough alone, so they've made an alliance with the Socialists. It's that coalition he has to beat and it's going to be close, but I suspect okay if we really get behind him. The Portuguese are Europeans, after all. The country is nine hundred years old and they have a tradition of common sense."

Alexis realized Arnold had come to sit beside her. He started to speak then looked at her closely.

"What's the matter?"

"It's all right, thank you."

"You've gone sheet white."

"I'm sorry. I don't feel well at all. Perhaps if you'll excuse me, I'll just lie down for a few minutes."

"You must. Harold?"

Upstairs, she was sick to her stomach. Missy came from the kitchen and took charge. She put a cold cloth over her forehead and pulled down the shades in the low-ceilinged bedroom. A cooling current of air came from across the stair landing through the open doorway of the guest bedroom beyond.

Harold wanted to know what she'd eaten at Sandy's.

"Lobster, potato salad. I'm sure it wasn't that. Please don't say anything to her."

"We ought to."

"Please."

She didn't mention the joint. She hadn't smoked marijuana for years because it always made her sick. But she didn't think it was that either. Not really. She didn't know what it was. She just knew she couldn't stand the Wildersteins. When dinner was ready she still felt nauseous. She sent down her apologies with Harold.

After dinner, she lay awake listening to the murmur of their terrace conversation just below the bedroom window. She didn't begin to feel better until Harold had finally come to bed and was asleep and there was no longer a light showing under the guest room door. Then the silent house began to belong to her again. She suddenly felt hungry. She got up quietly and went downstairs to the kitchen, poured a glass of milk, and got out some graham crackers. There were too many mosquitoes to be on the terrace without lighting the special candles they used to keep them away. She sat in the cool darkness of the living room, thinking of the unknown generations who had lived there, their loves and lives and hopes and dreams. She sipped her milk and listened to the faint creaking sounds the old house always made at night; to the deep resonant tick of the grandfather clock in the hall, the call of the loon up the estuary, and the high, spasmodic shrill of tree frogs.

Lying upstairs, feeling ill, she had made up her mind about two things. She had firmly decided she was going to find some way of getting Brigham Bay away from Arnold Wilderstein, no matter what the cost. It would be a wonderful place to raise children. She had also decided to persuade Harold that they shouldn't wait until he was no longer Secretary of State before having them.

Eight

David Farr was a black, in his midforties, who had once quarterbacked Arkansas. He was big, solid, and quick and acutely intelligent with a preference in his leisure reading for the better nineteenth-century English and French novelists. His wife, Susan, was seventeen years younger and also black. She had gone through medical school with his help and with prize money won as runner-up Miss America. She was now attached to the Naval Medical Center at Bethesda as a second-year resident neurosurgeon. They lived in suburban northwest Washington on a quiet, tree-lined street leading off Foxhall Road.

In the bureaucratic hierarchy of the FBI, Farr was well up the ladder. He was Deputy Assistant Director of the Intelligence Division and responsible for evaluation of all counterintelligence data, whether it came from the FBI's own units or from other sources such as the CIA. When recruited by the FBI, he had been admitted to the Bar in both New York and California and was planning to practice corporate law. When he married Susan, she was a senior in college and he had been with the FBI only three years.

David Farr had looked forward to lunch with Virgil Fein. They had been classmates at Harvard Law School and had kept in touch, but it was some months now since they'd met. Besides this, he enjoyed seeing people from

Langley and talking shop. It enlarged his perspective. His CIA friend was a little weak, perhaps. He had to be to put up with the sort of bullying he took from women, his wife or whomever he had as a current girlfriend, but he was intelligent and often interesting.

Farr, however, had not reckoned on what Fein wanted to talk about. They lunched at the Quorum, a favored spot with bureaucrats and congressmen, and as the meal wore on, Farr's dark and powerful face grew more and more somber. It wasn't the somberness of worry, however; it was annoyance. It went against his grain to waste time on suspicion when there was no clear line of evidence. Over the years, he'd followed so many false leads and had fruitlessly wasted so much effort and emotion doing so, that he'd learned not to. He required an unwavering finger which pointed concretely and concisely.

He carefully read Captain Shenson's memorandum twice and out of courtesy asked some routine questions. If all personal records of Professor Schaeffer, the drowned Joanna Volker's lover, were destroyed during World War II, had investigators tried to discover relatives or friends who might have known him before then? Had they also tried to find friends or relatives of the disappeared Marxist Melkin, General Volker's school friend, who could say definitely if Schaeffer was or was not Melkin reborn? Was any personal contact known to have occurred between Captain Shenson's murdered German agent and either Joanna Volker or her professor? Were they, for example, ever seen together by any neighbors or local tradesmen?

Fein insisted that all these lines had been carefully checked out. No new evidence of any kind had appeared to either strengthen or refute the memorandum's insinuation that the KGB had established, or tried to, a line to the American Secretary of State.

By two-thirty enough of the lunchtime crowd had left

the restaurant so that the FBI deputy felt it safe to raise his voice.

"Virgil, granted everything you say is true, agreed the good Captain may have been hedging his bets in this thing and may still be, accepting the fact you could possibly prove Professor Schaeffer is actually KGB, admitting the two deaths might be more than pure coincidence, you still don't have any line to Volker. Nothing."

Fein shrugged. He found Farr's negativism in a way more difficult to deal with than Helen Carson's suspicion. He weakened. "Look, David, admittedly I'm as confused as you and . . ."

Farr interrupted with a hard laugh. "Confused? Me? Correction. I'm not confused. It's all very clear." He glanced at the memo. "If one thinks in spite of everything that there is substance behind this suspicion, then the natural person to investigate is Volker himself, right? We try to uncover some ongoing connection with the KGB, right? We also try, if I understand some of what you've been saying to me, to catch him red-handed, deliberately setting up some of our foreign relations so that ultimately Russia benefits. Right?"

Fein didn't answer, so Farr replied for him. "Right!" he said. "Since it's what you've been thinking all along and are scared to come out and say." He added wearily. "Virgil, when we were in law school together, you gave no indication whatsoever of being totally insane."

He slapped his Visa card onto the check the waiter had brought. "Anyone who seriously considers investigating the Secretary of State for activities counterproductive to the interests of the United States needs to have his lunch bought for him. He's about to lose his job."

Back in his office in the Hoover Building, Farr briefly occupied himself with a small, highly-sensitive transmitter whose innards were a complex of microscopic chips and

51

whose motivation power was radium. The Bureau's laboratory on the 11th floor had received it yesterday from the State Department's Director of Security. Farr had heard about it from the lab director, who was a friend, and had asked to see it. A report accompanied the device. It said they had never seen anything like it. Analysis showed the steel to have come from East Germany, but they believed the transmitter itself might have been assembled in Czechoslovakia. Certain tiny screws were compatible with others traced a year ago to a machine shop in Pilsen. The report concluded that Czech manufacture didn't necessarily prove the device was KGB.

Farr put it away and noted the clumsy way the device apparently had been concealed and thus easily discovered. One thing stood out—Volker. Twice in one day.

And once yesterday.

Selecting a key from his key ring, he unlocked a drawer of his desk and pulled out a slim folder. Inside were two reports. The first was marked "Defector." In two concise pages it summarized information gathered during the lengthy interrogation of a KGB agent who six months previously had decided he preferred America. One of the things the defector said was that the KGB had successfully infiltrated both the Secret Service and the State Department Office of Security. Although no specific reference had been made to the special force protecting the Secretary of State, it had to be assumed the infiltrator could be one of the personnel assigned to it.

The second report, approximately the same length, was marked "Jesus d'Almeida." In the United States under the alias of General Alfredo Nasciemento, he had been murdered less than an hour after he had dined with General Harold Volker and his wife several days ago. David Farr glanced through it. The poor devil, he thought. They'd first trussed him up with wire and taken him to the dump where he was found. There, unquestionably to make an example of him, they'd emasculated him, then gouged out his eyes. While he writhed in agony, they soaked him with gasoline and left him to await the moment when smoldering garbage would set him afire.

Besides detailing this mindless brutality, the report mentioned d'Almeida's real occupation. Portugal had no espionage branch. But for years, under the previous dictatorship, he had been an exile working as an agent for various Western countries. After the revolution, he had returned home where he was now rumored to be helping build a new highly-secret intelligence cadre attached to the Portuguese Army. No reason was suggested for his visit to Washington; Lisbon clearly could not provide an answer or was unwilling to do so.

David Farr had not discussed either report with Virgil Fein. Nor had he mentioned the "bug" sent over by the State Department Office of Security. He had also not told Fein that because of the Defector report he had very carefully infiltrated one of his counterintelligence agents into the Volker household.

He took the Shenson memorandum from his pocket and spread it on his desk. Volker. Four times now. The possibility of a KGB agent on Volker's staff. His wife's office bugged by persons unknown. A Portuguese intelligence official murdered just after he'd spent the evening in Volker's home and when Volker was due shortly to visit Lisbon to help shore up the endangered moderate Prime Minister. Finally, some Army Intelligence officer suspicious Volker had KGB connections.

Was there a pattern somewhere? There didn't seem to be. The only common denominator he could see in any of it was Harold Volker.

He reread the memorandum, then read it again. He cursed Fein. All he wanted to do was forget the whole mess and go back to routine desk work. But he knew he couldn't.

He called his secretary and told her he didn't want to be disturbed. By anybody; for any reason. He had to think and think clearly. If nothing else, where Volker was concerned, there was one thing he couldn't afford and that was to make a mistake. Three hours later when the office closed, he was still sitting at his desk, staring at the memorandum.

Nine

It was eleven-thirty and Twenty-fourth Street outside Dr. Wyndholt's office was quiet. Most of the block had been converted into offices, but here and there rectangles of light from a few remaining residences slanted the dark pavement or contoured over parked cars. Occasionally, students from nearby George Washington University walked by, breaking the silence, or there'd be the single late worker moving, head bent, with the determined pace of one who wants to get home as soon as possible.

The two men had been waiting for over an hour in unrelenting heat for Wyndholt to lock up and leave. One was older and gray-haired, the other younger and balding. They were anonymously dressed in business suits. On the seat between them, there was a briefcase.

They were both miserably uncomfortable and getting nervous. The job they had to do would only take fifteen minutes, perhaps less. But they hadn't expected Wyndholt to work late and a cleaning lady for the building halls and lobby was due at twelve-ten. They'd cased the building for several nights and found her as regular as clockwork.

In low voices they considered calling the job off, but there was no way of reaching the man who had hired them to explain their problem. They had never met him, had no idea who he was. They'd been recommended to him a year ago by a friend who had given them a mail drop through which to establish contact. Once this was done, the mail drop was changed to another for each subsequent job. They'd been paid in advance for tonight and didn't want their employer annoyed. The money was good, the frequent jobs relatively straightforward and, as far as they could see, the connection between him and them so obscure as to make it impossible for them to be traced in the event he ever got in trouble.

The older man glanced at his watch. "We'll give him another ten minutes," he said.

Up in his third-floor office, Dr. Wyndholt remained unaware of their presence. His wife was with their children for the summer at her parents' home on Cape Cod and he spent several evenings each week at the office working on a textbook. Tonight he felt he'd written enough. He'd managed six clear pages. He added them to a thick manuscript lying in a folder, secured the folder with a heavy rubber band, and put it back on the bookshelf where he kept it. Then, he tidied his desk and pulled his jacket from the back of the chair. He checked his file case to make certain it was locked, turned off the light, and went out. His office door had a Yale mortice lock and a Ward lock. He secured both.

He washed his hands in the small bathroom off his secretary's office which doubled as a reception room. Once again, he automatically checked the locks on the two file cases there and when he went out into the hall, he double locked that door also. Wyndholt was very meticulous about patient security. In almost any of his files there was a virtual field day for a blackmailer. Tonight he was more careful than ever because his burglar alarm had broken down yesterday and he couldn't get it repaired until next week.

The two men waiting in the parked car gave themselves five minutes after he'd started up his Volkswagon and driven off. The older one checked his watch again. The time was eleven-forty. He got out of the car, his younger companion following with the briefcase.

The front door of Wyndholt's building had two locks. One was a night latch which could be opened with a piece of stiff plastic inserted between the door and the frame. Pushed hard, it forced back the lock's tongue. The other was a Ward and required a special Ward key. They had studied both the day before and had brought along several skeletons. The second one the younger man tried slid in easily, turned halfway, but no further. He murmured a request and the older man produced a small file from a pouch of neatly arranged tools in the briefcase. The younger man filed at the key. When he put it back in the lock, it worked. The door opened and they entered the building. Once inside, they put on gloves that might have looked suspicious outside and wiped the door handle, locks, and door frame free of any prints. They double locked the door behind them and put the skeleton on an empty key ring.

Upstairs was more difficult. A night latch was again susceptible to stiff plastic; a Yale mortice yielded to a skeleton. The third was again a Ward lock. They tried five skeletons before they hit the right one. When the door opened, they added the key to the ring with the downstairs door key, locked only the Yale and the night latch.

Inside the reception room, they ignored the two big file cases and went directly to the door to Wyndholt's office. They had discussed the files yesterday when, posing as telephone company technicians, they had cased the office. They had decided that Wyndholt would most likely keep general records in the outer office and immediate patient records in his own room. On the same case they fused the burglar alarm.

The door gave them problems. None of their skeletons worked on the Ward. It was now eleven forty-five. The younger man took two slender wire tools, each resembling a dentist's probe, from the briefcase, crouched by the lock and, inserting the tools, began to feel the lock's tumblers very carefully. There was complete silence. He worked by sound and feel. There were four tumblers and it took about a minute to turn each one, jam it open, and move on to the next one. When he was finished and had also snapped the night latch with stiff plastic, he was sweating hard. The "pick-locks" joined the two keys on the special ring.

He entered Wyndholt's office. The older man, coming behind him, wiped the door clean of any telltale smudges as the lock was mildly graphited.

Wyndholt's file was secured by a manufacturer's lock built into the file case. When they cased the office, Wyndholt had been busy with a patient. They had presumed it would be the same as the other files, but in case it wasn't, they had noticed the office equipment was modern and had checked out the types of locks used by some other major manufacturers and had brought along skeleton keys to suit. The file did indeed turn out to be unlike those in the outer office and they used one of those keys. It was eleven-fifty. It had taken ten minutes to get into the place. It would not take more than seven to get out.

Throughout the whole entering procedure they had employed a small pencil flashlight. Its beam now moved slowly along the line of red and green file tabs looking for one particular file. It found it and stopped and the older man removed it. The file was marked "Personal Finance." He took it over to the desk and from the briefcase got out a wide-lens camera loaded with infrared film.

He rapidly and efficiently began to photograph copies of Wyndholt's tax declarations, loan agreements, bank statements, and other data.

The younger man stood by a window watching the street. Whenever they did a job and whatever the job entailed, one always stood guard while the other worked.

When the older man seemed nearly finished, he glanced at his watch. It was five past twelve. He was about to say so when a car came down the street. It looked familiar. It slowed and he recognized Wyndholt's Volkswagon. The doctor had come back.

The two men were prepared for any eventuality. They moved very quickly. The camera dropped back into the briefcase, and the file into the file case which was locked instantly with the readily available key put onto the special key ring minutes before. When they went into the reception office, Wyndholt was getting out of the Volks. Again the key ring. This time the special tools. The younger man bent down, began to work it rapidly in the mortice.

One tumbler, two.

Downstairs, the front door opened.

Three tumblers.

Wyndholt's footsteps came upward, reached the landing.

The doctor fumbled with his own key ring, found all three keys to his office. He opened first the night latch, then the Yale, then inserted his Ward key. To his surprise, the Ward wasn't locked. He was certain he had done so when he left. He felt vaguely uneasy. Could someone have broken in? He opened the door carefully. Without stepping into the reception room, he reached around the door frame and switched on the lights.

There was nobody. Puzzled, he went to the door to his inner office and tried that mortice. He found it securely locked. He decided that he was overtired and his mind was playing tricks on him. He had obviously forgotten the other Ward.

He went to the bathroom and retrieved his watch from the sink. It was why he had returned. He came back out and put it on. Then a strange sequence of thoughts began to go through his head. Something was wrong.

Suppose he had indeed locked his outer office door.

That would mean someone had broken in and unless they had left the building before he returned, forgetting or not caring to double lock his office, they could still be there.

If so, where?

They could not be on the landing or stairs without his seeing them. There were two other offices in the building, a dentist on the first floor, a cartographer on the second. If he'd surprised someone, surely they wouldn't have had time to break into another office just to hide.

His heart began to beat violently. The back of his head felt exposed and cold. His ears rang.

They couldn't be in his inner office because the mortice couldn't be locked from the other side. There was only one place left. The bathroom. And only one place there. In the bathtub, behind the shower curtain.

He wanted to look, couldn't. Terror rose up his throat. Someone really was there. He could sense them now. Like an animal. Both mind and legs failed him. He couldn't bear to look. They might be armed. If he reached for the phone, it would be the same. He'd give himself away.

Then he remembered the pay phone at the end of the street. Just around the corner.

With enormous effort, he forced himself to behave normally. From the corner of his eye he could see through the open bathroom door. The shower curtain was reflected in the mirror over the sink. Did it move? Or did he imagine it?

Anyone behind the curtain could very likely also see him.

Try to appear casual. Don't let them know you know. Go to the door, open it, leave the office normally.

In the hall, he pulled the door closed gently behind him. His hands shook uncontrollably as he triple locked it.

He went downstairs quickly. Once outside the building he fought back panic and forced himself to lock the downstairs door to the street, too. Still controlling himself, he walked as rapidly as possible toward the corner.

His terror saved him, the fact that he couldn't bear to look. The moment they heard his footsteps on the stairs, the two men came from behind the shower curtain, the younger man pocketing a .38 revolver mounted with a silencer. They were quite aware of what might be going through Wyndholt's mind. They left the office at once, locking all three locks behind them, raced down the stairs and out, locking the front door also.

They made it to their car just as Wyndholt turned the corner. They saw no one else on the street. The older man slid behind the wheel, started the motor. He left the car lights off, pulled away from the curb, then put the car in reverse and backed rapidly down Twenty-fourth Street. When he reached H Street, he turned up it.

As he accelerated away, he had to slow for the cleaning lady as she crossed the street heading for Wyndholt's building. She didn't take any notice. They hadn't left behind a single clue. Wyndholt's office was as securely locked as when he'd left it at eleven thirty-five. When the police came they would find nothing to substantiate his anxiety. Absolutely nothing at all.

Ten

When David and Susan Farr
drove back to their suburban home in Chevy Chase, it was
well past midnight. They'd been to a concert at Wolf Trap.

Susan was ebullient and talkative. Her eyes shone and
there was laughter and delight in her voice. She didn't
have that many nights off from work and every time they
went out she was like a child going to the circus. She had
tucked her legs up under her on the seat and sat close to
Farr, her slender body straight and with one arm across
the seat behind him. From time to time while she talked,
she would very gently caress the back of his neck and head
with her fingertips.

Farr was very aware of her, of her sensuous young beauty
and her strong sexuality. At the same time his mind kept
leaving her and going back to his day. He had a rule not to
think about work when he was with Susan. It was the first
time he'd ever not been able to keep it, but he'd been
going around and around in the same circles since lunch.
The memorandum was what bothered him the most. Its
seemingly groundless suspicions were made conceivably
credible by his other evidence. Could he afford arbitrarily
to dismiss it? And if he decided he couldn't, then how
should he act? He doubted either his own boss or the FBI
director, a political appointee, had the courage to approve
an investigation of General Volker. On the other hand, if
something emerged by itself, he'd be blamed. Investigate
on his own? Covertly? One slip-up and he'd be ruined

there, too. The risk was too great. Susan was soon going to need money to set up a practice on her own and he was only just recovering from debts accrued putting her through medical school. Farr began to sympathize with the Army's Captain Shenson. The situation made you damned if you did and damned if you didn't. There was nothing concrete anywhere. It was all shadows and suspicion.

Their home was a one-story contemporary house set back from the quiet tree-lined street they lived on and from their neighbors, another doctor and an advertising executive, both white, by a lawn with shrubs and flowering bushes. Out back, Farr had flanked more lawn with a six-foot palisade fence to give them some privacy at their small pool. He drove into the garage and he and Susan went through the walkway into the kitchen.

"Do you want something to eat?"

"Maybe just a beer."

"I'll have one with you." She put her arms around his neck and her body against his and kissed the side of his neck. "You were the handsomest man in the audience," she said. "And you smell divine and I love you."

He found her mouth and kissed her gently. She responded in a way that said she wanted to make love. "Why not bring the beer to the bedroom," she said. She disappeared into the darkened living room.

He took beer out of the fridge and opened it, got down glasses, and went upstairs.

Where would one even begin an investigation of Volker? With a careful analysis of his past record, perhaps, for certainly Fein was correct about one thing. What an American public, humiliated abroad for years, hailed as triumphs, had indeed turned sour after the public's attention was focused elsewhere.

Uppermost, Farr remembered Venezuela where a military Junta put down Cuban-assisted peasant riots threatening a weak centralist government. Covertly planned by the

63

State Department in conjunction with the CIA, the coup was regarded as having saved huge American investments in that country's agriculture. In the resultant backlash, important political countergains for the Communists throughout all Latin America were obscured by other more pressing world crises.

Equally outstanding had been American Naval intervention in Southeast Asia when "terrorist" groups in East Timor helped the Soviets to establish rocket bases within range of the Indonesian capital city of Jakarta. Volker and the President were praised for their bold action so reminiscent of Kennedy and the Cuban Missile Crisis. When it turned out the terrorists were a legitimate resistance to the Jakarta genocide of a half-million independence-seeking natives, a wave of anti-Americanism brought down the Jakarta government, put a Moscow puppet in its place, and seriously threatened the Southeast Asia Treaty Organization. The CIA was blamed for bad intelligence gathering. Very few pointed a finger at Volker. Other world events again took precedence.

Political misjudgments? An overbearing Germanic way of doing things? Or skillfully planned misadventures. Was it reasonable or totally paranoid to suspect Volker of some dark Machiavellian scheme to injure his adopted country? And if in fact he were, what was his motivation? Money? Blackmail? How could his profitable friendship with Arnold Wilderstein ever be reconcilable with a connection to Marxism?

Susan was already undressed, seated at her vanity table, taking off her makeup.

"Are you going to shower?"

"You just said I smelled nice."

She laughed softly. He studied her body. She had a slender torso with full deep breasts and a long graceful neck topped with a small, exquisitely shaped head, emphasized by the way she kept her hair close-cropped in the

64

old "slave" style now back in vogue. Her nose was delicate, her eyes almond shaped, her cheekbones high. Farr thought she looked like a princess. Her seated hips were wide and feminine and her skin a rich cocoa color. It had always been a mystery to Farr why she had married him.

He brushed his teeth, shed his own clothes, and stretched out on the bed. Presently she turned out the lights and came and lay next to him, her head on his shoulder. She lay like that a moment, tracing small lines down his chest with one slender finger. After a while she said gently, "You've got something driving you crazy at work, don't you." It was a statement, not a question.

"I'm sorry, Susan." Even as he said it he tried to find some way to feel romantic. He couldn't. He felt like a fool. She was beautiful and he loved her. She loved him and wanted him. He couldn't respond. If he thought about nothing else but the actual physical act of making love to her with all its unleashed emotion and ecstasy, he still couldn't. He was too deep in the grip of anxiety. It was like being a cripple.

He heard her whisper, "Don't be sorry. And if you feel ashamed, I'll never speak to you again. Okay?"

She nestled close to him and was quiet. In a few minutes he realized she'd gone to sleep. He very gently eased away from her, covered her with the sheet, and went back to the kitchen. He got out another beer and sat in the dark living room, drinking it slowly.

Susan found him at four o'clock when she missed him in bed. "Whatever it is," she said, "you'd better tell me. This way we'll have you in a straitjacket."

He told her everything. They talked until dawn and she said, "I've heard Volker's marriage isn't so hot."

"Who said that?"

"She drinks and sees a shrink. If he really were up to no good, who could be in a better position to know than his wife?"

"You're crazy."

"Am I?"

"What's your source? Who says there are marriage problems?"

She knelt next to him on the couch, skin ebony in the faint light of dawn and against the white of the light summer nightgown she'd put on. She avoided the question. "She had a big affair with a man named Adrian James," she said. "They lived together for over a year. James broke it off. The word was he couldn't take her career. The next thing she was married."

He said, "I asked you a question."

She laughed softly. "I heard you. I read the gossip columns. A little from one. More from another. And doctors. James had some surgery on a trick knee. I know one of the orthopods." She laughed again. "A she. Wow! A real tigress. She eats up as many women as she does men. He took her to Paris for a week. I think with another girl. A threesome." She began to massage his neck and shoulders. "David, couldn't you figure out some way to get to her and somehow use her? For example, she's supposed to find it hard to say no. That's what James told my friend, anyway."

He felt a moment of pure outrage. "Are you suggesting I blackmail her?"

She gently kissed his shoulder. "No. Of course not. Nothing that simple. Or crude. I was suggesting she might want a friend, though. Someone to confide in. I was thinking of her background. She was a reporter, no? When you strip away all the cameras and glamour, that's what she was. An investigative reporter. So I thought if there really was trouble between her and her husband and the right suspicion was ever planted in her mind by the right person, she might do all your work for you. If you were careful, what would you have to lose?"

The thought appalled him.

"You're suggesting I use James to do it?"

"It was just a thought."

"And just how do I get him to go along with this?"

"I don't know," she admitted, "that's the flaw. But I suspect he deserves anything that happens to him. From what I hear, he's completely without morals."

"Doctor, you're crazy."

"You're probably right, but I'm on your side and you're giving yourself a nervous breakdown stewing over the problem. Shall I tell you why? Because when they wrote the book about National Security, they didn't include a chapter about the Secretary of State, that's why. Well, to hell with him. Under the title he's just another human being. Try to think of him that way. And try to remember that national security is what your job is all about." She kissed his forehead, then his lips. "It's dawn. I have to operate this morning and I can still get three hours sleep before I have to get up. And if you don't try to, you're the one who's crazy."

She disappeared leaving only the soft musky smell of her warm body behind her and the sense of her close presence. Farr tossed up mentally between beer and milk and decided mixing the two wouldn't kill him. He went back to the refrigerator and drank half a quart of milk. Then he followed her upstairs.

Eleven

The Watch Officer at the State Department Operational Center was the first to receive the news. It was telephoned from the American Embassy in Lisbon. He immediately relayed it to the Director of Operations at his home. The Director in turn put a call through to Harold Volker. It was four-thirty A.M. eastern daylight time, nine-thirty in Portugal.

Alexis had suffered through another sleepless night. She was sitting on the terrace watching the gray predawn turn slowly to a spectrum of blue and listening to early morning sounds, the awakening of house sparrows, the call of a redwing from the estuary, and the occasional scream of a passing gull. It was her favorite time of day, moments when she always felt filled with life and physically one with nature. Today was no exception. Neither the presence of the Wildersteins sleeping upstairs nor the security agents in the barn bothered her. The day was too perfect for any intrusion. She wanted to take off her clothes, run naked down the lawn to the little sandy beach by the boat house, and there throw herself into the estuary's warm water to float lazily on it, face down, as though embracing it.

The telephone rang in the barn's staff quarters as well as in the house. The agents, however, had orders not to answer unless it rang more than six times. Alexis insisted she be able to receive calls direct without interference. Brigham Bay, she said, was a home, not an office. She picked up the receiver on the third ring.

The Director of Operations apologized and said it was urgent. She woke her husband and he came downstairs in his short, summer, terry cloth robe. While he listened to what the Director had to tell him, she went to the kitchen to make coffee. She knew from the sound of Harold's voice there'd been a disaster someplace.

He hung up and entered the kitchen as she was getting down cups. He put his arms around her and nuzzled her neck. "I have to go to Washington."

She groaned and turned to face him. "Oh, Harold."

"Worse," he said, "I will probably have to go to Portugal this afternoon or tomorrow. The Premier has just been killed in a car crash."

"That nice man? Oh, my God." Alexis remembered a pleasant beefy man with a walrus mustache and a staggering knowledge of history. She had met him last summer when he'd paid an official visit to Washington.

"A truck ran a red light at an intersection. It took out one of his motorcycle escorts and then him. Nobody knows yet, but it could have been deliberate self-sacrifice, meaning an attempted assassination."

"Harold, it's awful. What will happen?"

"Politically?" He went to the refrigerator and got out orange juice and brought it back. "Well, unless the moderates can come up with a new candidate in a hurry, someone with real appeal, the Socialists and Communists could win the election. And time's short. There's only a couple of weeks left."

He drank some juice and they took their coffee out onto the terrace. First rays of sun filtered through the arched boughs of the massive shading elms. Alexis could feel its sudden, intense warmth. It would be another scorching day. They had planned to take the Chris-Craft out and picnic on a beach across the bay. The Wildersteins were going to a local antique show.

"When will they hold the funeral?"

"Sunday or Monday."

"Why do you have to go over tomorrow, then?"

Volker studied a pair of robins hopping on the lawn. He stretched out his suntanned legs, propped them on another chair, and opened his robe to let the sun reach his naked torso. He seemed unworried. "Two reasons," he said thoughtfully. "Show the flag. Let the Portuguese people know their principal ally is a hundred percent behind the moderates. That's one. The other is to see what I can do in the way of influencing those who are influential. Be sure President Luis Cabral appoints a caretaker premier who can win an election, for a start. To hell with ability—get someone who right now is really popular." He paused to smile. "And just to play really safe, I might also try to make a deal with the Socialist candidate to screw up his own campaign. I know the man. If there's anything he likes better than his Socialism, it's money." He laughed. "If I could get away with it, I'd take over a Treasury check for a couple of million bucks or so. Diplomacy will cost twice that in the long run."

When Arnold Wilderstein came down to breakfast, he was far more concerned about the new crisis than Harold Volker. "That bastard Socialist gets elected, you'll have Moscow commissars sharing the Estoril Palace with illiterate peasants. Portugal will go straight Red overnight, Harold. He won't be able to control them."

"It won't happen," Volker said calmly. "The Portuguese aren't stupid. And we have leverage. NATO and the common market. And the dollar."

But Alexis felt a chill of apprehension just the same.

Volker's departure for Lisbon was finally scheduled for the following afternoon. They drove into Washington together to have early lunch with the President at the White House. Volker would represent him at the funeral now planned for Monday to keep Communist demonstrators to a minimum. Most of the party faithful would be at work. After lunch they were flown directly to Andrews Air Force Base by presidential helicopter. It was one of those hazy days when clouds had no definitive shape, but merged with a sky more yellow-gray than blue. The weather service had announced air pollution at a hundred and nineteen, humidity at ninety-four percent. When he and Alexis arrived, Air Force SAM 70 had been fueled and ready since twelve-thirty. It was a Boeing 707 and Volker's favorite among the five Special Air Mission planes available to the State Department. Takeoff was scheduled for two o'clock.

There were very few people on the tarmac. Volker's arrivals and departures were so frequent they attracted only routine media attention. The Assistant Secretary had come, along with a handful of Department specialists who'd accompany Volker. They stood about, talking to the Air Force officers in attendance. There were also a dozen picked and privileged journalists and some necessary office staff.

Alexis found there wasn't a moment to be alone with her husband. If it was the ever-present Wildersteins at Brigham Bay, now it was officialdom and television cameras taping for the evening news. She gave him the kind of bright, noncommital kiss which would publicly state that she and Harold were a devoted couple, but at the same time would not embarrass anyone. When she spoke, she kept her voice low and her smile bright.

"Harold, please change your mind. I really want to come. I can pick up some clothes over there."

"I'm sorry, darling. It just isn't that kind of a trip. If it were a formal visit, sure. But it isn't. I must be free. If you were along, the Portuguese would feel they had to put on the diplomatic dog and entertain us both. I don't want that. I've got to be able to play it by ear and not be tied down to convention."

"But nobody would even have to know I was there. I could zip down to the Algarve and park myself on a beach."

"Darling, make sense." He laughed and gestured at a nearby TV camera. "You can't move without the world knowing it. Neither can I. That's the job. We're stuck with it."

"Please, Harold. It's important to me."

"Alexis, they're waiting." His smile had gone.

She glanced around. Close by, various officials were looking vaguely uncomfortable. The Under Secretary's eyes dropped to his watch. You presumptuous bastard, she thought, how dare you! She turned back to her husband.

"I'm sorry," he said. "I'll call you from Lisbon." He gave her another quick kiss, then joined the others.

She made a pretense nothing was wrong. She kept her cheerful, official smile as he went up the stairs and disappeared into the plane's interior followed by his security agents and staff and the journalists. Watching the plane take off and until it was just a faint smudge in the sky, she felt frustrated and vaguely rejected.

And suddenly very angry.

An Air Force staff car was waiting to take her back to the presidential helicopter. She ignored it as well as the young officer who had come over to escort her. She went instead directly to the official limousine which had brought the Under Secretary out from Washington.

"I want to use the telephone," she told the chauffeur.

"Yes, ma'am." Startled, he flung open the door. She got in. The phone was mounted on the wall separating the passengers from the driving compartment. She lifted the receiver. A State Department operator answered instantly.

"I want to call Brigham Bay," Alexis said.

"Is this Mrs. Volker?"

"Yes."

"Right away, ma'am."

On the fourth ring, Nettie Wilderstein's inane voice replied. "Hello?"

"Nettie, this is Alexis. Darling, I'm afraid there's been a change of plans. I mean where I'm concerned. I have to go back to R Street. Harold's given me something to do that I can't handle from Brigham Bay."

"Oh. Shall we not wait dinner for you, then?"

"I meant I won't be coming back at all, Nettie. I'm frightfully sorry."

"You mean not for the whole weekend?" She sounded incredulous.

"I have to stay in town."

"Oh. But we canceled antiques for today. We thought you could join us tomorrow. That way you wouldn't be alone."

"You're sweet. Would you tell Arnold how sorry I am. And if you need anything, just call me."

"Of course, dear. But what about your things down here?"

"I'll collect them the next time I'm there."

"But, Alexis . . ."

She put the receiver back and got out of the car. The back of her neck felt hot. She lifted her hair free from her shoulders a moment and smiled at the chauffeur.

"Thank you."

"Yes, ma'am."

She walked toward the staff car, taking long free strides, feeling wonderful for the first time all day, and saying all the right things to the young officer who, slightly taken aback, had rejoined her and hurried anxiously by her side.

She had no social engagements because it was expected she'd be at Brigham Bay. Sandy had the weekend off, so there would be no tennis. She was faced with Friday evening and Saturday night and Sunday alone and she'd never looked forward to anything so much in her life. There was nobody in Washington's social world she particularly wanted to see. She'd wash her hair, watch television, maybe go to a movie. Tomorrow she'd sleep late in the morning and then perhaps get in touch with some of her old friends in broadcasting.

It is wonderful. She'd asserted herself and broken free of the Wildersteins.

Five minutes later, the presidential helicopter lifted off and she was on her way back to Washington.

Twelve

David Farr had used his car to get across town to Folger Park. He found a place to leave it and again without trouble found the address he was looking for at the end of a rubble-strewn side street. The area was run down and slated for urban renewal.

The studio was in a converted warehouse. Once inside, most people forgot about the neighborhood. Farr did. He introduced himself to a curious Adrian James with whom he'd made an appointment that morning and while James poured him a cold beer, he sat on a wide, armless modern chair and looked around. High, floor-to-ceiling studio windows looked onto a charming Japanese-style garden replete with water, stepping stones, gravel paths, and exotic dwarf trees. Beyond, the windowless wall of a warehouse was painted light gray and gave the impression of a limitless landscape without horizon. Inside, above and behind him, was an open sleeping loft. Through its balustrade he could see a low king-sized platform bed covered with a Navajo blanket and with an antique, hand-sculpted wooden headboard. The stair going up was a tight spiral of ornate wrought iron reminiscent of New Orleans.

James, an art historian for the National Gallery, was also a painter and to Farr's practiced eye, a good one. There were two canvasses hanging on one huge bare wall, more standing in a corner, and one unfinished work on an easel. His style, Farr thought, was a rather dispassionate mixture of impressionist and early cubist. It was traditional rather than a radical departure.

"I like your work. Do you exhibit much?"

"I have a show this autumn in New York. My last show was in London. And before that San Francisco." James brought the beer over. It was in a tall Steuben-crystal glass, expensive as was everything else in the studio. As was James himself, Farr thought. He'd been struck at once by how like Harold Volker he was. Obviously Alexis Volker was attracted to a certain type. He wondered how much James and the Secretary were similar in character.

James sat down. He was tall, dark-haired, and tanned from playing tennis. He was barefooted and wore loose, Mexican-poplin trousers, a rough-weave cotton shirt, and wore a neck chain with some sort of medallion. Farr's first impression was of a Star of David. James's face was sensitive, his deep-set eyes dark and brooding. But he had a wide sensual mouth and he smiled easily and well. When he sat, he draped. It seemed to be his way. One leg fell idly over the arm of the couch, the other stretched out straight.

"I spend quite a bit of time in the National Gallery," Farr said. "It's an extraordinary place."

"I agree," James said. "But you didn't come here to talk about the Gallery. What can I do for the FBI?" He'd put Farr's card on the sideboard. He glanced at it. "And a Deputy Assistant Director at that."

It was getting to the point pretty quickly, Farr thought. Almost too quickly for his liking. But then he found the whole business going too quickly as well as against his grain. Ever since he'd lunched with Virgil Fein, nothing had gone according to form or routine. Or according to his nature. He felt caught up in something he couldn't stop or control. Swept along with it, whether he wanted to go or not. Fein's insistence of "just suppose" would not go away. Nor would Susan's comment about National Security. His mind flicked back to her, kneeling by him on the couch in the predawn of their living room. He had a vague sense of unease because he'd talked to her at all about any of it. It was the first time he'd ever revealed Bureau secrets to her.

Yesterday, he'd abruptly made his decision. No small part of it was based on the bug Sandy Muscioni had found in Alexis Volker's office. Clearly someone thought she might have something to say. Whether she did or not was another question and one that could not be left unanswered. It was like quarterbacking, taking the initiative in a split second and deciding to run with the ball when he couldn't find the receiver the play called for. Once committed, he went all out with no reservations and no holds barred. He'd only held back in one way. He'd told no one at the Bureau. If anything went wrong, he didn't want to look like a fool and expose himself to possible repercussions. His job was too important to him and Susan to lose. Until he had some sort of definite evidence to back up the suspicions of the Shenson memorandum, he was proceeding unofficially.

He looked at James, waiting for him to reply. "Okay," he said. "First of all, accept my thanks for letting me see you. I'm sure you're busy enough."

James looked slightly surprised at the courtesy. He tipped his glass in acknowledgment. "I'm sure you are, too."

"I'll come to the point then," Farr said. He shifted his frame on the chair, slightly awkward in his business suit, even though he'd taken off his jacket. "With the reminder, I'm afraid, that our conversation is confidential."

James shrugged faintly. He wasn't agreeing, he wasn't disagreeing.

"I understand you keep company with M. J. Lindley," Farr began.

James smiled. "That's public knowledge." His tone was slightly condescending.

Farr said, "Mrs. Lindley is separated from Arthur Lindley. He's the Public Relations Assistant to the White House Chief of Staff, am I right? Or is this another Lindley?"

"You're right. Does this have something to do with security?"

"Yes."

"In what way?" James frowned. "Mary Jane hasn't leaked anything. She never knew anything to leak in the first place. She and Lindley were separated before he went to the White House. Besides, she's completely apolitical."

"Do you call her M. J. or Mary Jane?"

James gestured impatiently. "Sometimes one, sometimes the other. Most people call her M. J. Is it important?"

"No. And it's not about her."

"Then what is it about?" James looked confused.

Farr said quietly, "It's about Mrs. Harold Volker."

He waited. James's eyes became immediately guarded. "Alexis?"

"Alexis Sobieski. Yes. You had an affair with her. Before she married."

"That's also public knowledge." James's tone was cautious now.

Farr knew he had him off balance. He glanced around the studio. "Did she live here with you?"

"Some of the time." James flushed slightly with anger. "But I don't see what possible business that is of the FBI."

Farr decided to retreat a little. "Fair enough," he said. "Would you mind telling me whether you still see her?"

"Yes. But I will. I don't." James's tone became nearly a sneer. "So if there's a leak in her direction, big state secrets she got from her husband, all that sort of thing, it hasn't come this far."

Farr said. "A good guess, but that's not why I'm here. I'm here because I want you to resume seeing her."

For a moment he thought James hadn't heard him. James was leaning slightly forward in his chair, forearms across his knees. He didn't move.

Finally he said, "Alexis? What the hell for?" A kind of ugliness came into his eyes. Farr could see him making a conscious effort to put tolerance into his voice. "Look, Mr. Farr. Once more. My personal life *is* my personal life and it certainly doesn't include being some sort of FBI errand boy, if that's what you're after. Now, if you don't mind, as you yourself suggested, I am busy."

Farr ignored the protest. "I want you to see Mrs. Volker again," he said, "and I want you to try to get her to regard you again as a trusted friend, someone she can confide in." He'd decided not to ask more of James at this time. He wanted him used to the situation first before he made the assignment more complex.

He was not surprised by James's reaction. The artist studied him briefly and said, "If you don't have a warrant that entitles you to be here, I'd appreciate your leaving. At once."

He came over to Farr, picked up his half-finished beer, took it back to the sideboard.

Farr cursed inwardly. He'd hoped almost desperately James would cooperate, but he knew he would not. Because he would not, what he had to do to James was dirty tricks and all the years he'd spent in counterintelligence had never completely hardened him to them. He'd do it not because anything could justify blackmail, but because, try as he could, he'd found no other way. Perhaps things would have been different if James understood what sort of suspicion Volker was under, no matter how vague. He could hardly be a Volker supporter. But he couldn't be told.

The words came hard. "The DEA," he said, "has had a close eye on Mary Jane Lindley's cocaine supplier for some time now. They haven't acted where she's concerned because she isn't divorced from her husband yet and they're reluctant to be responsible for any scandal which might involve a White House aide, even if just in name. They will, however, if I ask them to."

James turned from the sideboard, his mouth slack. "You rotten black bastard," he said. "She buys it for her guests. Half the stinking, two-faced politicians in Washington use it."

The insult helped. Farr was almost grateful for it. "I'm well aware of that," he shot back. "Just as I am aware half the Washington hostesses serve it with after-dinner coffee. But very few of them have two small children they could lose custody of."

He stood up, straightened his tie, and put on his jacket. It was partly a defensive move. He stood six foot two in his stocking feet and weighed a hundred and ninety, and in spite of his age it was all muscle still and looked it. He thought he'd let Adrian James see what he might run into if he lost his temper. He didn't want James to go that far. It would wreck everything else.

Oddly, James didn't. Instead, the rage in his eyes disappeared. He emitted a wry half-laugh, shook his head, poured himself another drink, and went and sat back down.

"I suppose you want me to go to bed with her?"

"I didn't say so," Farr replied. "I said I wanted you to become her friend. How you do that is your business. And hers."

"Okay," James said. "It won't be easy, but I'm not having M. J. or her children hurt by you or anybody else,

80

especially that prick Arthur Lindley. May I pour you another beer?"

The guy had a certain class, Farr thought. And poise. "No, thank you," he said.

"May I ask what this is all about?"

"Sorry," Farr answered. "Not today. Maybe later."

"Last question," James said. "Why me? I wasn't the only guy in her life before Volker. What the hell, when I met her she was hardly innocent. I can think of half a dozen guys in Washington I'm damn sure she slept with. Alexis likes sex."

Farr thought it a rotten remark. He remembered what Susan had told him about James and his orthopedic surgeon, their trip to France with a bisexual girlfriend. He suddenly disliked him and liked Alexis Volker. He suspected James had left her because he couldn't have his own way. He was the sort of man who could only behave decently when he was being pushed around and felt sorry for himself.

"From what I heard," he said, "you were the one she was in love with. Anyone else was just play. And anyway, in my books, nowadays, sex is a lady's prerogative as much as it is a man's."

James stared a moment. "You guys always have everything all figured out, don't you?" Hostility had crept back into his voice. And bitterness. Or was it self-pity? Farr wondered. James said, "Okay, I hope the hell you know what you're doing. When do you want me to start?"

"As soon as possible."

"Do I contact you? Or do you contact me?"

"Either way," Farr answered. "My home number is on my card. Give me a call after your first meeting, tell me how things went."

At the door, he looked back. "My suggestion is you at least make an effort to see they go well."

James didn't answer. After Farr closed the door behind him, he looked out at the garden. But he didn't see it. He saw Alexis Sobieski. She was sitting, a drink in one hand, her face white. "I can't understand why if you love me, Jimmy, you want to break us up. Why? Just tell me why."

Himself, shouting, "I've told you why. Because I can't stand having only half of you. Less than half. A quarter." He was fed up with her stardom, with people thinking of him as Mr. Sobieski.

"I could quit television."

"Alexis, please. Don't insult my intelligence. You're married to television."

"I don't have to be, Jimmy. I've been thinking a lot about it."

"Then go ahead. Quit."

She hadn't. And he'd been glad. He didn't really want marriage himself. Marriage meant the chains of children and soul-destroying responsibility where another person was concerned. Six months later she married Volker.

He glanced at his watch. Since Alexis, he had very carefully arranged his life so it would be undisturbed by anyone. It was uncomplicated, safe, and fun and he called the shots. In less than an hour, all that had been turned around by one man. Why? What the hell was really going on? What was he going to be asked to do next? He sprawled disconsolately in a chair. He was going to find out if it was the last thing he ever did. When he did, he'd have that bastard Farr hung for his pains. Meanwhile he knew when he was cornered. The most important thing was not to lose his cool, or his patience. Play it one step at a time and wait for his chance. At least he was in the clear. No one had anything on him personally.

He looked at the half-finished painting on the easel. Later on he'd change part of the color balance, he thought. The blue upset it. He picked up the nearby telephone and punched out a number. The phone rang. A woman answered.

"Hello?"

"Hi. I'm on my way."

She was annoyed. "Where have you been? You were supposed to bring some lunch."

"I got hung up. I'll explain. 'Bye."

"Wait a minute. Batman?"

"What?"

"Also bring some paper for joints. I'm all out."

He put down the receiver, checked he had his keys, locked the garden door, and left the studio. It occurred to him that Sandy might know something about Farr, or at least find out about him. At the right moment, he'd ask her.

Thirteen

The flight was quick. Washington simmered beneath them, splotches of light-colored buildings and dark roofs interspersed by trees, like islands in a river delta laced by green water. When they dropped down on the White House lawn, it appeared deserted. The President and his family had already departed for a weekend at Camp David and there was only the usual line of tourists filing into the east wing or waiting patiently the whole length of East Executive.

Before they landed, Alexis spotted her car. It had been brought right to the helicopter pad near the South Portico. A security agent waiting by it was identifiable by his suit and sunglasses.

She didn't recognize him as Steve Riker until she had landed and walked to the car. It was an unpleasant surprise.

"Good afternoon, Mrs. Volker." He held the door open for her, his expression candid.

She hesitated, then got behind the wheel. He closed the door and came around to the other side.

"I won't be needing you, Mr. Riker." She started the motor, put the car in gear.

"I'm sorry, Mrs. Volker. I'm under orders."

"That's your problem."

She let out the clutch. He stepped back quickly. She drove into West Executive, the closed-off street separating the White House from the monolithic Executive Office Building that once had housed the State Department. As she came through the security gates and headed for Seventeenth, she looked in her rear view mirror and saw a dark-gray sedan following her. It belonged to the security detail. Riker was driving. She felt the same anger she felt at the airport. Everything caught up with her at once and she slammed a hand furiously at the steering wheel. "Son of a bitch. Goddamnit!" A week alone with Harold ruined by the Wildersteins and Portugal and now, just when she was free, a sort of jailer to ruin a pleasant weekend alone. Approaching Georgetown, it crossed her mind to try to lose him. There was an ideal chance at the Washington Circle. But she didn't. Where would she go? Besides, she knew it would only serve to emphasize the unpleasant remembrance that lay between them—and to his benefit, not hers.

She drove up the gravel driveway of the R Street house and stopped before the door. When he pulled up behind her, she got out of the Lancia and before he could leave the sedan, went to its window, leaned down, and said, "I don't want to be disturbed this weekend, by anyone for any reason. Especially by you. I don't like you. Stay out of my sight. Is that clear?"

"Yes, ma'am." He smiled politely.

The smile infuriated her even more. In the front hall she took out her frustration on Everett. He asked her if she would be in for dinner. She didn't answer. She went to the living room, poured herself a drink, and took it to the safety of her office. Her desk was bare of letters waiting for her signature. Allison, of course, had signed them for her before she left Friday.

She preferred her office to the austere, unlived-in federal formality of the living room and decided to stay there. She closed the door, turned on the television, curled up on the couch with her drink, and began to watch the four o'clock news. The first thing she saw was herself kissing her husband good-bye. Herself, Harold, the smug Assistant Secretary, the TV cameras and journalists, and the big blue Boeing 707 SAM 70. She switched to another channel and "Sesame Street." It was nice looking at something children looked at. She often did. She loved the world they lived in. She could almost feel a child watching with her. When in bookstores, she often browsed the children's section, imagining she had children along or aching to buy books and take them home to read herself. She never did. Sometimes she'd feel foolish at the thought and lose her courage as though the salesgirl would know that she was the one who'd be reading *Winnie the Pooh*. Sometimes she'd decide a child's book at home would be a forceful reminder that there were no children there and that there might not be for some time. It would be painful to have around.

When her telephone rang, it caught her completely by surprise. Almost the only people who ever called on it were Harold and sometimes Sandy. She'd had it installed to duck Allison.

It kept ringing. It had to be a wrong number. She lifted the receiver anyway.

"Hello?"

"Alexis? Hi."

The tone was so familiar it jarred. But for a moment she couldn't place it. "Who's this?"

"Me. Jimmy." Vaguely indignant. As though he called her every day.

"Adrian?"

"Of course. How many Jimmys do you know? How are you?"

It was unreal. "I—I'm fine." On the TV set Oscar was emerging from his garbage can, complaining noisily.

"Good. Because in an hour I'm coming around to take you out to dinner."

"You're what?"

"Taking you out to dinner. So start thinking of where you'd like to go."

Alexis found her voice. "Jimmy, wait a minute." It couldn't be happening, she thought. It was the sort of casual call he used to make four or five times a day. It was as though four years simply hadn't happened.

"Maybe someplace close by in Georgetown," he was saying. "There's a new French cook in a basement in that mews just off Thirty-fourth Street, know the one I mean?"

"Jimmy, you're out of your mind. I can't go out to dinner with you. Not just like this anyway."

"Why not? Harold's off for Lisbon, isn't he? I just saw you kissing him good-bye on the box. Or are they sending out doubles these days?"

"Jimmy." She began to return to reality, to regain control. She was firm. "First of all, I am married and in the public eye. Remember? Newspapers write everything I do. And you are a well-known ex-beau."

"Lover."

"What?"

"Ex-lover. Beau is old-fashioned. What else?"

"Well, maybe I don't want to see you. Did you ever consider that? Five years and you call up, just like that. 'Alexis, I'm taking you to dinner.' And you don't ask, you just tell me."

He laughed. "Neither reason is valid and you know it. Put on dark glasses and a scarf and leave by a back door."

She kept her voice pleasant and calm. "I'm sorry, Adrian James, I've a prior engagement."

"Nonsense."

"Seriously, I do."

"Seriously, you're lying through your teeth, and if you are not, cancel it. I want to see you."

"Jimmy, this is impossible. How did you get this number, anyway?"

"I have friends in the FBI."

She began to laugh. "Jimmy, goddamnit . . ."

"I'll pick you up at seven."

"Jimmy."

It was too late. The receiver at the other end clicked and the line went silent. Alexis stared at the telephone as though it were bewitched. It was extraordinary. What on earth should she do? She couldn't see him; that was out of the question. She could call him back. He must still live at his studio. She tried to remember the number. Once she'd called it constantly. She reached for the phone book. Then she decided she wouldn't call him. She wouldn't give him that. They had said their good-byes five years ago. She'd tell Everett to say she wasn't home, if he really was crazy enough to come. And what could he possibly want, anyway? They had nothing in common anymore. Their worlds and friends were different.

She left her office for the living room, made another drink, and went upstairs and sat at her dressing table. Was the Alexis Sobieski looking back at her from the antique mirror any different from the one who had once made love to Adrian James? She started to remember their love-making, the sight and touch of his body, and the way he made her feel. She shook it off at once.

He'd say, "You're different, Alexis. You're not the same."

"I'm older."

The veiled look, then, of a man who realized the truth might be uncomplimentary and hurt his chances.

"I didn't mean that."

"But it's true."

She looked carefully. There were lines across her forehead and between her eyes and temples that hadn't been there when she'd known him. A weariness.

She tried her television smile. And hated it. It didn't work anymore. It was for a younger woman. Perhaps not younger in years, but younger in weariness. Someone on the make the way she had been. First UBC, then Harold Volker. It was too late for Adrian James—even just to be friendly. And even if he was the perfect answer to Riker, to the Wildersteins, even to Harold's cold refusal to let her go to Lisbon with him. To hell with him. Who did he think he was, anyway?

She ran a bath, got in it with her drink, and tried not to think of him. Or of anything, except Harold somewhere over the Atlantic, talking to journalists and his staff, having cocktails, chatting with pilots.

It didn't work. A sense of excitement had begun to run through her that stopped any thought. She laughed out loud, spontaneously and with a kind of relief that wouldn't stop. A thought had appeared to crowd all others from her mind.

Oh, God, she thought. We women.

She had found herself wondering what to wear.

Fourteen

Sandy sat smoking and thinking about herself and Adrian James. Her bedside clock said five-twenty. He'd gone out around five, brought back more wine, and now was in the shower.

They'd spent the whole afternoon in bed. But she thought, that's what beds were for. Men and women. Naked sexual bodies locked together in hot summer sweat and in a special world of their own where nothing and nobody else existed. Right now, a bed for the purpose of sleep seemed incidental. Her own body rejected any thought of it. She stretched out waiting for him, slender, blonde, athletic, and still languid from being made love to. The lack of femininity in her work, the self-effacement and low profile the job required, carrying a gun, practicing judo, always being alert for sudden violence, it all made her lose sight of being a woman. Now she felt like one and it was good. She didn't want the feeling to leave.

When he'd arrived at one-thirty, she'd produced some grass, they'd smoked, had some wine. He hadn't told her why he was late or what had happened. She hadn't asked. She knew it was important and that he'd tell her when he was ready to. He'd taken her clothes off, then his own, and they'd gone to bed.

One of the things she had done when she was first assigned to Alexis was check out her life. When protecting someone, it helped to know who their friends were, past

90

and present. That way, there were never any surprises nor embarrassments from perhaps being rough with the wrong person, especially on the telephone. She'd looked up a lot of people. James was one of them. She'd been professional, casual, but she'd felt the sexual chemistry at once. And so had he. Two days after they met, they went to bed.

At first it seemed all wrong, but after a while they were both able to disassociate what they had between them from Alexis and when they spoke of her, it was impersonally. She'd wanted to know about his affair with M. J. Lindley and he was candid.

"But if you're not in love with her," she'd asked, "then why are you living with her?"

"Not living. Not really. I keep a few clothes there, but sleep half the time in my own studio." He thought a moment. "She's convenient."

"That's all?"

"Socially speaking. Well, maybe a bit more, I'm very fond of her actually. She's become a way of life. She gives good parties. We get along. Being a bachelor in Washington is a bad scene. You need someone. It's just one of those relationships you drift into, I guess."

"How is she in bed?"

"No great deal, but okay."

They'd also talked about Alexis.

"She was great, but impossible. If it wasn't her goddamn career, she was driving both of us nuts looking for something."

"What do you mean, looking for something?"

"I'm not sure. She kept having the feeling she was missing the boat. That maybe broadcasting wasn't her final thing after all. She'd felt there was something else. She could never put her finger on it."

"Marriage?"

"I guess it must have been."

"Maybe you were scared when she found out she'd decided on you." She laughed.

"Maybe," he admitted.

"Were you in love with her?"

He'd been evasive. "Everybody says I was."

"Are you still?"

"If I am, I'm not aware of it."

"Is that because you never see her?"

"It could be."

"Or maybe you don't see her because you're scared you might find you still feel the same way about her."

"Let's just say I don't see her and I'm okay. I get whatever I need from M. J."

"And me."

"Most certainly you."

It worked both ways, what they got from each other. Their relationship was for sex and sex only, with no other demands. He frequently claimed she was the best lay he'd ever had. She knew he meant it and was flattered. What she got from him in return was beyond any of her expectations. He was uninhibited, liberated, sensitive, and very experienced. He knew a woman's sexual needs as well as he knew his own and a woman's body as well. Sandy didn't really see much in him as a person, but when they made love he'd lead her farther and farther into a kind of sexual limbo where her feelings became so intense and unending as to be almost unbearable. She'd never had any man do that to her. Sometimes she wondered if it was the same for every woman he went to bed with. She figured Alexis had picked the wrong guy. Sandy didn't accept love as a good factor in human relations. It always meant trouble. As far as she was concerned, outside of work men were for sex only.

She heard the shower turn off and he came out of the bathroom, bronzed and lean and beautiful and dripping wet with the towel slung around his shoulders.

She smiled at him. "You have a cock like a horse, do you know that? God!"

He grinned and lay down next to her. "Give it another five minutes." He lit a cigarette and said casually, "I had the FBI in my studio before I came over."

She kept the surprise out of her voice. "What did they want?"

"One FBI, actually. He wanted me to see Alexis."

"How do you mean—see her?"

"Resume seeing her."

"Oh? Why?" Sandy sat up against the headboard.

"He didn't say. He just said to resume our friendship and get her confidence. Any ideas?"

Sandy thought. It was a development she'd hardly expected. She tried to stall to have time to think clearly. "None," she answered. "But it's interesting. What are you going to do?"

"I don't have any choice."

"Why not?"

"If I don't see her, he pulls the plug on M. J. Cocaine."

She whistled. "Who the hell is this guy?"

"His name is Farr. David Farr. Know him?"

She got up. "Not personally. A black guy, right?"

"Yes. Is he important?"

"Yes."

"How important?"

"Next to top level. He's married to a neurosurgeon. You ought to see her. She's much younger. She was an almost Miss America." She laughed. "Maybe you could get revenge by introducing yourself."

She went into the bathroom and turned on the shower. James followed her in.

"Does it bother you if I see her?" He sounded worried.

"Alexis?" She felt vaguely irritated. It was his unexpected insecurity. "Why should it?"

"It's a bit close to home, isn't it?"

She thought again. She'd had a chance to get her mind straight. She didn't like the situation at all, but she'd be damned if she'd give him up. She'd have to try to play it very carefully, seem to care without seeming possessive. And, at the same time, not seem callous.

"Look, Batman," she said, "what you have with me is one thing. What your relationship is with her or with anyone else is another. I'm one part of your life only."

"It's not that simple, is it?" he asked. "She's your boss, no? And your friend, too, sort of."

She didn't answer. She decided to say nothing more for a moment. She soaped and rinsed herself aware of his eyes watching every movement of her hands on her body. That was a good sign. She didn't speak until she'd turned off the water and accepted the towel he handed her.

"Stop worrying." She made her tone friendly and reached up to brush her lips quickly against his. "Maybe she won't go to bed with you."

"The idea isn't bed. And for whatever it's worth, I certainly don't want to go to bed with her."

She shrugged. "That's up to you. As a matter of fact, maybe you should. You might do her a lot more good than Wyndholt." She kissed him again, letting her body touch his. "I mean it. I'm fond of you, Batman, very, but I'm not the jealous type. And don't ever think I might be, okay? I have my own life to lead."

She went into the living room and began to roll a joint. James poured them some wine. "I have to take her to dinner tonight."

"That's all right. What time?"

"Seven-thirty." He brought her wine glass.

She knew the worst was over. She lit the joint and passed it to him and brushed a hand slowly across his chest. "That gives us a whole hour and a half, doesn't it?"

Later when he was getting ready to leave, Sandy said,

"Have you figured out yet why they want you to be friendly with her?"

"No. Not really."

"I thought it was pretty obvious."

"Why?"

"They must be looking for a leak."

"You think so?"

"Well, they sure as hell don't want information on me or you or M. J."

They both laughed, James not as hard. Something had finally sunk in that an afternoon of sex hadn't been able to erase. He was into something over his head and had no control over it. He was okay with Sandy, but he still had to cope with Alexis. Perhaps worse, he had to cope with himself. Alexis was the only woman he had ever really been in love with and breaking up with her had been rough. To see her again might mean all the old wounds would open up. Going down to his car, he thought of David Farr again and cursed him. More than he had ever cursed anyone.

Fifteen

Two days later his feelings hadn't changed. It was nine A.M. Sunday morning and he'd been lying awake for some minutes listening to kitchen sounds. M. J. was getting her children breakfast. Outside her old Victorian house, the shady suburban street off Foxhall where she lived was quiet. The only sound James had heard, other than birds and a far-off muffled television, was a car passing slowly through. M. J. had gently wakened him half an hour earlier when she got up herself. He was supposed to move to the guest room when she did. She wanted to keep up appearances for the children's sake. This morning he hadn't. He felt completely out of it. The children were too young to know what it was all about, anyway, he thought. To hell with it. He tried not to think of what he had to do once he was up. Alexis had asked him to drive down to Brigham Bay with her. Yesterday morning when he called to thank her for dinner the night before, she said the Wildersteins had decided to go to Maine for a wedding, although she thought the real reason was that Arnold was bored. There wasn't any golf at Brigham Bay. Ever since, tension had built in him. Tension and anxiety. In a way, it was worse that Alexis had accepted him and wanted to see him again than it would have been if he'd been politely rejected. Last night he'd taken it out on M. J. as though she were to blame for all of it. He'd drunk too much and had been abusive. She'd left him in the living room and gone to bed in tears. This morning he couldn't remember what he'd said to her. That was bad.

He sat up and tried to organize his thoughts. He was picking up Alexis at eleven. He hadn't told M. J. yet, but he'd made up his lie. He'd wait until breakfast. He thought about Farr again. Since Farr, everything was a lie. Yesterday he'd called him at home. He remembered that while the phone rang, he'd stood at his easel daubing white onto the painting Farr had admired. He'd felt like wrecking the whole canvas just because he had.

A woman answered in a soft, educated voice. He asked for Farr and gave his name. There was no reaction he could identify from the woman. He thought it had to be Farr's wife and tried to visualize her. Sandy had said she was beautiful. Moments later Farr was on the line.

"How did it go?"

"I took her to dinner last night." He found it hard to say anything else. Inside he was raging.

"That was quick. Did she accept you?"

"You mean will she see me again?"

"Yes."

"No problem." He said it reluctantly.

"When is your next meeting?"

"Tomorrow."

"Lunch?"

"Yes."

"Where?"

"Brigham Bay. She wants to show it to me."

"That's good. Ask her about her husband's trip to Portugal."

"Portugal?"

"If she talks about it, remember if she mentions a General Figueira."

"What should I say?"

"Nothing. Just remember. And keep me posted."

He didn't bother to tell Farr how he'd planned his initial contact carefully, even rehearsed what to say to Alexis on the phone. She had a mind of her own. And pride. He hadn't wanted to give her a chance to think. He picked Friday afternoon for his first call because he knew with Volker just departed, she'd be low. But there was no way of being certain his approach would work and when he'd hung up, his palms were sweating. Later, the wait outside her house seemed interminable.

Would she come, or wouldn't she? All she'd said on the phone was no.

Finally, the door opened and the suspense was over. She appeared looking fresh and lovely in a light summer dress and silently got in beside him.

"Hello."

"Hi."

Four years disappeared in an instant. What remained was embarrassment over their estrangement. She sat sideways on the seat studying him, waiting for him to speak. He quickly made up something to say.

"What about your gorilla?"

She laughed. "It's usually a she and she's divine, but she's off. Her name's Sandy. I sent her replacement to buy some cigarettes you can't find anywhere except perhaps at the Portuguese Embassy. He's a real Nazi."

He hadn't expected mention of Sandy so soon. He drove off feeling acutely uncomfortable. It occurred to him that he was bound to meet Sandy in person sometime when with Alexis. The thought was nearly unbearable. He wondered if the same thing had occurred to Sandy.

They were awkward with each other, like kids on a first date, until they got to the restaurant. There, the intimacy of the place relaxed them both. When Alexis appeared hesitant to talk about herself, James let her steer the conversation to him and M. J. He asked her advice. He couldn't go on living with M. J. forever when he knew nothing would ever come of it. What should he do?

"If you walked out on her, Jimmy," she asked, "do you think she'd be badly hurt?"

"I'm not sure."

"Well, does she love you?"

Alexis had. He could see the remembrance of it in her eyes.

"I think she does," he admitted. "But she loves her children, too. More than anything. They always come first. I think she could survive on just loving them and nobody else."

"You can't spend your life walking out on relationships," Alexis said. Her tone became brittle.

"One for you," he said.

"I'm sorry. That wasn't fair, was it?"

Their eyes met and quite unexpectedly communicated the magnetism, all the violence and depth of old feelings.

A certain sadness came over Alexis. She was quiet for a moment, then she said, "I'm glad you called me. I missed you."

"I missed you, too." He wondered what to say next. They had wandered onto dangerous ground. He could tell she thought so, too. The waiter, bustling about with another course, saved them. The difficult moment passed. They began to talk about the political scene and after that in a sort of unspoken truce the evening went well and they caught up on four years of independent life.

Now he heard M. J.'s footsteps on the stairs and then she was sitting on the bed with a steaming mug of coffee and a plate of buttered toast. She wore a satin nightgown with a plunging neckline and her large breasts cleaved deep and stretched hard against the smooth material.

She smiled and kissed him and said good morning. "I'm sorry about last night," he said. He pulled her close and kissed her again.

"Forget it. That was last night."

"Honest?"

99

"Honest. It's the price I pay for being in love."

"You're not wasting your time."

"I hope not."

He decided it was now or never. He sat up with the plate of toast and began his lie. He told her he had to cancel the lunch they'd planned for today with friends. He had to go to New York for a meeting at the Metropolitan Museum.

"I know I should have said something last night. Obviously I got sidetracked being a bastard."

"But, Jimmy, it's Sunday." She looked confused and hurt. He wondered if she knew he was lying.

"I know that. But it's the only time the guy can see me. I'll try to get back in time for dinner. I'm sorry, Mary Jane." He put the toast to one side and pulled her to him, running his hands down her back to her hips. He suddenly wanted to make love to her. Not for sex, but to be very close. She was safety and he needed it. Even if just for a few minutes.

She resisted. "Jimmy, the children."

"Can't you give them some toys or something for half an hour?"

"Darling, you know I can't."

An hour later he left her for his studio. "I have to put on a suit and collect some papers."

Once there he changed into sneakers, jeans, and a faded Lacoste shirt, grabbed up an old sweater in case it rained, opened the roof of his sports car, and headed for Georgetown. Thank God Alexis wanted to go out to the country. If they had stayed in Washington, there'd always be the chance of running into M. J.

At ten sharp, he pulled into Q Street below R and between Twenty-eighth and Twenty-ninth. He parked in the middle of the block and waited.

At five past ten Alexis appeared, running. She took his breath away and made the web of lies almost bearable.

She looked years younger than she had the other night. She wore a light cotton skirt with a gold belt, espadrilles, and a white T-shirt emblazoned with "I Love Whales." She had a silk scarf tied loosely around her neck and was holding a canvas carryall. Her dark glasses were perched on top of her spilled-down golden hair. She was the woman and the face half America had been in love with. Himself included.

She got in his car, breathless.

"Did he see you?"

"No. He was in the hall and said good morning. I told him I was going to Old Alexandria for lunch and to bring my car around. I went to my office and turned on the TV and climbed out a window." She showed him a scratch on her leg and her laughter rippled. "Right into a rose bush."

Ten minutes later, they were on the Capitol Beltway swinging around South-West Washington toward the Potomac and Maryland.

Sixteen

Alexis had an overwhelming desire to share Brigham Bay with someone. It was quite obvious that the Wildersteins kept it only because it was valuable property. Their life was elsewhere. Harold, she knew, didn't care one way or the other. He seemed to have no feeling or sentiment about any property, no matter what it was. He would be as happy in a commercial hotel if there were good service. In view of his great interest in history, it was a side of him she simply couldn't understand. How could he be so oblivious to his surroundings as not to care about something as lovely as the old house with its gardens and lawns and moldering brick walks, with its stately elms and views of the estuary teeming with wild birds and marsh life.

Seeing Adrian James again, she had suddenly realized that where Brigham Bay was concerned, she'd found someone who would unquestionably fall in love with the place the way she had. He only needed it shown to him. When she had asked him to drive down with her, she'd had a twinge of guilt. After all, it was hers and Harold's home. In a way it was disloyal of her to share it with him.

The moment they arrived and he got out of the car, however, her misgivings were forgotten. James's face was a mirror of her own appreciation. Within minutes she was hard put to keep up with him as he impulsively explored every part of the house and the barn.

"Is this where the gorillas live? They would have done better to have kept cows in it. Or turn it into studios."

They filled some tall glasses with iced Chablis and found Samuel down at the old boat house.

"Mr. Wilderstein always said rum runners used this place during prohibition days."

"Do you have a key, Samuel?"

"I wish I did, Miss Volker. And I have no idea where they keep it, either. I could use that Chris-Craft come duck season, 'stead of my old leaky-bottom skiff. But them security people got it locked up all the time like everything else around here, ever since they came. Place gets like a jail sometimes."

They looked around with no success. Alexis went back up to the house and helped Missy fix sandwiches while Samuel talked marsh fishing and duck shooting with James. The old man got lonely sometimes for other men to talk to. The agents paid no attention to him except to order him around. Alexis had spoken twice to Harold about it. Samuel deserved better.

They ate on the terrace. Samuel and Missy took advantage of their presence to go into town to see a movie. They didn't get in often. Whenever she and Harold were there they were needed and they never would leave the house alone.

After lunch, they walked down to the estuary again to the little sandy beach. Adrian James rattled a cocktail shaker of iced white mint. Alexis held out her glass and he refilled it.

"I'm seeing double," she said. It wasn't strictly true, but a rock a few yards offshore was definitely blurred. The branches of one huge oak stretched out over the water. She lay back on the sand and through half-closed eyes looked up through leaves at the dancing amber light which was the sun.

At lunch there'd been no awkward moments or fear of

past unhappiness the way there was Friday. They laughed like school kids and talked about mutual friends they'd had, what had happened to them, where they were now and whether still partners with the same person.

Toward the end of lunch James, with Farr always in the back of his mind, found to his surprise a certain fascination in gathering information. He began with Washington protocol, the White House staff. He asked questions about congressmen.

"When I used to do the news," she said, "most of them were just faces and names. I saw them as the public saw them, even when I was interviewing. Now it's different. The President's a guy with a cold or a hangover or mad at his wife. Or me because I beat him at tennis."

"Is it true he screws around a lot?"

"I guess he does. She's a cold bitch. But he's very discreet."

After a while they talked about her. James didn't start it; Alexis did. Looking at his lean Semitic face and his intense eyes, she'd suddenly wanted him to know.

"It isn't Harold," she said. "He's the one thing that's right. It's the goddamn life. It's not what I quit television for. I quit it for a home and babies. I'm not getting either. Harold wants to wait until he's out of office, but if he goes for another term with the President, then I'll be too old. That's a problem men don't have. Age and childbearing. That's a nightmare which was handed out exclusively to women."

"What are you going to do?"

"I don't know," she said. She looked up again at the sun shimmering through the leaves and branches. "The other day I decided to hell with him, I'd get pregnant. Now I'm not sure."

James poured them both more white mint. Alexis drank hers, then held out her glass for another. She was beginning to feel drunk and didn't care. She could get drunk

104

with Jimmy, as drunk as she wanted. He'd seen all the worst in her. She didn't have to make any pretenses.

When he lay down, putting his head on her lap, she didn't protest. It was like old times. She ran her fingers through the thick shambles of his hair and said, "I don't know whether to cheat Harold and just do it or play fair and try to change his mind, or, just give up."

"Give up how?"

"Maybe go back to television. Part-time anyway. I could go back to UBC with my tail between my legs, maybe. Or maybe accept an offer from another network. Who knows? Maybe they wouldn't even have me. I hardly see a face I know on the box anymore."

James propped up on an elbow and turned to face her. "Aren't you confusing marriage with Harold with marriage in general? Maybe you made a mistake and picked the wrong guy. Millions of women have. You have to figure out what's more important to you. It doesn't have to be Harold or back to television. It's maybe Harold or someone else who doesn't mind washing dishes and taking care of babies and the shitty mess they make all over the house."

She giggled. "You make it sound so awful."

"Babies are."

He lay back down and curled a free arm around one of her upraised knees, elbow between her thighs, hand on her knee.

Alexis felt his touch race up into her. She thought, I shouldn't be down here with him. I ought to tell him to sit up. Or move away from him. She tried to think of Harold and couldn't. What would he be doing now? He seemed to be on another planet. There was only the shimmering sun and the leaves and James whom she knew she still loved in a funny way. And wondering how you could love two men at once.

She heard him say, "Are you sure you're not confusing

105

love for Harold with an obsession to make marriage work out the way you wanted it to. Just the way you were obsessed with getting to the top in television?"

"It's a different thing," she said. "I really want this and I didn't really want television."

"That sounds like *Alice in Wonderland*," he said. "The Red Queen. It takes all the running you can do to remain in the same place."

"It's *Through the Looking Glass*," Alexis said. She half sat up. She felt she had to defend Harold. "Anyway, you don't just walk out on someone you love. Well, maybe you do, Adrian James. I don't. Why do you find it so impossible that I might love Harold?"

"I don't find it impossible. Just improbable. He's not like other men."

"I'm not married to other men."

She thrust out her glass angrily. He took it, removed the lid from the shaker, and handed the shaker itself to her. She drank directly from it. She couldn't see the offshore rock anymore. Even the water looked blurred.

"He's brilliant and charming," she said, "and he's good in bed. I'd be lying if I said he wasn't."

"And best of all he's Secretary of State."

"You bastard. That was plain nasty." She tried to get up. He gently pushed her down.

"You're right. It was. I'm sorry. Let's change the subject."

She didn't resist. She was suddenly fed up with even thinking about her marriage. Or anything else. She only wanted to enjoy the interloping weight of James's head on her stomach, the feeling of his hand on her thigh, the blissful irresponsibility of being drunk. The water was shallow and sandy right there. Once more she wanted to strip and throw herself onto the water, just the way she'd wanted to the last time she'd been there. Now she would. Missy and Samuel would be gone for hours. The sun had moved slightly, its rays fractured into golden wheel spokes. It was hard to speak, her words were slurred. "You know something. You really are a bastard and I love it out here with you."

"You're drunk, that's why."

"That's not the only why and you know it."

He rolled over to stretch out beside her, propped up on one elbow, searching her face. She turned her own head to look at him. His tanned face was suddenly very close to her and his dark eyes swam out of focus. She knew he was going to kiss her.

"Jimmy, no. We mustn't."

But she wanted him to. More than anything. He blurred completely. She felt the warmth of his skin, then his lips and the coolness of his open mouth against hers, his tongue soft against hers, the old kiss she knew so well and had nearly forgotten. And then the gentle pressure of his fingers covering one of her breasts.

She closed her eyes. She didn't want him to stop. She stayed motionless, not even breathing, letting her own mouth begin to respond to his, letting herself flow with the sensations she felt.

Then she felt him move away.

"You're worse than a bastard," she said. She meant it. "Now you're going to walk off and leave me again."

"I have to, don't I? You're married."

"Oh, Jesus. You pig." She started to sit up again. He pushed her back down quickly and kissed her hard, forcing a response. He said, "Don't you dare move. Don't you dare. And don't say no."

He began to pull up her T-shirt. She saw his eyes were dark and uncontrolled.

It was like the old days. When he wanted her, he'd just taken her. No matter where they were. Or what the obstacle. Her heart began to race, and a weakness spread through her limbs. She thought, I've drunk too much and

107

got myself into a mess. This isn't the old days, this is now and I'm married to Harold and I love him. Everything in her cried out. She had to stop it, but she knew she couldn't because she didn't want to. Sometime during lunch she'd suddenly wanted more than talk. She'd wanted the strength and masculinity of his body making love to her, the security she knew she'd feel the moment he entered her. The way she'd always felt it. To hell with afterward. She wanted him.

His hand was on her breast once more. She pressed it close, feeling the warmth it poured down into her body, saying yes with her own hand.

She accepted his mouth again and when his weight moved over her she tightened her arms around his neck kissing his face and hair. Wanting him had become everything. She felt the long hardness of his sex against her, his hand between her thighs. She fumbled blindly at his belt. She could think only of being filled by him completely.

Later, there would be time for slower love, for her making love to him. For doing all the wonderful, loving things a woman could do to a man. For swimming together and making love again on the sand. They could make love all evening and all night if they wanted. She'd find an excuse for Missy and Samuel. Harold was away and she didn't have to go back to Washington if she didn't feel like it. She owed this moment to herself. For the past and for the present, too.

Seventeen

Only three days later M. J. Lindley received an anonymously posted envelope containing a dozen photographs. She knew quite a bit about photography. She used a good camera and took excellent pictures of her friends and family. After studying the photos a few minutes, she very carefully placed them side by side on the dining room table. They were 8 by 10 glossies and were very clear, every detail distinct. It was extraordinary, she thought, considering they must have been taken with a 500 millimeter telephoto lens. Some of the views were through a window into a semidarkened bedroom and taken from a tree or another house, probably. The photographer would have used extra high-speed film.

Emotionally, she was numb. When she first opened the envelope, she was so surprised at what they were that she'd thought they were pornography sent to her by mistake. It had taken half a minute for her to realize the male was Adrian James and then she was so shocked that although she recognized Alexis Volker at once, she couldn't fit the familiar face with a name.

The really terrible thing about such pictures, she thought, was that nobody could bear to look at them, but always did. There was no question of when they had been taken. There was one nonsexual picture of Adrian and Alexis walking past his parked car on their way into some lovely old country home. The car's license plate was clearly visible. It established the year as now. Because the trees were in full leaf and Alexis was wearing a light summer skirt and a T-shirt saying "I Love Whales," it had to be this summer. Five of the pictures were in the bedroom and seven were taken on a small beach.

Who had taken them? Why were they sent to her? She found it difficult to breathe. It wasn't so much the infidelity itself, or the sexual intimacy. It was the open look of rapture on their faces.

She put the photos back in their envelope. In a few minutes he would arrive. She'd called him at his studio immediately to say she had to see him. It was urgent. Just that. He'd said he'd come right over. She tried to think of what she would say, but she couldn't. She couldn't even think of how she felt. And it was important to recognize her real feelings, not stand on false pretenses. Wasn't sexual infidelity common with nearly everyone? If she was hurt, was it because of whom he was unfaithful with? Did the pictures say Alexis still had emotional priority in his life?

She couldn't find answers. In one picture they were doing something she'd always thought she shared exclusively with him. That was now destroyed.

A painful knot in her stomach grew still tighter. She knew she should try to concentrate on why the pictures were taken, and why they'd been sent to her. But she couldn't. What was in the pictures overwhelmed everything else.

She heard the sound of his key in the front door. The door opened and shut, his footsteps were in the hall.

"Darling?"

She heard him go into the living room, call again, then run up the stairs. His footsteps were overhead, his voice muffled. He came down again, went into the kitchen.

"M. J.! Where are you?"

110

He burst into the dining room, stopped short seeing her so unexpectedly. "Oh. There you are. What's up? I came as fast as I could." When she didn't speak, a wary look came over him. "What's the matter? M. J.? Hey! Are you all right?"

She had begun to cry. She couldn't help it. She felt the tears brim silent and scalding from her eyes. She felt the wet taste of their salt in her mouth. And she felt short and dowdy and old. Alexis was slender and beautiful. She was not.

"For Christ's sake, speak to me. Is it one of the children?"

She handed him the envelope and waited.

"What's this?" He stared at it blankly, then held open the flap and peered in. He couldn't see and pulled the photographs out, impatiently throwing the envelope on the table.

He looked at them one by one. In silence. It seemed forever. The only sound was once when she sniffed hard and hated herself for it. It made her seem like a child. Her body shuddered with the effort not to break down completely. She couldn't bring herself to look at him.

When he finally spoke, his voice was harsh with shock and fear. "Who sent you these?"

She didn't answer.

A chair scraped. He put the photographs back in the envelope and sat down.

"I'm sorry," he said. "Believe me, I'm desperately and deeply sorry." After a moment he said, "Oh, God, how awful for you." And then, once more. "Who sent them? Don't you know? Goddamn them!"

She found her voice, surprised at its controlled coldness. "I wouldn't know. There wasn't any letter. I suppose whoever took them. When was it? Last weekend when you were in New York?"

"Something like that."

She began to laugh. "I Love Whales," she said. And laughed harder. It felt good, a release.

He jumped up, seized her by the shoulders. "M. J., listen! We couldn't help it. We drank too much and it just happened."

She shook him off violently and suddenly she was screaming. "Take your hands off me. Don't touch me." That felt good, too, to scream, to let it all out. She kept on. "Son of a bitch. Don't you dare touch me."

"M. J. It doesn't mean anything. It won't happen again. Ever."

She took the envelope and went into the living room across the hall. He followed. She said, suddenly calm, "Jimmy, I don't really care whether it does or not."

She poured herself a stiff drink. It made him angry, but he tried not to lose his patience. "Look, I know you're hurt. You should be. You probably hate me. Okay. But we've got to talk about these things. Who took them and why? And why did they send them to you? There could be a lot of trouble here."

She shrugged and turned her back.

"M. J., for God's sake don't shut me out. We've got to talk."

The fury came back, tight-lipped, controlled. He was right. There was serious trouble somewhere. But that didn't matter. What mattered was him and Alexis. She heard herself say, "I just want you to do one thing. Pack your clothes. Right now. I want you out of here before my children come home from their gym class."

James lost his temper. He grabbed her arm and spun her around to face him. "Look, you stupid idiot. Forget all that shit. We're in trouble. Now let's start with the reason I went to see her in the first place. It wasn't my idea. I went because I had to. Because of you. And that's the only reason."

"Oh, please." She laughed again. "Because of me?"

But something in his voice made her stop and look at him, finally. His eyes were frantic. "It's true," he said. "The FBI got hold of me and told me to start seeing her again. Do you think I'm crazy? After what I went through leaving her?"

M. J. experienced a sudden draining weariness. It had to be a lie and in a way that was worse than the photos. "You don't have to make up stories, Jimmy."

"I'm not making it up. They told me if I didn't, they'd take action against you for cocaine. They said Lindley would be the first to know."

M. J. sat down slowly. It was the truth. Nobody would invent that. She'd thought nothing could be worse than the pictures. And it was. The room stood still. Adrian James was frozen motionless before her. She heard her own heartbeat. She heard him say, "Somebody must have talked." And finally her own voice. She asked the question aloud. One word. "Who?"

"I don't know. Maybe the guy you get it from?"

Maybe. But did it make any difference? Her mind leapt. Imaginations. People were at the door. Police. She was arrested. Photographers. A courtroom. A judge. Lindley taking the children away. The bars of a cell. Caught for coke when everyone in Washington used it. It wasn't fair. Only she was caught.

She heard him saying her name. From far off. She didn't reply. She thought of Oregon and her family's home outside Portland. They'd have a tough time getting her back from there. But she'd have to be careful. She couldn't let anyone know she was going. How long would it take to move? A day? Two days?

"I'm going to try to get out of it, M. J. Honestly. I'm going to tell them it just isn't working."

"It doesn't make any difference, Jimmy. It's over. I don't want any part of this. Did you really expect I would?

113

It isn't just you and Alexis. It isn't just that. It's what you've done to my life. One day, there's this, the house, the children. Us. Maybe marriage, I don't know. The next day, it's dirty pictures in the mail and the FBI and possibly getting busted on a drug charge."

"But can't you see, it's none of it my fault?"

She laughed. All of a sudden, he appeared ridiculous. "Is it mine?" she demanded. "Well, is it?"

A veiled look came into his eyes. "I'll pack up," he said. He walked out of the dining room and she heard him go upstairs.

How long would it take? He didn't keep much there. Some toilet articles. Jeans, some shirts, underwear, socks. He'd never really moved in. They'd agreed he wouldn't. People who came to dinner always seemed to pry about. She didn't want to go public with James until she and Lindley were officially divorced. Besides, there were the children. She wondered briefly if Lindley used coke, too, now he was at the White House. He had when they were still together. If he did, she'd never prove it. And even if she could, they'd whitewash it.

The envelope was on the sideboard and seemed almost a thing of the past. The coke had taken over. The coke and now, unexpectedly, Jimmy packing up and leaving.

She felt the first hurt of it. A stab of fear. Wouldn't it be better, perhaps, if they did stay together? He was right. They had to find out who sent the pictures. Maybe together they could work it out better.

An ache grew. She went into the hall and waited. Maybe she'd reacted wrongly. She loved him, that was something she had to face. And if you loved someone, you forgave them. He'd been desperately in love with Alexis when he'd left her four years ago. To see her again, to pick up again, must have been very hard. And he was weak, she'd always known that, deep down. And everyone fell from grace once in a while. The really hurtful person

114

was the one who took the photographs. Why would someone do something so awful? Why?

He came downstairs, face set, carrying a suitcase and what he couldn't get into it slung over one arm. She tried to speak, but she couldn't. She saw him in the photographs again. With Alexis.

"I said I was sorry." He studied her, eyes forgiving. "I meant it. When you want to talk let me know."

Then he just stood there, waiting. All she had to do was reach out. He'd take her up to bed and everything would be all right. Somehow together they'd get rid of the FBI and the drug problem, too. Somehow.

She couldn't move.

"Suit yourself," he muttered. "You just half-killed me, but that's your prerogative."

The door closed behind him. When she finally reached out, he couldn't see she had.

She sat on a hard chair in the hall and began to cry again. After a while she went back to the living room and collected the envelope of photos from the sideboard. She took it to the kitchen, got a pair of heavy shears from a drawer, and very methodically began to cut the envelope and the photographs into tiny pieces, dropping them in a sporadic shower into the garbage disposal.

There was tomorrow. She'd find a way to let him know it was all right.

Eighteen

Daylight slowly ebbed away. Adrian James sat before the open, sliding-glass doors of his studio's garden. Beyond its Japanese symmetry the light-gray brick wall of the warehouse was now dark shadow.

He saw neither. His glass was empty and warm in his hand. Instead, he saw himself and Alexis, naked and starkly revealed in the maelstrom of their sex, their bodies pale, awkward, obscene, the visual antithesis of everything they felt. How had he ever been stupid enough to let it happen? And who had been watching? What nameless sick horror had smirked and pressed a camera's shutter release again and again and again. And why? Why take photographs? Why send them to M. J.? Would more be sent to someone else? And when?

Mentally, he once again ran down an endless list of his friends and M. J.'s friends, trying to think who might be an enemy. Once again, he got nowhere. It had to be someone connected with Alexis. But again, why involve M. J.? Around in a circle. Back to square one.

He rose to put more ice into his glass and more vodka. This morning and M. J. seemed a lifetime ago. Her rage and misery, his own shock and guilt. Could it have been Lindley? Private detectives? Looking for evidence in a custody suit? If so, did Lindley know about him and Sandy? That could be even worse. For him, for Alexis, for everyone.

The studio was nearly dark now. He turned on a light and shivered. Someone could be watching him right now from the far shadows of the garden. He drew the drapes and punched in his stereo. Vivaldi's *Four Seasons* whispered from every corner.

He had to pull himself together. He'd put off calling Alexis all day, but she had to be warned at once. Had they sent pictures to her, too? She would have called him. And what about Volker? Suppose he got duplicates when he came back from Portugal. And Farr had to be notified. Tonight. He dreaded it, but he had to do it. Right now.

He went to the telephone, lifted the receiver, hesitated. Maybe he should call M. J. first. The photos were too serious for them to be fighting. They had to stick together, think it out. But calling her had to be timed just right. She needed time to seriously reconsider, but not too long. Too long and she would resent his not calling sooner. Too soon and she'd still feel she had to stand on pride.

He hesitated again. No. Once more, do it. Now.

He started to dial. The doorbell rang. Once, twice. The sound shocked him. He was expecting no one. Who was it?

He got a grip on himself. It could be a parcel, a delivery he'd forgotten, a neighbor, anything. He went to the speaker by the door to the hall and asked. There was no answer. There were two apartments above him. Someone must have rung his bell by mistake.

The bell sounded again. He went into the building's carpeted foyer to the front door and looked through the peephole. He could see nobody. He called, "Who is it?" There was no answer. He yanked the door open. There were only the empty front steps and the empty street beyond. His fear fled. He laughed with relief. They'd given up, gone away. Or discovered they had the wrong building. He tested the door to make certain it was locked and

117

went back to his studio, locking its door behind him and putting on the chain, softly humming to the Vivaldi.

When he turned and saw the two men standing by his easel, the sheer surprise of their presence tore a cry from his throat. They were hatless and wore ordinary light summer business suits. One had gray hair and was older. The other, younger and stockier, was getting bald. They'd come through the garden. It was the only way. Distracted him with the bell and slipped down the narrow alley that flanked the building and vaulted the garden wall. He knew immediately he was in serious trouble. They were wearing gloves.

He found his voice. "What do you want?" And simultaneously wondered what he could use for a weapon. There was a poker by the fire, but the younger man was standing close to it. Under the overhang of the sleeping loft was the kitchenette and a knife rack. Better still, there was a cleaver slotted into a butcher block. If he could get to it and back to the stairs, there was a telephone by his bed.

Then he saw the revolver, its round cylinder exposed above the older man's half-clenched gloved fingers which curled around the butt. A thick dark steel tube projected from its barrel. It had to be a silencer.

He managed to speak again. "Listen, what do you want? Who are you?" There was no answer. He tried to sound unafraid and reasonable. "Help yourself, then. The silver's over there, it's not worth that much. There's the stereo, I don't use television." He pulled his wallet from his hip pocket and tossed it onto the nearby couch.

The younger man came over, picked it up, looked through it.

"Seventy-five dollars," James said. "That's all. Sorry. And I'm up to my limit on the MasterCard."

The younger man silently handed the wallet to the older

man who flipped it open, glanced at various credit cards, and spoke for the first time. "Your name?"

"James. Adrian James."

The older man nodded, waved the revolver at the desk. "Please sit down." He had a flat voice, neither uneducated nor cultured. His sallow skin nearly matched his graying hair. James noticed his tie for the first time. It was the same color. And he was sweating. Beads of it dotted his forehead.

"Sure. But can't you tell me what you want?"

The revolver waved at the desk again.

James sat down. Both men came to stand just behind him, one to each side.

The older man said, "You will write a note."

"To whom? What for?" His skin prickled with the feeling he would be hit on the back of the head. He shrank forward.

"Just write what we tell you. Get some paper."

James pulled a sheet of paper from a slotted cubicle over the desk.

"A pen."

He found a Bic in his pencil tray.

The older man produced a small notebook from his pocket, opened it, and prepared to read. "You will write the following, 'My darling.' Go ahead. Write it."

James obeyed. "I wish to Christ you'd tell me what this is all about."

" 'My darling. I am deeply sorry for what I have done but I couldn't help it.' "

He waited. James wrote. He went on.

" 'Please try to forgive me. Kiss the children and take care of yourself. I love you, Jimmy.' "

James finished writing and waited again.

"An envelope."

He found one.

"Write on it, 'For M. J. Lindley.' "

"That's all?"

"Just that. Now put the note in it."

He obeyed once more.

"And now, please stand."

He tried to speak and couldn't. A terror had begun deep inside him and had risen in his chest to choke back all sound. He did what he was told, his legs so weak he didn't think he could make it.

"Your hands behind your back."

From the corner of his eye he saw the young man produce a scarf and step behind him. He felt the cloth wrap expertly around his wrists and tighten. There was a jerking sensation as a knot was pulled tight.

"Now upstairs," the older man ordered. "Don't try anything foolish. I don't want to have to shoot you."

The revolver appeared close to his face, its silencer pressed against his cheek, pushing his head around. He turned, felt something prod into his back. The same revolver? Or another?

"Go ahead."

He went to the stairs and started up them to the loft. The spiral was steep and it was hard with his arms behind his back. He stumbled awkwardly. Hands held him firmly, urging him upward. They'd leave him there while they got away. He couldn't come down by himself, not tied the way he was.

When he reached the top, the older man handed the revolver back to the younger man. He showed James a folded handkerchief. "I'm going to have to gag you. We can't have you calling out. Do you understand?"

There was no chance even to nod. The revolver pressed against the back of his neck. "A little discomfort. Don't resist. It will make it worse."

It had to be just robbery. He clung to the thought. It couldn't be more than that. Just a holdup. But why the

120

note to M. J.? He couldn't think further. Terror was like a silent barrier.

"Open your mouth."

The dryness of the handkerchief made him gag. He tried to wrench away and for the first time knew they could do whatever they wanted with him. A hand shot between his legs, grabbed his genitals. Another pushed against a nerve just beneath his jawbone. The pain numbed. He was lifted to his toes.

The older man's voice was sharp. "Don't struggle."

He forced himself to balance, not move. A scarf was tied across his face to hold the handkerchief in his mouth. He gagged again, cried out. The sound muffled silent before it reached his lips. Something tugged at his ankles. He looked down. The younger man was tying his feet together. If they'd only lower him to the bed, let him rest.

Now nausea. In hot waves. He wanted to vomit. And then something light and narrow circled his head, falling, striking his shoulders. Hands turned him to face the loft's balustrade. And he saw the nylon cord. The younger man wasn't quick enough leading it back from his neck to the corner radiator.

He saw and simultaneously understood. A wildness seized him, a panicked violence. He began to leap and buck and smash with his body. He had to get away. He had to.

Arms pinioned him.

"Hurry up." It was a hiss. The older man.

"Jesus God, no, no." He thrashed, fell, the older man crashing down on him. "No, no, no."

He heard the screams, animal-wild and distorted in his ears by the gag. There was a darkness before his eyes.

The screams went on and on.

Suddenly there were two faces close to his, the younger man had finished with the rope.

"His legs. Quick."

121

One face disappeared. The older man's. He felt his legs jerk from under him, fly up, his whole body lift.

And seem to hurtle outward over the balustrade. He saw the floor of the studio below him, his couch, and the painting on the easel.

They flew at him. There was a terrible blow on his neck and blackness.

Nineteen

A cleaner found his body in the morning, hanging by the neck from the balustrade of the bedroom loft, feet only inches from the floor. Death had been instantaneous. The third and second cervical vertebrae were shattered, the atlas torn half out of the skull. As though to make certain, the thin nylon cord had bitten deep into the flesh, crushing the larynx and shutting off the trachea and the carotid arteries as well.

The hands hung limply by the thighs, the face had turned black, the tongue protruded. A pool of blood, urine, and fecal matter spread out over the studio's polished floor, slowly drying.

The Homicide Division of the Metropolitan police took charge. Forensic experts busied themselves. Photographs were taken. Although there was no sign of breaking and entering or of any struggle and although James's death was immediately accepted as suicide, the whole studio was routinely dusted for fingerprints. The note to M. J. Lindley was soon discovered where it had been left on James's desk. She was questioned the same day and afterward, until the funeral, was placed under a doctor's care. The coroner issued an immediate statement that the deceased had committed suicide while under severe emotional stress.

The police also briefly interviewed Alexis Volker, the wife of the Secretary of State. As Alexis Sobieski, she had once virtually lived with the dead man and had been seen in his company the previous weekend. She did not cancel any official engagements and dined at the White House the night after. Through her appointments secretary, she issued a statement saying she was deeply grieved at the tragedy. Nothing more. The following weekend, she attended a performance of a Tennessee Williams play at the Kennedy Center in the company of State Department friends and afterward went to a party for the playwright.

This was the basic information gleaned by Susan Farr from *The Washington Post* and *The New York Times*. Clippings from both newspapers lay on the cocktail table and the floor of her living room. There wasn't that much. James was not known to the public, there are scores of suicides every week in America's big cities, and his connection to Alexis was too obscure for a feature story. Susan had also glanced through a copy of the coroner's report her husband had brought home.

It was late in the evening, she'd read all of it when she'd come home from work, letting her husband get dinner. Since then she'd simply sat and tried to help him with his anxieties and the guilt he obviously felt. She wondered if anyone down at the FBI ever saw that side of him. She doubted it. He had been wearing a track in the living room rug for two hours. Back and forth, back and forth. A caged animal, seething with frustration.

James's suicide was not acceptable to David Farr. He told Susan bluntly that Adrian James had been murdered. "He was bound, gagged, the rope put around his neck," he said, "and then heaved off the loft. They must have used scarves to tie him. Silk probably, so there weren't any marks. And some sort of material as a gag that wouldn't shed any lint we could identify."

"But there wasn't any struggle."

"Snake and rabbit," Farr said. "He was psyched from the moment they walked in."

124

The horror of it numbed Susan, even though as a doctor she was used to violent death.

"Do you want some coffee, David?"

"No thanks. I'd never get to sleep."

"How about a drink?"

He stopped pacing to glance at his watch. It was just past midnight. He grinned wryly. "Too early in the day."

"Well, then a glass of milk and don't say no."

"Okay."

She slipped out to the kitchen and poured a tall glass of milk and thought how lucky she was to have him. He was a man who cared. When he committed himself he did so all the way with no reservations. There weren't many like that. She took back the milk and stood close to him while he drank it, gently rubbing his back with one hand. He was so big, she thought. She only came up to his shoulder. She always wondered how a man like him, in the blind passion of love, never seemed to lose control and hurt a woman with his weight and strength. She wished he'd make love to her tonight, it had been weeks now, but she knew he wouldn't. He was still too immersed in the Volker business. She must be careful how she handled him and not add to his anxiety.

"Thanks," he said. "That was good." He handed back the glass, and sank down on the couch, forearms across his knees, head in his clasped hands. Susan knew some of the tension was finally going out of him. She stood next to him to massage the knots from his neck.

"David, I understand where you've been coming from all night, but you've got to stop it."

"How can I? I got the poor bastard into it."

"Correction. If I've read correctly, he was a guy whose life-style was heading him straight for disaster of some sort, anyway. You were just the instrument. Did you talk to Fein?"

125

"Yeah. Scared the hell out of him, too."

"Who does he think did it?"

"Same as me."

"Are you sure?"

"No. But we have to presume it's KGB, don't we? For security's sake. We have to presume it just the way we have to presume they linked James to me somehow and were sure he might sooner or later pass on something they don't want me to know."

"Like evidence to back up the memorandum?"

"Could be." He shook his head. "This mess makes it look less and less of a joke, doesn't it?"

Susan shivered. She'd thought of James again. How could one not? Bound, gagged, thrown off the loft. Had he realized what was happening?

She heard her husband. "I blew it, Susan, but I didn't just blow Adrian James. I blew a lot of other stuff. For a start I blew any inside link to Volker." When she started to protest, he held up a cautioning hand. "No, I did. But you're right, feeling sorry for myself is no solution. I've got to move. And now. I'm not sure of how or where, but I've got to."

"Will you take it to the Director?"

"God?" Farr laughed. The Director had no law enforcement background. His only qualifications for his job were an inside track to the White House and influential friends on the Senate Committee that had cleared his appointment. He was completely dependent on the Bureau's career professionals to keep from making a public fool of himself and few had any respect for him. "I'll have to, won't I?" Farr said. "Among other things there's Alexis Volker to think about. Suppose they decide I'm hooked into her, too."

Susan's eyes widened. "They wouldn't dare."

"You think not?" He grimaced cynically. "A 'suicide' for James, how about a 'car accident' for her?" He rose from the couch. "I'm going to bed. Coming?" She kissed him lightly. "I want to watch the late movie."

His eyes were worried. "Don't you operate in the morning?"

"Yes, a malignancy on the first temporal. A woman. It's all right. I work better with my eyes shut."

He laughed and went off. Susan felt let down. She wanted to talk more. There were still unanswered questions. How had the KGB, if they really were involved, linked James to the FBI, for example? Had James talked to someone he should not have talked to? But she knew David Farr well enough not to pursue the matter further. He'd shut off. When he wanted to, he'd tell her.

She felt very tired and hoped he'd go to sleep quickly so she could go to bed, too. She'd only stayed downstairs to keep the pressure off him.

She turned on the television and curled up on the couch and tried to forget about James and concentrate on the movie. It was hard to. In spite of the warmth of the night she shivered and clasped her bare shoulders with her hands. Something that had begun in such a nebulous way had become very real and very ugly. She had a feeling it was going to get worse.

Twenty

At eight o'clock the same morning, David Farr commuted into downtown Washington. He didn't go to the Hoover Building. Instead he drove to the Executive Office Building, which had once housed the State Department. He showed his security pass at the gates of West Executive and waited patiently while it was checked out on a computer.

The guard pointed at a long line of cars, parked nose into the curb. "You'll find a place about halfway down, sir."

"Thank you."

The barrier rose. Farr drove on, parked, and went to the building's main East entrance. He showed his pass again and waited for a second check out before he was admitted. His appointment was upstairs and he still had five minutes to make it. He crossed one of the open courtyards in the building's center, climbed a broad marble staircase, and went down a long, high-ceilinged corridor. The architecture was among the best of Washington's eloquent Victoriana. It had style. Farr thought that Adrian James must have appreciated it.

At the end of a corridor, he reached a massive oak door with a high ornate transom. He knocked. There was no answer. He swung it open and entered what had been the State Department's reference library and now was a frequent meeting place for the National Security Council. A relatively small but well-proportioned room for such a place, it was dominated by the long conference table in its center and by a double tier of balconies which rose above it and housed shelf after shelf of beautifully bound books.

Farr sat down at the head of the table. What decisions must have been made there and how many important government figures must have climbed the narrow stairs to those balconies in search of information. Lost in thought, he was unaware of Sandy Muscioni coming in until she pulled out the chair next to him.

"Hi." She looked hurried and flushed. "Sorry if I kept you waiting."

He returned her greeting. "Where did you park?"

"On East Executive." She smiled. "I did a few traffic tricks. Just in case."

Farr nodded. He hadn't wanted to take any chances on their being seen together. Any contact between them since he'd first dummied phone threats five months ago to Alexis Volker as the way to put Sandy on the inside, had been made with utmost caution. When she telephoned and said she wanted to see him, he had arranged they park in different places and at different times. Sandy was supposed to arrive first. Her access from the East Executive to the Executive Building would have been across the White House grounds. It was unlikely that anyone hostile would have seen her come over to join him.

"Okay," he said. "What's it all about?"

On the telephone, she had only told him she had information pertaining to James's suicide.

She was thoughtful. Then she said. "Well, it occurred to me if there was anything suspicious about James's death that I might be the reason." She waited, meeting his eyes with a level look.

Farr took it in. It was quite a revelation already. He said cautiously, "Tell me first what you thought suspicious."

"He wasn't the type to kill himself, that's all. Certainly not over Alexis Volker and most certainly not over M. J. Lindley. He was murdered."

Farr smiled. "I take it you knew him, then. How did that happen?"

"When I started the job," she explained, "the first thing I did was run a thorough check on anyone Alexis had ever known. Well, at least for the last five years. I did it for two reasons. First of all, I wanted a complete picture of her life. Secondly, and more importantly, because that's what you put me on the job for, I wanted to see if there was anyone who had been in her life at one time who had reentered it recently."

Farr nodded. "In case the KGB did what I wanted to do with James. Infiltrate socially?"

"Exactly."

"And?"

"I found nobody. When Alexis left broadcasting, she really left it. She hasn't seen one friend from the old days. Nobody reentered her life."

"Which means if the Defector Report is right and there is someone on the inside, it definitely has to be staff or security."

"That's correct. Which would also fit in with the bug I found. You probably heard about it. I turned it over to the Security Director."

Farr grinned. "He sent it to our lab."

"My boss thinks Nasciemento was responsible."

"Do you?"

"I didn't try to tell him he was wrong."

"Does he suspect your connection with us?"

She smiled. "No. Not at all."

"Good. Go on."

Sandy, Farr thought, suddenly looked embarrassed. She said, "You're probably not going to like this. You'll think it very unprofessional of me. I don't think so myself, under

130

the circumstances, because at the time I had no idea in a million years you'd ever use James. Why should I? As far as Alexis was concerned, he might as well have been in China." She took a deep breath and continued. "When he told me you'd contacted him, it really threw me a curve. It seemed a fantastic coincidence."

"Ah." Farr finally understood.

"I'm sorry. I honestly didn't see anything wrong with it. I mean, how it could affect my job in any way. He hadn't seen Alexis in years. He was single. So was I. And the chemistry was pretty strong."

Farr cursed inwardly. Just the same, he had to be fair. It was true, there was no way she ever could have known and people were entitled to their private lives. Even people in her profession. The fact that she was a counteragent didn't change anything, certainly not human nature.

He said, "All right. These things happen. It would have been better if you'd told me right off, but I understand why you didn't feel you needed to. Meanwhile we must both have come to the same conclusion about linking James to me. If it is the KGB, they couldn't afford to see your relationship with him as innocent. Anyway, people in our business don't tend to look at things that way. They would have had to presume, because he contacted you away from the Volker home, that he was possibly affiliated with us." He paused, frowning. "I don't like where that now might leave you, Sandy."

She grinned wryly. "Neither do I. Much."

"We'll have to pull you out."

She shook her head. "No. It's too late."

"Why?"

"Because that would blow it for anybody else you put in, wouldn't it? I mean, pulling me out now would in effect be an admission that I was a plant in the first place, so anyone replacing me would be instantly suspect."

Farr knew she was right. He told her so. He said, "I'm

131

sorry to ask this, but do you think James went to bed with Mrs. Volker?"

She thought a moment. "I don't know. I rather suspect he did." She smiled. "It's all right, we weren't that close. Not to shock you with too much women's lib, it was quite honestly just physical between us. Nothing more."

Farr decided not to comment. He thought first of the world of lies and half-lies Sandy lived in, a world where almost anything would seem moral. Then he thought of Susan. Had she ever said that to another man about him? He thought of their life together and her gentle sympathy and tact about his recent sexual failure and was sure she never had. He asked Sandy, "When he told you about me, did he seem upset?"

"I think he was. A little."

"Did he tell you what kind of persuasion I used?"

"Coke? Yes. But it wasn't that, so much. He was a pretty cold-blooded guy. He was mostly upset because he was afraid of seeing Alexis again. It took him a long while to get over their affair."

"I always understood he was the one who'd busted it up."

"He was. But it was self-defense. He was crazy in love with her. It's just that she was going through a whole identity crisis and he couldn't take it."

"I see. What's her reaction been to all this?"

"On the surface, calm. Alexis is tough. But I think she was really hit hard. She hasn't talked to me about any of it, but that's not unusual. I think most of the time she tries to confine very personal confidences to Dr. Wyndholt."

"Do you think James told her about you and him?"

"No. I don't." She smiled, but her eyes looked slightly hurt. "We traveled in different worlds. I don't think he would have told anybody about me."

So much for just plain sex, Farr thought. It could never

be that way a hundred percent. Like it or not, people get involved.

Sandy rose abruptly. "I'm meeting Alexis. She wants to go shopping."

He went to the door with her. "For what it's worth, Sandy, if I had an affair with you, I'd go around with a ten-foot banner announcing it to the whole damned world."

She glanced up at him, surprised. "Thanks, boss man. I appreciate that."

"Take care of yourself," he said. "You're important."

She touched his arm and was gone.

Farr waited a few minutes to give her time to clear the building and make it back to East Executive. Then he headed down to his own car.

Twenty-One

It was a scorching day. The suburban street was oppressively silent, its trees and shrubbery wilted. M. J. watched the sweating men carrying the couch out to the moving van and realized that tonight she'd sleep a last time in Washington and at a friend's house. The children had been there since yesterday and the flight which would take them to Portland was at nine-thirty in the morning.

She'd decided the day of the funeral. When she phoned her father, he'd offered the family summer place near Cape Lookout, a rambling cottage set back from the water amidst windswept pines and looking southward down the wild coastline. She'd told neighbors she was moving to Arlington and asked the moving company to say the same if anyone asked. She'd told no one else. If Arthur Lindley heard she was going so far away, he could try to stop her from taking the children. She doubted, however, in view of his job, that he'd do anything once she was there.

Adrian James had been dead less than ten days. She felt remote from all that had happened and sometimes wondered why she didn't grieve more than she did. Something in her had clicked off at the funeral. The black despair she'd experienced when told he was dead had miraculously disappeared and she was left with an odd sense of relief. Was it because she had never really loved him, only thought she had? Or was it because his death right after those terrible photographs was so awful as somehow to make him undesirable?

Or was it because of the cocaine? Jimmy had been too frantic to be telling a lie. She still remembered his eyes. Nobody from the FBI had come to see her yet. Would they? And if they did, when would it be?

She left the front hall and walked through the dining room to the kitchen. The house seemed larger without furniture. Her footsteps echoed on bare floors. In the kitchen, there was a carton of unwanted food which the real estate agent would take. She made a cup of instant coffee and sat at the kitchen table, waiting for the men to finish loading the van.

In ten minutes, one of them came in with some papers to sign and then the van left. She checked the house a last time and drove away herself. The car was rented. She'd sold hers yesterday. She didn't look back. It had never been home, just somewhere she and the children had slept and where Adrian James kept a few token articles of clothing.

Driving through suburban North Washington, her sense of anticipation grew. Every time she stopped for a light, what she was about to do seemed more impossible. But she carried a burden that had become too intolerable to carry alone. She had to share it and there was only one person she could do that with.

She drove into Georgetown and up Oak Hill to R Street and the Volker home and parked in the shade behind a smart, blue Lancia convertible. There was an attractive young blond woman in tennis clothes leaning against one fender. She flicked at blades of grass with her racquet. "Hi," she said. Her smile was warm. M. J. returned the greeting and went up the front steps to ring the doorbell. She resented sun-bronzed youth. They made her feel far older than she was.

When the door opened, she found herself looking into the expressionless eyes of a butler.

"I'm Mrs. Lindley. I have an appointment with Mrs. Volker."

"I believe madam is in her office. Someone will be out in just a moment." He went to a house phone to announce her.

M. J. was surprised at how quickly a secretary appeared. She'd turned to examine a picture of Venice, wondering if it were a real Canaletto or a copy, when she heard the sound of a door. Turning, she saw a tall, attractive young woman smiling at her.

"Mrs. Lindley? I'm Allison Palmer. Would you like to come this way?"

She was led down a carpeted corridor. Allison made small talk. "Did you have trouble finding us? So many people do. They always expect the Secretary of State to be living in some huge official building."

M. J. said she hadn't. They reached what was clearly Allison's office.

"May I get you some iced tea?"

"I'd love it."

Allison knocked and pushed open a door leading into a second, far larger and more luxurious room and said, "Mrs. Lindley."

"Thank you, Allison. No calls, please." Alexis came from behind her desk, hands outstretched, smile gracious. She looked younger than M. J. expected, and more beautiful. She tried not to think of the photographs. The wantonness of the woman in them didn't match the well-dressed dignity of this woman at all.

They got comfortable on the couch and bridged momentary awkwardness with talk about her move to Oregon. Alexis was the only person she'd told. Allison brought in the tea. Alexis raised her glass and said, "Well, here's to you. I'm dreadfully sorry, you must have had a rotten time."

"Thank you." M. J. reminded herself it was up to her to get to the point. "Look," she said, "you cared very much about Jimmy and there are things about his death I think you ought to know. It would trouble me a lot if I left Washington and didn't tell you." When Alexis made a deferring gesture, she added, "Please believe me, I'm not the offended 'wife' or anything like that. In some strange way, I don't think I love Jimmy anymore. Although God knows I did. I'm just worried."

She saw something flicker in Alexis's eyes. Expectancy, perhaps anxiety. She realizes I must know, she thought. She'll think he told me.

She went on, "You spent an afternoon with him, shortly before he died. At Brigham Bay." She rushed on quickly. "It's all right. When you've had the sort of love affair you and Jimmy had, it isn't buried overnight. Not even by getting married. I understand that. But something absolutely awful happened because of it. Did he get a chance to tell you?"

Alexis's reply sounded small and pained. "No. What?"

"The photos?"

"Photos?"

M. J. told her. It was hard. Hard for her to think of them herself, hard to explain to Alexis how bad they were without embarrassing her into total silence. She kept going doggedly and against the horrible realization that Alexis might think she were a blackmailer. Alexis, as pale as death, stared back at her with wide eyes.

"I destroyed them," M. J. said. "And obviously I didn't tell the police. I don't know who took the damn things. Or who has the negatives. There was no letter. Just pictures."

She felt less nervous now. Beginning had been the worst part. "I lost my head with Jimmy," she continued. "We had a hell of a row. I told him I never wanted to see him again. That's what the note he left referred to."

One of Alexis's slender hands went to her throat. M. J. suddenly felt deeply sorry for her. In the last few days, she'd wondered what it would be like if someone you loved died and you had no one to tell or to turn to for comfort. Alexis might be in love with Harold Volker, but her face revealed she also still loved Adrian James.

"There's more," she said. "Jimmy still loved you very much and didn't want to see you again at all because he knew seeing you would be painful. For both of you."

"Why did he, then?" Alexis's first words were hoarse.

"Because the FBI forced him to," M. J. said. She waited until some of the shock in Alexis's eyes ebbed away. Then she said, "Making love to you was something else. They didn't ask for that. And he certainly hadn't planned it."

Alexis burst out. "The FBI forced him? Forced him how?"

M. J. told her about the cocaine. Alexis rose. "I don't know about you," she said, "but I could use a drink." She pressed the speak switch on her intercom. Her hand was shaking. "Allison, we'd like a couple of vodkas, please. Right away."

She came back and sat down. Some of her color returned. "I'm sorry. It's a lot all at once. Who else have you told this to?"

"No one," M. J. answered. "No one at all." It was nearly all out on the table now and she felt exhausted.

"But what the hell does the FBI want?" Alexis demanded. "That crowd! Jesus! Did Adrian say?" There was anger in her eyes now.

"He wasn't specific," M. J. answered. "He was told to gain your confidence. He thought it must concern your husband's staff. Maybe a leak. They mentioned Portugal."

138

"But that's crazy. If they think there's a leak, why Jimmy? He's hardly qualified to dig out that sort of thing. Siccing him on me, that's despicable. It really is."

Learning about the FBI had brought Alexis off the defensive. She was no longer an adulterous woman trapped by obscene photographs. She was again the Secretary of State's wife and didn't have to accept being pushed around.

"Are you going to check it out?" M. J. asked.

"Yes," Alexis replied. "But don't worry. It will be in a way that won't involve you." She smiled thinly. "After all, Jimmy could have told me all of this. In a way, I wish to God he had."

"Be careful," M. J. cautioned. She took a breath, getting ready to say what she'd been leading up to. She'd thought a lot about it last night. Sleeping alone in the empty house without even the comfort of the children, she'd been frightened. "Jimmy's dead, isn't he?" she asked pointedly.

There it was, she thought, all the dark fear she'd suffered alone finally out in the open. She felt a wonderful relief.

"Oh," Alexis said. Her eyes narrowed. "That means you don't think Jimmy killed himself."

"Do you?" M. J. asked.

"No. I don't," Alexis replied quietly. "I never have. He just wasn't the type. And certainly he wouldn't have killed himself because of a woman. Any woman. Jimmy? Good God!" She smiled faintly and said, "So that leaves us with a real nasty, doesn't it?"

M. J. nodded and shivered. "Yes," she said. "Whoever killed him probably took the photographs. His suicide note was to make them look like the reason. The photos and our fight."

Alexis said, "Do you think the FBI and his death are connected?"

"I don't know. I've thought about it so much I can't anymore. But they must be."

Allison Palmer knocked and came in with glasses, tonic, and some expensive Russian vodka. "I thought I'd spare you Everett," she said.

"Thank you."

Allison put down the tray, shot a quick glance at M. J., and went out again. Alexis silently poured herself and M. J. a drink. Then she said, "I don't like this, Mary Jane. Any of it. Is this another reason for your leaving town? I mean besides cocaine?"

"Yes."

"Then go away with one thought in mind," Alexis said. She took M. J.'s hand warmly. "I'm going to be careful. Very careful. For both our sakes. I don't want you to worry I might blow it."

There was nothing more to say. They sat drinking quietly, making small talk.

Ten minutes later, Alexis watched M. J. drive away. She felt sad. There was an unbreakable bond between them, a tragedy and a life shared. For a few minutes she'd wondered if M. J. hadn't in a strange way unburdened herself as a form of revenge. She'd dismissed the thought. M. J. was too decent a person. But she'd been right in calling Jimmy a bastard. He was. Why were so many women often attracted to that sort of man?

Sandy was still waiting by the Lancia, talking now to one of the other agents. Alexis called out. "Sorry. I'll be ready in ten minutes."

Sandy waved.

Back in her office, she went immediately to her desk and picked up her private phone. She flipped through her telephone index and dialed a number.

When it answered, she said, "I want to speak to William Rupert, please. This is Alexis Volker."

William Rupert was the Director of the FBI and Alexis had known him personally and well for the past six years. So had her husband. Rupert had been an usher at their wedding.

Twenty-Two

Less than twenty-four hours later, she was seated in William Rupert's office and confronting not just Rupert, but also David Farr.

Sunlight streamed into the deep-carpeted room. The tip of the Washington Monument just visible past the tower of the old Post Office building seemed to David Farr an incongruous intrusion and as unreal at the moment as William Rupert himself. The Director was acutely nervous. He felt he'd been compromised and was trying not to show it.

His tension showed in the way he compulsively rolled a pencil back and forth between thumb and forefinger. It was in the way he moved restlessly in his chair each time he spoke or whenever Farr said something that made him more uncomfortable than he already was. It was in his eyes, too. They were evasive. David Farr wondered if Alexis Volker saw, or if she was too much on the angry offensive to notice.

He found himself staring at Alexis's slender suntanned legs, one crossed over the other. They were like Susan's, but lighter. He had a feeling that in some ways their characters might be similar. Certainly they had the same clothes sense. It could have been Susan there in an expensive linen suit, the skirt narrow-belted, the pale orange silk blouse opened casually two buttons down from her throat, a cool summery frame to the gentle contour of her bosom.

And it could have been Susan's canvas and leather Gucci shoulder bag slung so casually over the back of the chair and her light Givenchy perfume filling the room.

He brought his mind back to what Alexis was saying to Rupert.

"But for God's sake, Bill, why the secrecy?" Some of her initial anger had subsided. She sounded almost indignant now. "Once more, why couldn't you have told me or Harold about this? After all, you are talking about people who work for us."

Farr decided it was time to speak. Rupert had avoided putting his foot into it so far, but he was getting flustered. Bad enough they had to confess they'd used James because they didn't know how much she knew and couldn't risk denying it. They could not under any circumstances let her discover they were after her husband. The name of the game was to lead her astray. They had to make her feel she had an inside track without realizing it was a wrong one. It wasn't easy. Both were very aware they were dealing with a woman who for years had been an investigative reporter.

He said abruptly, "Mrs. Volker, there's something I'd like to clear up."

She turned, surprised. Except for formalities, he'd been virtually silent ever since she came in. Rupert had explained they thought there was a leak by someone on Volker's staff to some of the foreign press. Especially to a Lisbon paper. Farr knew she didn't really accept it. That kind of a leak would have been a State Department security problem and not in the province of the FBI.

He went on. "I made an error with James. Right from the beginning. I was incorrectly briefed about him and had no idea you and he were once quite close. He gave me no hint of it when I interviewed him. He told me you'd been casual friends only."

Her eyes said she didn't quite believe that either. He

went on quickly. "I know what you're thinking," he said. "Why James in the first place?"

She said coldly, "I presume you had something on him and he had to."

"You presume wrong," he replied. Inwardly, he smiled. She probably knew they did, but perhaps not precisely what it was. He said, "James had done work for us from time to time. His connections were useful."

"Adrian?" Her astonishment was genuine. "I find that hard to believe. He hated the police. And that's what you are, aren't you?" She waved at the luxury of Rupert's office, "Disregarding all of this."

Farr shrugged. He liked her. The more he talked to her, the more he was beginning to find her very real. He said, "That's true and James didn't think much of us. But he had some serious problems with the IRS. We were his way out."

The lie upset Rupert. A claim of venality between the Bureau and Internal Revenue could come home to roost. He rolled his pencil even more furiously. But he kept silent. He couldn't think of anything to say.

Farr saw his discomfort and didn't care. He thought of how bad things could have been if his young assistant hadn't burst into his office at five o'clock last night with Xeroxed copies of a half-dozen letters.

"Volker correspondence."

Routinely, Farr had ordered a Post Office intercept on Volker's personal letters abroad. A correspondence between Volker and Gunter Schaeffer, the dead Joanna Volker's lover, had shown up ten days ago, but first excitement had ended in disappointment. The Bureau's cryptoanalysis unit had discovered nothing. The contents were just what they seemed, the two writers apparently settling details of the dead woman's estate of which both were executors.

"Catch me some other time." Farr wasn't in the mood

for anything concerning Volker. He knew he stood a good chance of being fired. William Rupert and Harold Volker were friends and Rupert, only too aware of his limitations, could be vindictive when he felt the need to justify his position.

"But, sir. They've finally come up with something."

Farr took the letters. "It better be good," he said.

It was good. The dates on the letterheads, both Volker's and Schaeffer's, didn't match the postmarks on the envelopes. Letters postmarked July and August were dated inside, January and March. Cryptology could make nothing of it. It was just enough hard evidence to lend real weight to the Shenson memorandum, to the Defector statement, the Nasciemento murder, and to his own certain belief James had been murdered.

The Director had surrendered with surprising speed. The implications of what Farr might be onto pushed any other thought from his mind. As Virgil Fein, then David Farr before him had done, he succumbed to the thought "what if." It also took him less than a minute to decide the safest way to handle the whole mess would be to pass the buck. He had already made an appointment with the Oval Office for tomorrow and was going to take Farr with him to do the talking.

Alexis was saying, "Can you tell me just what Adrian was supposed to do? And why him, of all people? Why not one of our security people, for example?"

Her tone was truculent. She doesn't like to lose, Farr thought. He knew the moment had come when he had to let her think he was surrendering inside information. It was risky, but not as risky as stonewalling.

"We've had information," he said carefully, "that someone working for you or for General Volker may not be who they say they are."

She stared a moment, then exclaimed, "My God, you're talking about a mole."

"We hope not," Farr said, "but one is never certain. Anyway, that's why we couldn't use any existing personnel. And a counterintelligence replacement for any one of them would have been instantly suspect."

"But Adrian was hardly trained for that sort of thing. And he didn't live at R Street."

Farr shrugged. "I agree. His activities would have been limited. We wanted him to photograph every employee for study down here at the Bureau. We gave him a special camera," he held up a thumb and forefinger, "this big. That's all we wanted."

"So somebody suspected anyway and good-bye Adrian," Alexis stated matter-of-factly.

It caught William Rupert flat-footed. It didn't catch Farr. He was prepared for it. From the very beginning he'd thought she knew.

He tried bluffing. "I don't follow."

Alexis smiled coldly. "Surely you don't think Jimmy killed himself."

"In view of the coroner's report, would I have reason to think otherwise?" It sounded hollow, but if he could keep it going a little longer, admission it was bluff would seem more sincere.

Alexis said, "Mr. Farr, up until now you were doing fine. But I once lived with him, remember?"

Bill Rupert fidgeted again. "Alexis, the coroner's office . . ."

He got no further. Her eyes flashed. "Oh, please, Bill, spare me."

Farr decided the moment right. "Okay, Mrs. Volker, I agree. I don't think he killed himself either. Where does that leave us?"

"It leaves us," she said, "with Jimmy being murdered because he was working for you and planning to spy on my husband's staff. Or mine. Someone obviously didn't want him doing that. It leaves us with someone working

146

for Harold or me who is doing something bad enough to kill to prevent it being discovered. That's where it leaves us."

She unslung her shoulder bag from the back of the chair and stood up.

Too accurate for comfort, Farr thought. He sensed she knew more about James's death than she was saying and wondered what it was. "If you are correct, Mrs. Volker," he said carefully, "and I'm not saying you are, I'd appreciate your keeping this interview between ourselves."

"That's asking quite a bit, isn't it?"

He picked his words carefully. "No, it's not. If you're right about why Adrian James died, I wouldn't want whoever killed him to decide *you* were cozy with us, too. Which is precisely why we never discussed our worries with you or General Volker in the first place."

He was waiting for a fear reaction. He didn't get it. Instead he got a slight smile. "I'd like to give you that one, Mr. Farr," she said. "It was well played, but to be honest, I've already thought of it."

Farr kicked himself for not realizing that of course she would have. He acceded, "Fair enough, I'm sure you have."

"Where do we go from here, then?" she asked.

"We don't," he replied. "We cool it. If we mole hunt at all, we'll set our traps in the KGB itself. We have our moles, too. Where you're concerned, you have your bodyguard. She's the best, I understand. If you're worried about anything or want to talk to me, I'll be right here. I'd like to think I'm someone you can call on if you feel like it. And vice versa."

A warmth came into her face. She took his hand firmly. "Thank you, Mr. Farr," she said.

Rupert rose to make polite noises. He looked relieved. He said he hoped they'd cleared things up. Alexis managed courteous replies. Once she caught Farr's eye and

Farr had the impression she almost winked. He remembered Volker was due back from Portugal in a few hours. He knew she was on her way to Andrews to meet him. He would probably have heard about James and must know James and his wife had been lovers. What would she say to him about it?

She went out with Rupert. The door closed behind her. Then, she suddenly reappeared, leaving Rupert in the secretarial office. She said quickly and in a low voice, "M. J. Lindley. Cocaine. I'd appreciate it, personally, Mr. Farr, if you could get her slate wiped clean."

He nodded. "Count on it."

She studied him a second, smiled, then left as quickly as she'd entered.

Clever woman, Farr thought. She'd held that back through the whole meeting, not planning to use it unless she had to. It made him wonder how long it would be before she realized it was Volker himself they were really after. For there was no doubt in his mind she would.

When Rupert came back, he spent a few necessary moments with him. Then he went back down to his own office, ordered coffee, and added things up. How now to find out if Harold Volker was indeed in some way involved was more problematical than ever. That was the minus side. He would have to depend on the CIA for whatever they might ferret out in Portugal and that could take forever. He would have to go back to routine and exhaustive investigation of everything from the original memorandum to renewed scrutiny of anyone ever involved in Volker's life, including the dead James and M. J. Lindley. Police work—dull, slogging. All done once already. Perhaps his best hope was that the cryptoanalysis unit might have a brainstorm.

The plus side was that he no longer had to be covert about it. He could openly use the full resources of the Bureau. There was nothing like being official.

Unless, however, the President said no. That, of course, was a distinct possibility. Modern history was littered with the names of traitors and defectors who had held high office. It was also marked by the treason of those never named because the office they held was so high that revealing their betrayal could be political disaster. Such might be the case with the office of Secretary of State.

Twenty-Three

The Lancia pulled up out of the Hoover Building executive garage. It turned left on Pennsylvania, then swung around the Capitol on Third Street and onto Independence. Sandy drove.

Alexis looked at her watch. "Are we going to make it?"

"No problem. But if you'd stayed in there another five minutes, I'd have started a war between the services to get you out."

Alexis knew that was Sandy's way of trying to find out why she'd gone to see William Rupert. "Bill Rupert likes to talk," she said. "I asked him to do a favor for M. J. Lindley who came to see me yesterday. For the privilege of having him say yes, I had to listen to all his so-called funny stories."

"How did Mrs. Lindley tangle with the FBI?"

"She didn't," Alexis said. "It was a DEA situation. I don't know anyone there, Rupert does."

"Oh." Sandy's expression acknowledged that further information was none of her business. Forty-five minutes later, they drove through the main gates of Andrews.

Harold Volker's return to Washington was even less conspicuous than his departure. The media had not yet chosen to make Portugal very prominent in the consciousness of the American public. His meeting with Alexis when he came down the stairway from the plane was warm and personal. He quickly fielded routine questions from whatever journalists were present, then walked her away from officialdom so they could be alone for a few minutes. Outrageously, he wore jeans, boots, and an old Windbreaker over an open-necked shirt. He was heavily tanned.

He kissed her hard. "I really missed you this trip. I wish I'd let you come."

"You look wonderful. You've been on the beach."

"Every afternoon for two hours while they were all recovering from too much wine at lunch."

Ten minutes later, they drove off in an official limousine. Security agents and aides followed in another. They held hands, his arm was across the seat behind her shoulder and he toyed with her hair. "At the risk of facing a divorce," he said suddenly, "I have a meeting tonight."

Alexis hid her disappointment. She mentioned some old friends she'd asked for dinner, a retired Air Force General and his wife, a New York couple in the arts. They were people he liked and could relax with.

"I'm sorry," he said. "I should have telephoned from the plane. Can you manage them alone?"

"Of course."

He pulled her close. "It's the damned Portuguese Ambassador," he explained. "I'll finish him off by eleven."

"At the Department or the Portuguese Embassy?"

"The Department."

Alexis said, "Actually, you're just trying to escape Everett one more day."

He laughed. "You're right."

When they pulled into the courtyard of the State Department's Twenty-first Street entrance, he motioned to the chauffeur to leave the door shut for a moment. He was thoughtful, then said, "Alexis, I hear Adrian James killed himself."

"Yes, he did." Caught by surprise, she mentally braced herself.

"I'm sorry. Was it very upsetting to you?"

She studied his eyes. They were warm and concerned. She touched his cheek. "It was a shock, but don't worry about it."

"You had seen him?"

"He called. He was having terrible problems with M. J. Lindley, the girl he was living with. I took him down to Brigham Bay and gave him a picnic. He was pretty desperate, the poor darling."

He smiled. "I'll see you later. Don't fall asleep."

When he'd disappeared into the building, Alexis told the chauffeur to take her home. She hated the lie. Worse was the dull ache of sadness she constantly felt and which she had to hide from everyone. The only companion she'd had in her grief, the only person who knew and cared was M. J. It was bitterly ironic. At the funeral she'd worn a black veil and stood well to the rear of the other mourners. She'd felt completely alone. It was as though her whole past had ceased to exist and with it any final security she always drew from it. James had been a last link.

Back at R Street she threw herself into routine. She had a meeting with the National Women's Arts Committee, dictated letters, made household arrangements and caught up on her phone calls. From the time she'd got up that morning, her husband's imminent presence had seemed unreal, an intrusion. She'd tried to change her feelings so it would be the other way around. She'd tried even harder not to think of Adrian James. It was impossible. Remembrance of their ecstatic afternoon of love crowded in on the nagging guilt she felt because of it. Her terror of the photos shared the horror of his death. Someone had the negatives. Where and when would they show up?

At dinner, in spite of her guests, she kept remembering her meeting with Farr and Rupert. No matter how she'd tried to maneuver, Farr had been in charge from the moment she'd walked into Rupert's office. Somehow, he had steered their talk in the direction he wanted it to go, answering her questions without ever replying directly. The more she thought, the more she knew she'd been put off. But why? Something didn't ring true and she couldn't put a finger on it. Why so much heavy espionage to ferret out a suspected mole? Why the complication of Adrian James in a plot that snared even poor M. J.? Why not just fire the whole staff and begin anew? And if there really were a mole, why bother with household when the critical staff were all at the Department?

Finally, there was the biggest question of all. Was any inside track on Harold's wide-open diplomacy worth murdering for when he was notorious for making most of his plans at the last possible moment?

She was pouring coffee, playing hostess with half her mind and trying not to think at all with the other, when Everett appeared. She was wanted on the telephone. She excused herself and took the call in the library.

It was someone called Francisco José Catarino. His name and accent were Portuguese. He was a Colonel and said he was an aide to General Figueira. Alexis searched her mind quickly and remembered Figueira was Army Chief-of-Staff. The General Nasciemento who had come to dinner had also been one of his aides.

"Do you know where I can reach your husband, Senhora? I am due to meet him in half an hour at my hotel. My flight from Lisbon was late and I am still at the airport."

"He's at the State Department. He has a meeting there this evening with your Ambassador."

"Ah? But our Ambassador is still in Lisbon."

"Lisbon? Are you sure?"

"Oh, yes. General Figueira and I had breakfast there with him today."

Alexis thought quickly. Obviously Harold or his staff had made a mistake. It was most probably Harold. Official calls for him at home came in on a special phone constantly attended by a security agent. The fact that Catarino was calling on their personal phone meant Harold must have given him the unlisted number. Nobody else would have.

She apologized. "I'm afraid there's been a mix-up somewhere," she said. "I suggest you first call the Department. If they tell you he's on his way home, is there someplace he can reach you? Sometimes he doesn't answer his car telephone."

The Colonel hesitated, then gave her a number. "Thank you very much, senhora, and I am sorry to have disturbed you."

"It's quite all right."

Alexis rejoined her guests and organized bridge. They played three rubbers and she was on her way to bed when Harold finally came home. He hadn't had dinner and they went to the kitchen so she could make him something to eat. She nearly forgot the call.

"Oh, Harold. Someone named Colonel Catarino called. On our private line."

"He caught up with me."

"He said the Ambassador was still in Portugal."

"I know. The office got things backwards. I could have dined at home with you, after all. But by the time I found out, it was late and Operations had a load of Task Force stuff for me to make decisions on. They thought they had movement on the Libyan hostages, but it turned out to be the usual dead end."

After he'd eaten they made drinks and went upstairs, his arm around her.

154

"You must be very tired," Alexis said.

"Never felt better."

He thrived on it, she thought. On the shuttling from one capital to another, on sleeping aboard SAM 70, on the nervous energy spent in maneuvering one head of state against another, on the political intrigue always raging between Congress and the White House.

Halfway to their bedroom, he stopped and kissed her.

"It's been exactly fourteen days since I did that properly. To the hour."

In spite of everything, she had a surge of romantic feeling. When later they made love, she stopped feeling guilty about Adrian James for a few moments. It had been just one of those things that happens. She forgot David Farr and all the anxiety he represented. She loved Harold. And for a few precious moments she also forgot the fact that he had just lied to her.

But when he slept, when their room was in darkness except for the faint slant of light across the ceiling from a street lamp down R Street, she couldn't ignore it any longer. For years she had learned to sense any nuance, any shadow behind which people tried to hide the truth. Tearing the shadows away had become habit. Colonel Catarino, she remembered, had been quite positive about his date to meet Harold and it was almost inconceivable that Harold would have been misinformed on the Ambassador still being in Lisbon. It meant that when Harold told her this morning he was seeing the Ambassador, he knew he wasn't. He knew he was seeing Catarino.

Why hide it? Why the lie? Had there been others? Vague and unexplained contradictions came back to her, things about policy and maneuvering which didn't quite add up. At the time she'd ignored them, because they seemed totally unimportant. Now she couldn't. They began to form a pattern that fitted into all the rest of her worries.

From it a thought emerged, one that had constantly lurked in the back of her mind and that she had chosen to ignore.

She was on her back, Harold was on his side next to her, one leg across her hips, his head against her shoulder. She very gently disengaged herself and sat up. Although the room was hot, she pulled her side of the sheet up over her body protectively. The thought at first diffused was now very clear. It made her stomach tighten with a fear she couldn't control because she knew it could explain Adrian James and all the complex search for a supposed mole. And why she'd been put off by Farr.

The person they were really investigating could be her husband and James was a perfect choice to influence her to reveal whatever she might know of Harold's affairs.

Her heart thudded. Next to her Harold muttered in his sleep. That meant he would awaken in a few minutes. Whenever he woke soon after making love he always wanted to make love to her again. And usually she to him. This time she knew she couldn't.

The headboard felt hard against her naked back and she felt as though a heavy spike had been driven right through her, nailing her to it.

Twenty-Four

For the sheer weight of meetings held and things planned, David Farr thought, it had been a rough day. He hadn't got home until ten o'clock. Now it was eleven. It was still eighty-five degrees and even Washington's dull-red glow against the sky failed to extinguish a three-quarter summer moon.

He was in his backyard swimming pool with a beer in one hand and both elbows hooked over the pool's edge, glancing occasionally at the moon, talking to Susan, stopping when she would duck under the water to watch her slender naked body flit like a shadow across the bottom lights before she surfaced with a faint splash. Waiting for her, he would draw in his breath to inhale the smell of the roses and the jasmine they had planted two years ago when they bought the place.

They talked in low voices so their neighbors wouldn't hear.

"But what was he like personality-wise?" she asked. "I mean besides being President, he's theoretically also human. You can't tell from television."

Farr laughed. The day had begun at seven-thirty with a one hour meeting in the Oval Office. Besides himself and Rupert it had included the White House Chief-of-Staff, Lanard "Duke" Chancery and the National Security Adviser, Bernard Kornovsky. And, of course, the President.

"You say something and he doesn't respond. So you never really know what the hell he's thinking."

"No reaction at all?"

"None. Poker-faced. He just stares at you. Or at something else. Then says something totally unrelated. It can really throw you."

"Who did most of the talking?"

"Well, first the 'Duke.' Rupert briefed him yesterday and he summarized the gist of it. Then the President turned to me and asked if I realized the seriousness of the situation. When I said I did, he wanted me to go into detail on what got me started. He asked exactly what I'd come up with for evidence since. Also my gut feeling about the outcome."

"Were you surprised by his decision?"

"No. He's a weird guy, Susan, but he's got guts. And it's not just the Office. He's very strong."

"What about the others?"

"Kornovosky nearly had a nervous breakdown."

"He was for a cover-up?"

"He and the 'Duke' both. They wanted to bury the whole damn thing. Coal mine deep. And from day one. Silence everybody, me and Fein included, destroy any copies of the memorandum, the works. And find some way to get rid of Volker. A reason for him to resign gracefully." He paused, remembering their panic, then went on. "Old fish-eye just sat until they ran down. Then he told me to go ahead with what I was doing. He said, 'Let the fucking chips fall where they may.' That's a quote. He said he didn't want any Watergate in his Administration."

"But what about Volker meanwhile?"

"He stays. The decision was to keep him right where he is until we can prove something. The President said if it ever got out why he was forced to resign and we didn't have proof, the repercussions would wreck the Party. Volker has powerful friends."

158

"Wilderstein."

"Among others."

"It's taking a terrible chance, David, isn't it? I mean if your suspicions turn out to be true, he could really do some harm before you get him."

"I suspect the President weighed that."

Susan drank some of his beer. "And then what?"

"What do you mean, then what?" He kicked his feet, churning up waves of tumbling silvery bubbles.

"You were booked into the Oval Office for an hour. You've been home for thirty minutes. That means thirteen and a half hours to explain."

"Dr. Farr, I don't want to talk about it."

"Well, you're going to."

"Oh, Christ. I come home dead tired, fix a drink, climb into the pool with a beautiful naked young woman, and some damned doctor wants me to tell my life story."

"And allows you just fifteen seconds to organize it." Susan ducked under the water and swam slowly past the lights on the bottom. She came up and stood provocatively between his legs, her forearms resting across his thighs. "I'm listening.

He surrendered. "Back to square one," he said. "Exotic ideas of ladies telling on their husbands, that's out. Flat-footed policemen are in."

It took time and he skipped a lot of it. There were things you didn't even tell your wife. Sandy Muscioni, for example. Somewhere in the middle of it all, when he'd been in the pool too long, she wrapped him in a beach towel and took him to the kitchen where she cooked him a steak and tossed up a green salad and poured some imported Burgundy.

He'd been put in charge of the Volker investigation, he told Susan, and the first thing he did was classify anything pertaining to the Secretary of State as top-secret. Next, he created several special units to conduct specific investigations. One would check out all previous clearances of everyone working at the Volker home, security agents as well as secretarial and domestic staffs. Somewhere some heretofore unconsidered aspect of someone's life might lead them to a mole. And the mole possibly could be forced to lead to bigger game.

Fein came over and spent an hour with him. Fein took charge of looking into Portuguese politics with emphasis on General Figueira. They also arranged for a joint FBI-CIA unit that would work closely with the BKA, the Bundeis Kriminal Amt, West Germany's equivalent to the FBI, and try again through agents in East Germany to find some new lead which might indicate whether Schaeffer was or was not the missing Horst Melkin. Army Intelligence was asked to have Captain Shenson come to Washington by first available military flight to help.

Early in the afternoon, Farr met with detectives of the Metropolitan Police Homicide Bureau. They discussed James's death as murder, and a secret exhumation of James's remains was ordered for further autopsy. The staff of the cryptoanalysis unit was doubled and the laboratory was asked to expedite efforts to trace the transmitters Sandy had discovered in Volker's office.

Finally, Farr sent three agents to Frankfurt to lead yet another exhaustive search into Volker's pre-American past. Their work was to be independent of the Schaeffer investigation and cover ground already gone over not only by the CIA and themselves, but also by the Senate Committee that had confirmed Volker's appointment.

He set himself the task of an in-depth investigation of all of Volker's foreign policy record. Somewhere amidst the mass of correspondence, taped meetings, testimony, speeches, and media reporting which accompanied two years of diplomatic negotiations both secret and public, there might be some clue pointing to skillfully planned misadventures.

160

Long after most of the Hoover Building was in night-time silence he still was at his desk. The last thing he did before he left was to roll a sheet of paper into his secretary's typewriter and carefully peck out a progress report which first thing in the morning would be placed on the President's desk. There would be one sent to the White House every day from now on.

When he and Susan were finally in bed, lying close together, the night air stirring the curtains of their bedroom and soft on their bare skin, he once more experienced the acute humiliation of disappointing her. Once more he couldn't shake off the day. The burden of proving a United States Secretary of State guilty or not guilty of treason now officially rested on his shoulders. One slip and his career would be in ruins.

But how long could his marriage take his failure? He somehow had to get a grip on himself. Resigning wouldn't help. There was Susan's medical future to help set up, and at his age getting reestablished as an independent lawyer might be a long haul.

He thought again of Alexis Volker. In an odd way they'd become partners. She'd had time to think about her meeting with him and Rupert, to add it all up, and decide she hadn't been told the truth. She'd had time to realize it was Volker himself they were after.

Farr wondered how long it would be before the investigative reporter in her overcame the woman in love with her husband.

Twenty-Five

Looking at Andrew Taylor from across his memento-littered desk in the UBC Washington offices, Alexis thought he seemed desperately tired. And in the last few years he had aged. His hair was no longer gray, but white. His round, generous face was lined and there were dark circles under his eyes. She knew it was partly her fault and felt guilty. He had counted on her and she had failed him.

Shortly after she'd quit television and in a flurry of publicity, he'd found another young protégée. Valerie McCullough had been the weather girl from his home town of Grand Island, Nebraska. She was young, red-headed, and had a dynamic personality to match her beauty. She was, in fact, the image of herself, Alexis realized, when getting to the top of UBC had been her most dominant thought. But she also knew that to Taylor, no matter how good, Valerie wasn't the same as Alexis Sobieski.

His greeting when she entered his office told her so. There were tears in his eyes as he rose silently from his ancient Smith-Corona to take both her hands in his and just look and look at her. When he finally spoke, it was to tell his awed secretary he was to be disturbed only in the event of nuclear war or a presidential assassination. He fixed her a drink, made sure she was comfortable in a deep chair, and hung on every word she spoke.

She told him everything, from her anxiety about her marriage and Dr. Wyndholt to her afternoon at Brigham Bay with Adrian James. "I was drunk," she said, "and I turned Jimmy into a sort of surrogate husband who would give me what I wanted—Brigham Bay, children." She told him about M. J. Lindley, the photographs, and the FBI and Farr. She revealed worries about her husband's politics she'd not recognized herself until she'd caught him lying to her.

"But I can't believe Harold would be involved in something he shouldn't be," she protested.

"And if he was?"

"I don't know," she answered. "I'd have to face it, wouldn't I? What I do know is that I can't go on like this—not knowing."

Andrew Taylor's face betrayed an inner struggle. He was silent, then he said, "I can't tell you what to do, my dear child. Or even advise you. It's not my business to and I am not certain I would want to even if it were. I am too old now to face the sort of pain involved in the decisions you have to make."

He paused, again thinking. Alexis waited dully. He went on. "But I am going to help you help yourself. And you will have to trust me."

"Of course."

"Blindly? It's going to hurt."

Alexis nodded. What did he mean?

He studied her. "All right," he said. He flicked on the intercom to his secretary. "Ask Valerie to come into my office, please. Right away."

It left Alexis speechless. For the last four years she'd carefully avoided meeting Valerie McCullough and she was certainly the last person she wanted to see right now.

Andrew Taylor read her mind. He smiled. "Now calm down, Alexis. You said you'd trust me. You're going to have to do this one my way." He thrust an index finger at her. "And, like it or not, she is going to have to trust you. She won't want to, by the way, but I suspect she will decide to."

It was only moments before Valerie got there, so short a time Alexis was certain he'd arranged it beforehand.

A sharp knock, the door opened abruptly, and she stood on the threshold, smaller than Alexis had imagined and thinner and with an odd almost touching air of vulnerability in spite of overall self-assurance.

She's as frightened as I, Alexis thought. Their eyes met and Alexis saw expressed in the younger woman's everything she knew she would feel herself if she had been in the same position. It was all there, awe and admiration of Alexis Sobieski the legend, jealousy and resentment because she knew she could never replace Alexis in either the affections of Andrew Taylor nor those of a nation of viewers. With all that there was also a hint of vindictive triumph at something she knew which Alexis did not. The conflict raged only a second, then vanished behind a curtain of self-control. Valerie McCullough came into the room with a smile, hand out. Andrew Taylor let her greet Alexis warmly and was patient through some short, polite small talk before he came abruptly to the point.

He said, "Valerie, for a number of reasons, I'd very much appreciate it, as would Alexis, if you would tell her about your current number-one project. All about it. Everything."

Whatever Valerie McCullough expected, it wasn't this. She was as surprised as Alexis had been. She lost all composure. She seemed to hold her breath. She turned wide eyes on Alexis and there was real anxiety in them. Andrew Taylor held up a soothing hand. "Please understand, my dear. You are under no obligation to do so. None."

He smiled gently. In the silence, Alexis realized he was counting on Valerie's need to prove herself a worthy successor. It was clever. It was also frightening. If Valerie

164

had something to say that could equal her own best, it had to be something big. Alexis waited, aware her smile was frozen and false.

Valerie McCullough walked into Taylor's trap. "Of course," she said, finally. And to Alexis, "I'm afraid it won't be easy for you. I'm sorry."

Alexis deferred. Her fear grew.

Andrew Taylor said, "It has to do with General Volker." It was a way of getting things started. "Valerie has stumbled onto something through her FBI contacts." He turned to her, "Alexis recently met with Bill Rupert and David Farr to protest their using Adrian James to get information on what they said is a possible leak by someone on General Volker's staff."

"I felt there was more to it than that," Alexis said.

"A good deal," Taylor said pointedly. He and Valerie exchanged looks.

Valerie plunged in. "All right, I might as well come right out and say: It's not staff they're investigating, Alexis, it's your husband."

Alexis felt the same numbing shock she had when told of James's death and the photos. Her darkest fears of the other night weren't as bad as having them confirmed. What Valerie told her, took away hope. She heard her explaining the contents of an Army Intelligence memorandum which possibly linked her husband to the KGB.

"I must emphasize," Valerie insisted, "they have no hard evidence. Only suspicion. And if their suspicions are correct, they still don't know what's involved, if it's money or blackmail or what. Of course," she went on, "they have more than just the memorandum." She told Alexis about the Defector Report.

Alexis kept her prior knowledge of a mole to herself. "But why does a suspected mole add suspicion?" she demanded.

"Because," Valerie explained, "they think it's a 'shepherd.' That's a mole who's there not to spy, but as an ally or a control." She went on to the date discrepancies on the intercepted letters, to Nasciemento's murder, and the worry that something might go wrong in Portugal. "They think there may be a deliberate pattern to many past diplomatic successes which later turned into reverses," she explained.

Alexis took a deep breath. "It's a lot to come from an informant," she said to Valerie. "He could go to jail for what he's told you. Why has he?"

"My informant is a she." A faint smile flicked Valerie's eyes, then vanished immediately. "And she owes me a big one."

Alexis didn't speak for a moment. She remembered deals she'd had with some of her own informants. Presumably Valerie was smart enough to have double checked her information somehow. Looking at her, it briefly crossed her mind that she might be a lesbian. If she were, she hoped Andrew Taylor never found out. She asked if she had a copy of the memorandum.

"I'm afraid I don't," Valerie said. "But I saw one. I don't think it was so much its contents that motivated the investigation as the thought of where they might be if its suspicions ever turned out to be well-founded and they had *not* investigated." She smiled. "I suppose all three of us would have done the same. I mean it's the way we track down a lot of stories, isn't it?"

The phone rang. It was for Valerie. She spoke, hung up, and asked if she could go and apologized.

Alexis rose and thanked her. For the first time there was real warmth in the other's eyes. "I know this has been worse than bad for you," Valerie said. "Please, if at any time I can be of any help, just call. I'll drop everything."

Alexis knew she meant it. It made her feel better. She spent a last few minutes with Taylor. She told him Valerie McCullough was great, he hadn't made a mistake. They talked about the old days. When she kissed him good-bye, he asked, "What will you do?"

"I can't live with a man," she answered, "I'm always wondering about, can I?"

"I guess that's more or less what prompted David Farr," he replied. "He's the one running the show now."

Going back down in the elevator, she thought about Farr. He was strong, kind, and intelligent. He wouldn't be in this sort of thing unless highly motivated. The thought slammed a final door on ignoring the truth.

In a way it helped. She knew now exactly what she had to do. She had to find out for herself if Harold were guilty or not. The fact that life might become meaningless if he were, was a bridge she would have to cross when she got to it.

Twenty-Six

A few mornings later, David Farr drove out to Langley to see Virgil Fein. Fein had offered to have him briefed on Portugal and its current political problems by CIA specialists. Farr had decided to take advantage of the offer, figuring the CIA with a vital station in Lisbon was probably more up on the Portuguese than the Bureau.

It was raining, but rush-hour traffic had lightened. He'd risen late. Susan had called last night to say she might have to spend the night at the hospital and hadn't come home. He had coffee alone, not fully realizing how much he'd missed her. At nine-thirty the phone rang and it was her again, this time to say good morning. He felt better, checked with his secretary for telephone messages, then got his car from the garage. The trip from Chevy Chase took only twenty minutes.

Fein was already in his shirt sleeves, his tie loosened, when Farr came in. He stood up to introduce a slender, dark-haired young woman. "Helen Carson," he said. "Helen's in charge of synthesizing political information for this department."

Farr nodded. That meant she was given a pile of research to condense into a short, readable report. He would have preferred to meet the research specialists themselves and to be briefed verbally. He took her in, straight hair, no makeup, a braless well-shaped bosom, a runner's body, and an expression that was aggressively activist on her rather delicate, attractive face. He knew the type. You appreciate their looks and they call you a sexist.

He took off his own jacket and sank comfortably onto a couch. A secretary brought them coffee, then left them alone. By way of getting started, he reported on his meeting the day before with Captain Shenson, who had arrived in Washington and after being briefed by the Army had shown up in his office. He'd spent an hour with him. His promotion confirmed, the Captain had been quite talkative.

"What does he look like?" Fein demanded. "What did he say?"

"Flat-footed. Round-shouldered. Think an average-height Charles de Gaulle except you could meet him twice and not remember him. He said the German agent they found shot was totally efficient and one-hundred-percent trustworthy. The agent was convinced Schaeffer was Melkin. This was a guy, mind you, who apparently knew the KGB inside and out."

"Shenson wasn't able to turn up anything the agent might have had? An old notebook or anything?"

"No. Nothing. Someone beat our side to his room. Shenson tried to run down a family, a woman, whatever. Nothing there, either."

Fein shook his head. "Probably the only way we'd ever get anywhere with this is to have Schaeffer himself tell us."

"Well, why not?" Helen Carson asked. It was the first time she'd spoken.

Fein laughed. "You mean make Schaeffer talk? Have you thought of the political consequences if it ever got out that the CIA had quote interrogated unquote a German academician? To play safe we'd have to liquidate him and that could be even riskier."

Farr said, "Let's move on to Portugal." Fein hadn't mentioned the immorality of murder, just the impracticality. Intelligence made too many people lose all perspective, Farr noted.

He took the twelve-page report she handed him. She kept a copy for herself.

"I think you'll find everything you want in there," she said. "If not, I can answer any question you might have. You're probably already up on most of it." She glanced at the first few pages. "Portugal, as you know, was a dictatorship and a police state for nearly fifty years until 1974 when the Army revolted and arranged for free elections, a constitution, and a parliamentary system of government with a national assembly. That's all covered on pages one through four. On five through seven I summarized the country's economy."

Farr scanned quickly.

"Roughly," Helen Carson said, "the hilly north is comprised of small independent landowners and industry; the south is flat with huge estates worked by a half-starved peasantry. The north is moderate or mildly Socialist and will probably stay that way for a while if the recession doesn't affect factory workers too badly. The south is predominantly Communist."

Farr decided to slow her down. "Why?" he demanded.

She shrugged. "Because hungry, hopeless people these days usually are."

Okay, Farr thought, so I'm an idiot.

She went on. "After the revolution, all the huge estates were confiscated and offered to the workers, but in such small parcels nobody could make a living from them. So the peasants turned them down. They wanted communes. The government still has the land and any peasant who wasn't already a Communist became one."

"How about the Army?" Farr demanded.

"The Army is very important. It's highly political and plays a watchdog role. If things don't go right, there's

170

always the threat it will step in. In 1975, the Army nearly went Communist, but it's predominantly moderate now.

Farr shuffled more pages.

She followed suit. "Seven through twelve is the present crisis," she said. "I've tried to state it as simply as possible."

"I'm pretty aware of it," Farr replied. He'd suddenly had enough of her expertise. He knew now and without a doubt where the original suspicion of Volker had stemmed from. He wondered what her personal and unofficial scenario for Portugal would be. Her report made no prediction. It only stated the existing situation: that the Portuguese president with full U.S. approval had appointed a highly popular premier and that the Socialist-Communist coalition had slipped badly in the latest polls. Volker's recent low-profile trip to Lisbon seemed to have been just what it was touted to be, a very successful blow for moderation.

"In view of your current investigation," he said, "what do you see for Portugal in the near future?"

"The Communists," she replied, "are close to getting what they want and I can't see them giving up easily. Nor," she added acidly, "our friend in the State Department."

"The Army is controlled by General Figueira and he's a rightist," Farr countered. "Wouldn't that pretty much rule out a Communist coup d'etat?"

"Not if there were covert elements involved we didn't know about," she said stubbornly.

"What sort of elements?" he insisted.

"I don't know," she answered. She obviously didn't like his challenge and didn't bother to hide her annoyance. "I don't know for example how much pressure the Portuguese Reds might be getting from Moscow."

"If," Farr demanded, "there were a successful Communist coup, do you think we'd have the Russian Navy in Lisbon?"

She shrugged and favored him with a condescending smile. "The Portuguese Communist party isn't like the rest of the Eurocommunists. They follow a strict Moscow line."

Farr held his tongue. It was one thing to make accusations and arouse suspicions, another to try to prove them. There were too many Helen Carsons in the world.

She rose abruptly. "Now, if you'll excuse me, I have another meeting. Virgil, if you need anything further, you know where I am."

Fein looked slightly embarrassed. He had to be sleeping with her, Farr thought, but that wasn't the hold she had over him. The hold was her aggressiveness. Out of kindness, he spent a few more minutes with Fein to let him resume a pretense of running the show. When he was leaving, Fein asked him if he had a tail on Alexis.

"Let's just say we're keeping a close eye on her. Of course."

Fein smiled, "Did you know the day after she saw you at the Bureau she went over to UBC and saw Andrew Taylor?" There was a touch of vindictiveness in his tone.

Farr cursed inwardly. He'd been caught on that one. So much for being nice about Helen Carson. Sandy hadn't told him. Alexis must have gone there when she was off duty. That or lied to her. Or possibly Sandy just hadn't seen the importance.

He kept a straight face. "How did you know?"

"Same source who told me you've got a leak at the Bureau," Fein said quietly. He went on. "Friend, Valerie McCullough knows half of what you're doing. Maybe more."

This time Farr let his feelings show. They were surprise, anger, and worry. "Thanks. Now you tell me."

Fein shrugged. "Now, or half an hour ago and ruin your coffee. What's the difference? I only heard last night."

"Who's your informant?"

"One of the UBC news producers. Helen knows him. Apparently he and McCullough occasionally play a number together and he says she's also into girls and has some heavy friend whose husband works for the Bureau." He grinned. "Forget your Victorian sensibilities, David, if you have any left. This is the 1980s and Washington's a small town. Half the guys we know play around or aren't totally straight. Why should the women be any different?"

Coping with traffic entering Washington, Farr chewed it over and over. It was bad. If McCullough aired what she knew, the Administration would have political mayhem on its hands. Heads would roll, his among them. He hoped Andrew Taylor still had a firm hand on things. He'd know enough to keep the lid on. But it was scary to have to pin one's hopes on another man's intelligence.

And who was the leak itself? He tried to think of which agent's wife could be guilty. He knew them all and couldn't see any of them in a lesbian connection, even part-time. Or informing. Besides, none of the agents really knew the overall picture. Just their own section of it.

He parked in the Hoover Building garage and went upstairs to his office. He was going to find out if it killed him. He had to.

He was in the elevator when it hit him. His secretary thought he was ill and followed him into his office. He told her he was all right and didn't want to be disturbed. He closed his door, and sat at his desk and tried to find some way of not facing it. He couldn't. The plain facts were there and wouldn't go away. The Bureau wife in the best position to know about the Volker investigation was Susan. She was young and beautiful and passionate and had an easy way with people. She had known everything about Adrian James and was friendly with one of the girls he took to Paris with him.

In that sort of fast world, knowing one key person led to knowing others.

Farr forced his way back through the twisting shadows of his mind. It wasn't just recently that he'd failed her. There had been occasional other times. There'd been times, too, when he'd sensed she felt chained to quiet suburban evenings with a tired man seventeen years older than she. Times when he felt she wanted desperately to break free and fly.

He thought of last night when she'd phoned and said she had to stay at the hospital. There had been other nights, when she'd called to say the same. He kept telling himself he had no proof, only suspicion. It didn't do any good.

After a while it became too painful to think of anymore and he slowly went back to work. Nothing would ever be the same again.

Twenty-Seven

Dinner at Brigham Bay was on the terrace. Twilight crept across the dead-still water of the estuary, first purple and mauve, then in a soft hush of velvet dark. The lawn smelled richly of fresh-cut grass. The air was warm. There was no moon. Candlelight flickered gently, reflecting from the leaves of the towering beech and elms.

Alexis had arranged the guests at three tables, six persons to each, putting the Portuguese Foreign Minister with her husband at one, herself with General Figueira at another, and Arnold Wilderstein in charge of the third.

Cocktails were served on the lawn. Everett had come down from R Street with two maids because General Figueira and his wife were spending the night. The presence of the butler seemed a travesty to Alexis. She'd had to speak twice to him about his overbearing rudeness to both Missy and Sam. There was also a full complement of agents in the barn. She'd offered Sandy the weekend off to escape this, but Sandy had said she'd stick it out. A state police car was parked where the dirt driveway turned off from the county road and two police boats were anchored at a discreet distance down the estuary.

They sat down to dinner at eight-fifteen. Alexis tried hard not to let her emotions show. She felt the presence of Adrian James everywhere and with the feeling, persistent sadness and guilt. Then, also, since she'd seen Andrew Taylor and talked to Valerie McCullough, she felt halfway back to her old life as a correspondent, and protocol had become harder than ever to bear.

Figueira was a graying, cold-eyed man with steel-rimmed glasses. He had come over ostensibly on an arms purchasing junket, but in reality to give the Portuguese people additional reassurance that their government was closely backed by the United States. Alexis found him very difficult to talk to. By the time dinner was over he began to represent to her all the resentment toward her duties as wife of the Secretary of State she realized she'd long harbored and half-buried. She felt not much more than a convenience. But glancing at her husband in animated conversation at the next table, some of her resentment ebbed. She found herself asking whether her feelings might not be exaggerated because of the suspicion he was under. She made every effort to throw herself back into being a good hostess.

Her resentment rose up again, however, when after dinner Harold unexpectedly announced that the men would retire to his study for brandy and cigars and she was left to serve coffee to the women in the library. He had agreed never to do this. For a moment, listening to safe inanities concerning language differences or Portuguese impressions of America, Alexis felt as though she were in the nineteenth century.

A Marine Corps string ensemble was setting up in the living room. She left the women for a moment to speak to their leader and turned back to hear the young wife of the Senate Foreign Relations chairman ask a question she would not have asked if she were more experienced. Diplomats didn't usually discuss politics at any but very private functions.

"Are the Communists really going to be a threat in your elections?"

It was addressed to the Foreign Minister's wife, a

haughty doña in her late middle age who forced a smile. "Of course not. There is no threat from them at all," she replied. "Especially not since General Volker's recent trip to Lisbon."

The young woman realized she'd probably said the wrong thing and tried to back away. "We'd heard they were so well organized," she said. "But our media never gets anything right. I'm sure they couldn't be."

Nettie Wilderstein had neither that tact nor intelligence. "Communism," she pronounced in her high nasal tone, "is always a threat. Whether organized or not."

She appealed to the Foreign Minister's wife, but it was General Figueira's wife who answered. She was a brittle woman with narrow features and a superior air. "It depends on the country," she said in a humorless tone. "Our Communists have numbers, yes, and perhaps that has been misinterpreted. They have numbers, but no force. After all, they are just workers, peasants. Most of them can't read or write."

"Animals," the doña assented in a murmur.

The General's wife's voice rose slightly. "You have to see the way they live. Dirt floors. They cook outdoors on charcoal fires. Plumbing? They don't know it exists. Some don't even have oxen. Who pulls the plow? The women." She laughed. "That's your Portuguese Communist. The eleventh century. We don't let them worry us. Besides, the Army wouldn't stand for their nonsense if it ever became serious."

Alexis was surprised. It was not an attitude she had ever found among the many more modern and liberated Portuguese women she knew. She wondered at the woman's vehemence. Later, during the concert, she remembered a Colonel Catarino who had called Harold the night he got back from Portugal. She had refrained from ever asking Harold about him again, not wanting to be reminded of the distress that his lie had caused her. Senhora

Figueira was seated next to her and during an interval she casually brought up his name. The reaction she got was another surprise. The General's wife looked completely taken aback for a moment. Then her eyes narrowed warily. "A Colonel Catarino? Here? In Washington?"

"He called my husband one night. He said he was on your husband's staff."

"There must be some mistake. I've never heard of him." Senhora Figueira had regained her composure and laughed. "I'm afraid our Army is overloaded with Colonels, all ambitious and claiming an importance they do not have."

Getting ready for bed, Alexis decided to discuss the woman with Harold. She was at her dressing table taking off her makeup. "What's Figueira's wife's background?"

He came from the bathroom. He'd been brushing his teeth. "Wealth. Millions. Her father was the second biggest landowner in Portugal. He owns half the Alentejo. Wheat, cattle. The property was in the family for seven generations."

Alexis knew the district he spoke of, a vast hot area to the southwest of Lisbon, an area of cork and pine trees, a burned-out granary. There were few towns or even villages and for hundreds of years the peasants had lived in virtual serfdom.

"Like most big estates," he said, "it was confiscated right after the revolution." He draped his towel around his shoulders and sat beside her on her dressing table bench. "Did she tell you what animals the peasants are?"

"She told me women pulled the plows."

"You can bet *she* didn't. She had her own maid to dress and undress her and went to finishing school in Switzerland. She skied at St. Moritz and gambled away fifty men's yearly wages every night at Monte Carlo."

She laughed. "You don't like her either."

178

"Can't stand her." There was anger in his voice. Alexis had heard it before, rage and bitterness about the downtrodden, cynical skepticism at any hope of alleviating the misery of the third world. At the same time he embraced Arnold Wilderstein and his banking cronies, who if not actually waxing rich on the plight of the less fortunate, chose to turn a blind eye to their despair.

"I don't understand something," she said. "If they were such big landowners, how did Figueira survive the revolution? Why wasn't he exiled? Most of his friends were and I always heard he was the most right wing of all."

"He is. And he came close to it, I guess. Especially when the Communists dominated the Army in 1975. But he commands the loyalty of several key divisions and they didn't want to risk alienating them. At the same time he kept a very low profile and avoided stepping on anyone's toes. Figueira's always been a pragmatist. He wouldn't go to the wall for any political ideal. Position and money come first."

Alexis without turning, watched him in her mirror. He was relaxed and in the soft bedroom light she felt a surge of intimacy toward him. She wanted to rise from her dressing table and lead him to bed and make love to him, but she couldn't. The gulf between them was too wide. Knowing the truth had become a compulsion. She had to know. She began to brush her hair and suddenly found the nerve to ask where Catarino fitted in.

"Catarino?" He looked at her blankly.

A touch too blankly, she thought. Why? And why didn't he seem to remember the name?"

"The man who called you the evening you came back from Lisbon."

"Oh. That one."

"I asked General Figueira's wife and she'd never heard of him."

"That's not surprising. He's not important. Just a courier. He was bringing me a message from the new premier. He went back the next morning."

Alexis hid a wave of spontaneous anger. The man who had talked to her on the phone had not been just a courier. Couriers did not have breakfast with ambassadors. What would Harold say if she called him on it? It was the right moment; he was off guard.

She was phrasing questions in her mind when he rose, slipped on his robe, and began to rifle through his dispatch case. It was too late. The intimacy that made her feel safe to ask was gone.

"Have you lost something?"

"My *Heidelberg Review*. I thought I'd slip downstairs and catch up on it. Would you mind?"

"Of course not."

She came from her dressing table to help him look and found the magazine in the top flap of his suitcase. He kissed her and went off downstairs with it, looking, she thought, like a small boy with his favorite comic book. Sometimes it surprised her he could read it. It was in German and she would remember he was German, or had been. It was practically the only reminder she ever had.

She went to bed and turned out the light. A half-hour later she got up again. She had to talk to him. It couldn't be put off any longer. She would go downstairs into the quiet of the study and sit by his chair and tell him everything that was happening. She loved him, she was his wife. No matter what he was involved in he had to share it with her. Now was the time. Now, before he took steps that were irrevocable. There might never be another chance.

She stood in her housecoat on the landing outside their bedroom listening. The house was silent. They'd all gone to bed. From far away she heard momentary faint sounds of activity. A door slammed. That would be the agents in the barn, or the servants. The landing window looked over the estuary. Lights flickered on one of the security boats anchored there, reflecting on the still water.

He could resign, she thought. Change his course. Whatever. But do it now before Valerie McCullough or the FBI came up with evidence that would make doing anything impossible.

She went silently downstairs without turning on any lights and made her way across the dark hall. The grandfather clock ticked with slow methodical resonance. There was a light under the study door. She reached for the handle and stopped. There were voices. Her husband's and then she recognized the other. It was General Figueira.

She went slowly back upstairs again. What she wanted to say to Harold would have to wait. The moment had passed.

Twenty-Eight

"I managed to line up one of the small screening rooms," Valerie said, "so we don't have to get stiff necks from bending over a Movieola."

"That's wonderful," Alexis said. She had swallowed her pride and called Valerie McCullough to ask for help. To her surprise, she sensed none of the resentment in Andrew Taylor's new young protégée she'd felt on their first meeting. Valerie was warm and had bent over backward to be helpful. When Alexis arrived midafternoon, she presented her with an 8 by 10 glossy news photo.

"Francisco Jose Catarino," she said.

Alexis found herself looking at the tough, square, weathered face of a prematurely-gray, crew cut soldier still in his thirties. The mouth was wide and determined, the jaw solidly firm, the eyes were dark and intense.

"He commands an armored division," Valerie said, "and what do you want to bet he's got a playmate in every town in Portugal?" She laughed. "He can have me anytime. His biography is on the back."

Alexis scanned it. One word stood out among all others —Communist. He was a militant party member and in 1975 had been one of the principal leaders in an abortive Communist coup. She felt the old excitement every correspondent feels when stumbling onto something important. So much for anonymous courier, she thought.

Valerie handed her a stack of other photos. "Every politician we have a record of," she explained, "and half the Army."

They spent an hour familiarizing themselves with faces, and refreshing their knowledge of the 1974 Portuguese revolution from a short summary the news department had provided. Then they left Valerie's office to go downstairs to the screening room. It was a slow trip along the hall to the elevator. People kept recognizing Alexis and stopping her—correspondents, news editors, cameramen. Once or twice, Alexis found herself close to tears. She was grateful when the elevator doors closed and she could laugh when she had to ask Valerie for tissue to wipe her eyes and blow her nose.

She apologized. "I'm sorry. I didn't expect this."

"Nonsense. Enjoy it."

"It's like being home again."

The screening room had a dozen comfortable lounge chairs, each with its own telephone for reaching the outside or the projectionist. When they came in, the latter emerged from his booth at the back. He was large and perspiring and authoritative. He'd been with UBC for over thirty years. "Got the whole damn library in there, Miss McCullough. Not enough room for a Portuguese midget, let alone me." He thrust a typed list of the films at her, then did a double take on Alexis. "Gawd Almighty, look who's here!"

Alexis found herself welcomed all over again. It was nice, but it was even nicer to see how much the man liked her successsor. Valerie's position and authority made what they were doing far more bearable. Professionalism took some of the edge out of the nastiness.

"I ordered all the news footage we have on the Portuguese Army," Valerie told her, "as well as footage of the revolution. From now right back through 1974. About three hours' worth, I think, on a straight run. I didn't think you'd want to go back beyond that." She glanced at the list. "Where do we start, day one?"

"Sounds right to me."

Valerie returned the list to the projectionist. "That would be April twenty-fifth, 1974, I guess. Reel 43."

"Okay; 43 it is. If you want me to stop, just pick up the phone."

The projection booth door thudded heavily behind him. Alexis and Valerie took seats. The lights dimmed; the screen lightened. Numbers flicked across it, seven, six, five, four, and there was Lisbon in bright color and sunshine. A sea of people filled streets and plazas, joyously celebrating unexpected freedom from fifty years of iron dictatorship. There were laughing, smiling soldiers, thousands of them, in tanks, in armored cars, on foot, and everywhere surrounded by well-wishers. Red carnations peeped from silent gun barrels. On walls, long bare of any written sentiment, red paint blossomed into every kind of political symbol with the word "Liberdad" dominating all else.

"Stop." It was Valerie on her phone to the projectionist. "Back a few feet. The balcony shot."

The film flickered, reversed, stopped, framed. The revolutionary Junta, a half-dozen high-ranking officers looked down onto a huge plaza packed with cheering people.

"There's Figueira," Valerie said.

"You're right." Alexis had missed him. She warned herself to be more careful. "He doesn't look any different than he does now."

"It's the guy on the far right," Valerie told the projectionist. "The one with the gray hair and the steel-rimmed glasses."

The projectionist's voice came into the theater on a speaker. "He looks like one of Hitler's crowd."

184

"I think he'd like to have been. If you see him again, would you stop?"

"Sure."

"We're also looking for a much younger officer," Alexis said. "He ought to show up a reel or so from now. He's prematurely gray, has a crew cut, and is really tough. He'd most likely be with tanks or armored vehicles, but possibly at Communist meetings."

"We'll find him."

The screen moved again. Country scenes with armed soldiers at road blocks, village squares filled with milling peasantry, the Air Force roaring overhead, Naval ships in Lisbon's harbor. Public figures addressed banks of microphones or emerged from crisis meetings. And there were the fallen, the dreaded secret police and the informers, the petty and bullying bureaucrats of the dictator now filling the jails they had once haunted in a different role.

They saw Figueira twice more, always with senior officers and keeping in the background. Then Catarino finally appeared two reels later as Alexis had guessed. It was early in 1975 when the Communists had begun serious domination of the Army.

"There he is," she said. The film stopped, freezing five young officers outside the Headquarters Building of an armored division barracks in Lisbon. One of them was Catarino. They ran the reel again. The sound track reported growing division in the Army as it leaned farther and farther toward Communism. The officers were "young turks" who would throw their loyalty behind the Communists if a coup d'etat were attempted. It was January of 1975.

Turbulent political scenes followed. Mobs again milled Lisbon's main avenues. Massed red flags choked streets like rivers of blood. The hammer and sickle dominated graffiti. In the countryside there was rioting and sporadic shooting. The nation staggered through a long and frightening summer. But slowly, nine centuries of national common sense prevailed. Catholic and moderate resistance to the Communists grew. Saner heads in the Army, horrified by imminent civil war, broke Communist dominance.

Throughout, there was no question of where Catarino stood. In scene after scene, he appeared at Communist rallies or with officers who were leading the Communist takeover of the Army.

It was not until late in the evening, however, that the ninth reel of the film they ran produced the electrifying scene Alexis's hunch told her she might find, but which she hoped she would not. The scene was the Alentejo, the dry southern flatlands. The time was two years later. An armored column arbitrarily blocked tourist traffic heading south to the beaches of the Algarve. Junior officers, arrogantly amused, ignored the pleas of anxious French, Germans and English who emerged from cars loaded with beach paraphernalia. One tank was splashed scarlet with the hammer and sickle. In the background an Army limousine appeared and stopped. Two senior officers got out. Although camera emphasis was on tourist harrassment, it was clear who both officers were. One was Colonel Catarino, the other General Figueira.

"Can you slow it down?"

The scene crawled. Figueira waited by the limousine. Catarino went to shake hands warmly with the column commander. They discussed the holdup and Catarino ordered the commander to move his vehicles. He then rejoined Figueira.

The scene switched to the armored column as it pulled off the road. Tourist vehicles began to move again. In a final shot, the limousine drove away.

"Okay," Alexis said. "That's all I need."

186

Later, back in Valerie's office, they had coffee and discussed the connection between the two men.

"A Communist and a neofascist," Valerie said. She whistled astonishment. "Two impossible bedmates and from what you tell me obviously still very much in touch. What do you figure it means?"

"I wish I knew," Alexis replied.

But she knew very well. A desperate last loyalty to Harold was all that stopped her from telling Valerie what he'd said to her about Figueira the past weekend. Young Communists motivated by near religious fanaticism didn't sell out. They preferred death. But a compromising old General who liked wealth and position better than ideals, and who had a wife's fortune just out of reach, might well make a deal which would give him that fortune. Figueira was due to retire soon. He controlled key divisions in the Army. It was his last chance to use that leverage. The Communists in turn were about to lose a last chance to take over the government and turn the southern flank of NATO. Things were going against them in Portugal and because of their mole in her household they might also realize they were rapidly running out of time where help from her husband was concerned.

The ingredients were all there. It remained only to be seen how they were to be mixed.

And when?

The Portuguese President was due at the end of the week. His visit had been carefully orchestrated to achieve the maximum influence on the approaching Portuguese elections. He would benefit from the impact on the Portuguese voters not just of his arrival in the United States, his highly publicized stay at Camp David and his departure, but also from his arrival back home in Lisbon and his report to the Portuguese Parliament only days before the polls opened.

If there was to be a coup d'etat, what better time than during his absence? And if Figueira was to be part of it, what better screen to his treason than his presence in Washington with his president?

From her experience as a correspondent, Alexis knew the only thing she could do was wait and watch and hope that something of substance might soon happen which would tell her what her husband's role was. She would not know what to do until then, nor how to use that knowledge to extricate him and her marriage from the jeopardy both were in.

Exhausted by what she thought, she promised Valerie to keep in touch, kissed her warmly good-bye, and left. She'd finally realized that Valerie was using her. Her young successor had greater faith in Alexis Sobieski getting the story than in herself. It was cynical, but a back-handed compliment and Alexis found she didn't mind. Each to their own. Valerie was tough and she liked her. I would have done the same in her shoes, she thought, when I was fighting my way up. Exactly the same. And it was strange, it seemed only yesterday that she was.

Twenty-Nine

Portugal's President Luis Cabral arrived midmorning. His plane, a Portuguese Air Force 707, barely touched down at Andrews Air Force Base before an ugly squall line preceding a fast-moving cold front swept the field. He was met by the President of the United States. Inspection of an honor guard of Marines was canceled due to near torrential rain. Umbrellas shielded both presidents as the American read his salutatory remarks citing Portugal as one of his country's most honored allies and underscoring the critical role it played in NATO's shield of a free Europe.

President Cabral responded with an expression of his delight at being in the United States, a great nation that was an inspiration to democracy everywhere. He got polite laughs for injecting ad-lib humor about the weather when he suggested the summer White House be moved to the Algarve, the perpetually sunny Portuguese southern coast.

Metropolitan and state police motorcycle police phalanxed the presidential convoy back to the White House at siren-screaming speed. A small group of cold, wet Portuguese supporters of the Socialist-Communist coalition, mostly students, were kept several hundred yards down Pennsylvania Avenue so their placard-waving demonstration would not cause embarrassment.

After an informal lunch in the relatively intimate atmosphere of the "President's Dining Room" in the West

Wing, the weather began to clear. Both presidents with their accompanying wives left by helicopter for a weekend of talks and relaxation at Camp David. They were accompanied by the Secretary of State and his wife.

Alexis, approaching the weekend skeptically, to her surprise found herself having a delightful time. President Cabral's wife was a modern woman and the direct antithesis of the two wives she had entertained at Brigham Bay. Just turned forty, she was passionately interested not only in Portuguese politics, but in everything political, in the United States as well as in Europe. She was well read and well informed, spoke four languages, and was clearly involved in her own career as well as her husband's. She was a marine biologist, one of her country's leading conservationists and an outspoken advocate of women's rights. She played good tennis, too. Alexis ruefully found that once more the only person she could beat was her old rival, the American President. She was sorry when the presidential families came back to Washington Sunday afternoon and she and Harold had to do the same.

They had tickets to a ballet at the Kennedy Center. They ate an early light dinner, dressed, and were ready to go when Harold was called to the phone. He came back from it to tell her he had to go to the Department.

"That was Operations. There's been some kind of movement by the Libyans on the hostage situation. They need immediate advice."

Alexis didn't try to hide her disappointment. Looking forward to the ballet had lessened the letdown of returning from the escapist atmosphere of Camp David to be alone with her husband and having to face again the reality of what he might be involved in.

She tried to disguise the growing hostility she'd begun to feel toward him. "Oh, hell, Harold. Couldn't you tell them anything they need to know on the phone?"

"I'm afraid this one's a bit more complicated than that.

You go ahead with Sandy. I may be able to join you for the last act."

Alexis protested he'd undoubtedly end up at the Department for the whole evening. "If you don't mind," she said, "I have a good book. I'd just as soon stay home."

"Darling, it's not that easy. One of us has to go. And I can't. The tickets are complimentary and the show is standing room only. It would be damned impolite not to."

She remembered the Kennedy Center manager presenting them with the tickets the last time they'd been there.

"He's a nice guy," Harold said. "And useful. We can't afford his feeling put out."

He kept at it and she gave up. Fifteen minutes later she was on her way into town with Sandy.

"You get to see the ballet," she said acidly.

"Until General Volker comes anyway," Sandy protested.

Alexis knew she was secretly delighted.

"He won't," she said emphatically. She clashed gears accelerating too fast coming out of a corner.

"Just the same, it's very nice of you to let me come," Sandy said.

She sounded vaguely hurt. Alexis realized she was being unfairly ill-tempered, but couldn't help it. She sensed she was being got rid of. It was the same feeling she'd had at the FBI office when Farr and Bill Rupert had fobbed her off. She told herself she was being foolish. It was hardly Harold's fault he'd been called out. But her uneasiness would not go away.

They parked the Lancia in the area reserved for officials and went into the lobby. It was crowded. Alexis spotted the manager and presented her husband's apologies. The bell sounded for the first curtain, and she and Sandy entered the auditorium. They were going down the aisle to their seats when she realized it was Harold's seeming anxiety about the manager that didn't ring true. It had taken only seconds with the man to realize he didn't mind at all if she missed the performance. He'd already won his points in presenting the tickets. Surely Harold wouldn't have misjudged him so.

Why had he been so insistent, then?

There was only one answer: because he wasn't going to the Department. He was staying home and didn't want her to know. And the only reason he'd do that would be because he planned to meet with someone he could not safely meet elsewhere and he didn't want anyone who would understand the meeting's implications to know. Not even her. Perhaps especially not her.

Alexis hesitated. Was she being paranoid? The usher was waiting, smiling. People had risen to let her and Sandy reach their seats.

"Excuse me. I'm sorry." She grabbed Sandy's hand and ignoring her surprise, dragged her back up the aisle and out into the lobby, now nearly empty.

"Look, Sandy. You've got to do something for me. Go back in and watch the ballet. I'll join you for the second act. Or maybe the third."

"Where are you going?"

"Home."

"But you can't."

"Why not?"

"Not with me staying here. I'm under orders. I've got to stay with you. You know that."

"Please, Sandy. I don't want both seats empty. If you're in yours, people will think I'm in the building at least. The bar or the ladies' room."

"But Alexis, if anything should happen to you, I'd lose my job. Permanently. And it isn't just that. I'd have you on my conscience for the rest of my life."

Alexis tried not to let rising frustration get the better of her. "Sandy, be reasonable. I'm only going straight to R Street and coming back. What could happen to me?"

"A lot."

"No. Nothing. You know as well as I we haven't had a crank call since the original one. Nor anything which would require a bodyguard. We're stuck with bureaucracy. Sandy, dammit, we're friends and I need your help. If I get mugged or shot or God knows what, you must know I'd never blame you or hold you responsible."

Sandy hesitated.

"Darling, please. This is important to me. Really important."

The final bell rang for seats.

Sandy smiled wryly. "What do I say if the General shows up?"

Alexis kissed her impulsively. "You'll think of something."

She slipped quickly out of the Center and went to her car. She drove up the Potomac Parkway toward Georgetown and then up through Georgetown toward R Street. Fast. But not too fast. She didn't want an accident or an alert police cruiser tying her up. When she got to Q Street and Twenty-eighth, she parked. She recognized the spot. It was where Adrian James had waited for her the day she'd taken him down to Brigham Bay. A hundred yards up Twenty-eigth Street was an old back-garden servants' entrance she'd used to evade Steve Riker.

She locked the car and started toward it.

Thirty

Twenty-eighth Street was narrow and tree-lined and descended steeply from R Street and the Wilderstein home where the Volkers lived. Where the property ended a hundred and fifty feet down from the corner, the grounds were ten feet above the sidewalk and supported by a massive brick wall half-covered with moss.

The gate there was very narrow, perhaps just wide enough for a delivery boy with a carton of groceries. With ivy spilling down both sides, a person could walk past without ever noticing it. The rusty iron work was simple, six straight square vertical bars with dangerously sharp tips held rigid by the three crosspieces, the middle one with a night latch. Past the gate, narrow brick steps rose steeply to the back garden. Light from the nearest street lamp near R Street was partially blocked by a line of trees. But Alexis could still see that since she'd last used the gate, which opened easily from the inside by simply lifting the latch, a chain with a heavy padlock had been added.

Stymied before she'd even begun, she chewed her lip, wondering what to do, hoping no evening stroller or car would come by. The brick wall ran smoothly in both directions. Tree branches extending over it began out of reach above the street. She had to scale the gate itself. She tied up her skirt and got a foot up onto the middle crossbar between two vertical ones. Then she seized the bars and pulled herself up. Standing on her toes, she could just reach the top of the wall. Her fingers groped and found what seemed to be a solid hold. She raised one foot up to the gate's top traversing bar and pulled herself up again to a precarious crouch. The sharp tips of the bars brushed against her stomach. Her heart thudded and her mouth was dry. If she slipped and lurched forward, she'd be speared.

She had to move. Arches and calves screaming, she slowly stood. She glanced down. The street seemed a mile below her. She quickly took her eyes away from it. The top of the wall was now at her waist, but it seemed higher. Immediately beyond was dank, thick shrubbery. She hooked both her elbows into the ground and bellied her way up and forward, face thrusting into branches and cobwebs. Something skittered across her neck and arm. She just managed not to jerk back. In a moment, she was standing with a scraped knee and a torn skirt. Holding onto bushes, she moved alongside the rising steps until she was on a weed-choked flagstone path leading to the back of the house and the kitchen.

The kitchen lights were on. She stopped short in shadows as a man in his shirt sleeves walked past the windows. Everett. He had a coffeepot and went with it into the adjacent butler's pantry, on the opposite side of the kitchen from where she stood. She knew that the cook who lived out had already departed.

For the first time, she faced the problem of how she was going to get in without being caught. Up to now, she hadn't even considered it. It seemed ridiculous; it was her own home. But if Harold heard she'd left the ballet and come here, she'd never be able to make up a story he'd believe and any chance to help him and their marriage might be destroyed forever. Before she did anything, she had to be certain he was there and that all of this wasn't for nothing. She left the flagstone path and keeping beyond white squares of window light on the lawn, headed toward the west wing.

She began to worry about security. Had she already disturbed a motion or sound detector? She'd heard no alarm, nor seen any of the agents. The house itself was wired, but the system was never turned on until both she and Harold were in bed. When they'd first moved in, they had too frequently set it off with unexpected evening sorties.

She reached a point opposite his study and stopped. The room was dark. The curtains were open. But almost as she wondered what to do next, the door from the corridor opened and a man stepped in. Everett again. He turned on the lights. He was wearing his jacket now and carrying a tray with cups and a silver coffee service. He put it down on the desk, looked around, and left. His action meant one thing: Harold was indeed there.

She didn't have long to wait. Within minutes, the study door opened again and her husband appeared. Her immediate discomfort at spying on him was partly assuaged by the presence of the man who followed him in. It was General Figueira. She waited while they made themselves comfortable, Harold pouring coffee, then moved back the way she had come.

She knew now precisely what she had to do. Harold's office was officially bugged. Whenever he wanted, his secretary could keep a taped record of meetings. The Akai machine was in the adjoining secretarial office and could be turned on simply by flicking a switch. She would rewind and collect the tape early in the morning before the secretaries came in.

Everett had reappeared neither in the kitchen nor the butler's pantry. That meant he was in the dining room, setting the table for breakfast. Alexis knew her time had nearly run out. If she was going to use the kitchen door, she would have to move quickly and decisively. If she set

196

off an alarm, she would have to think of a suitable story for whatever agent appeared. She had the advantage. She was Harold Volker's wife and they wouldn't see her as an intruder.

She braced herself, walked quickly to the door, and tried the handle. It opened. A second later, she was in the kitchen with its bright overhead lights. Across it lay a hallway leading to the office wing. As she headed for it past the open pantry, the door to the dining room swung in and Everett appeared, backing through it with a heavily loaded tray. She leaped forward. By the time he turned, she had closed the door to the hallway softly behind her.

On the other side, she paused to pull herself together. That one had been too close. Entering the corridor, she hadn't known whether anyone was in it or not. There hadn't been time to listen. It was a short passageway with doors on each side leading to utility rooms. At the end was the door to the west wing. She heard nothing and opened it carefully onto the plush-carpeted corridor beyond.

The corridor was empty, its light on. At the far end, the door to the front hall was closed. The open doorways of the offices, and the theater and projection rooms across from them were dark shadows for possible safety. If someone came, she could duck into one. She headed for the secretarial office next to her husband's study.

The Akai was on its own table by the desk closest to the door between the two rooms. When Alexis went to it, she could hear the faint muffled voices of her husband and General Figueira. She hurriedly explored the machine. To her dismay, both its reels were empty of tape. She looked around, eyes adjusting to the near darkness. She tried desk drawers. They were locked. So was a steel cabinet. So were file cases. There were no reels on any of the book-shelves. Obviously, they'd been put away for the night and probably in the safe she remembered stood in one corner and could now even begin to see.

The disappointment was acute, her fear more so. Sustained by a goal, she had managed to control rising panic that said forget the whole business, turn, and run. Now she had to force herself to listen at the door. The voices were still unintelligibly muffled. She tried kneeling head down to the threshold over which came a faint sliver of light.

She rose, defeated. She couldn't stay there. The risk was too great. A visitor in her husband's study could mean a routine security check on adjoining rooms. She started to retrace her steps. The best way out, she decided, was through a window of her own office.

She was halfway back down the corridor when her husband's study door opened. She barely had time to duck into the theater. He came out and went to the front hall, leaving both doors open. Peering out, she could see him talking to Steve Riker. His back was turned and Riker was facing her. But Riker was looking at Harold, not down the corridor. She took a chance and ran for her own office suite.

She waited tensely by Allison Palmer's desk. Had Riker seen her or not? She didn't dare look. She heard the hall door shut and after it the one to the study.

Then silence.

It was because of the silence that something suddenly struck her. Harold's office had been silent, too. It was a cool evening and he had not turned on his air conditioner. Voices might carry through its ventilator shutters or even through the window itself.

She went into her own office. In a bottom drawer of her desk was the tape recorder she'd used in television. By modern standards it was large and clumsy, the size of a heavy book, but she still used it for dictation and the batteries were good. She got it out and slipped in a new one-hour cassette. Then she went into her bathroom to repair herself. She pulled the blinds, turned on the lights,

198

washed her dirt-caked hands and elbows, combed her hair, and fixed her makeup. She found safety pins and closed the tear in her dress. With luck, she could get back out without further damage. She grabbed a towel to put on top of the wall and returned to her office to listen carefully a moment in the dark before she quietly unlocked and opened one of the windows. Outside, the garden was equally silent. She stepped over the windowsill into a flower bed and closed the window behind her.

Staying close to the protectively dark wall of the house, she edged along until she reached the first window of Harold's study. The curtains were pulled shut now. She listened. Harold's voice came faintly but clearly through the air conditioner. She put her tape recorder directly beneath the window, under a concealing laurel bush, and hung the microphone from one of the branches so it was inches from the air conditioner's grill. She doubted that anyone would come close enough to find it. She pressed the button to record and turned the volume up full. She couldn't see if the tape was turning, but the recorder had never failed her. How and when to retrieve it was a bridge she would cross later. Not now. Now, she had to get back to the Kennedy Center as quickly as possible.

She returned along the side of the house. When she was midway between the study and the still-lighted kitchen, she ducked across the lawn into the shrubbery and trees beyond. She turned and waited. She saw nobody. She carefully made it back to the brick steps leading down to the service gate, tied up her skirt once more, and again edged along the brick wall until she was just above the gate itself. She put her towel down on the dirt under the bushes and cautiously lowered herself into the bushes and onto her stomach, easing her legs down off the wall and feeling for the top of the gate and the sharp projecting tips of its upright iron bars. One jabbed at her ankle. She moved her foot down it until her toes touched the traverse bar, followed with her other foot, and let the bar take her weight.

What happened then took seconds. And seemed forever.

The rough hand that clamped around her ankle and the voice were simultaneous.

She heard the voice and what it said even as a kind of total terror paralyzed the scream that rose instantly to her throat.

"Freeze. Don't move until we have a look at you. Don't talk and don't move or I'll pull you right down onto the spikes, understand?"

She looked back under her arm. Half-light from the street lamp shone on Steve Riker. He had his revolver out. He held fast to her ankle, shoved the revolver into his waistband, and pulled a small flashlight from his jacket.

He flicked it on.

Its beam swung toward her. But suddenly flew into a wild twisting arc as the flashlight shot over the gate onto the street.

One moment Riker was standing. The next, a body piled down on top of him from the head of the steps and smashed him against the iron bars. An arm swung. Something glinted. There was an audible crack, his legs collapsed, and he was an unconscious huddled shadow wedged between the gate and the bottom step.

Sandy Muscioni straightened and caught her breath. "Stay put, if you can, until I get onto the street." She dropped her .25 automatic into her evening purse and ran back up the steps. Bushes rustled, there was the sound of her dropping off the wall onto the street. She reappeared at once on the other side of the gate and climbed halfway up it.

"Can you reach my hand?" She stretched up. "Okay, now go slow. Right foot first. Jesus, he must have scared the hell out of you."

Alexis used her steadying grip and in a moment was back down on the street.

"Okay?"

"Yes." Alexis was shaking too hard to say more.

"Wait a minute," Sandy said. She scooped up Riker's flashlight and shone it at him. A trickle of blood ran down his temple. "I whipped him with my automatic," she explained, matter-of-factly. She reached through the bars and lifted one of his eyelids. The eye moved. "He'll be all right. Just confused." She straightened. "Let's go. And quick. But don't run."

They walked down to Q Street and the Lancia.

Alexis drove. "What made you come?"

"I smelled trouble. You gave me the impression you weren't going in the front door. Riker doesn't like you and I knew he'd be happy as hell to embarrass you somehow."

"Do you think he knew it was me?"

"I don't think so. He didn't see your face and you being where you were would have been completely out of context for him."

Sandy took her .25 automatic from her purse and put it back in its holster on the inside of her upper thigh.

Alexis said, awed, "My God, you really move when you move, don't you. When did you get there?"

Sandy laughed. "About ten minutes after you. You were just coming out your office window."

"Thank you, Sandy." Alexis reached out and touched Sandy's shoulder.

Sandy squeezed her hand. "No problem, boss lady. Unless General Volker ruins everything by knocking off early and finding two empty seats."

But he didn't and they made it back in time for the third act. It seemed impossible to Alexis that she'd been gone for less than an hour. Glancing at Sandy seated next to her and immersed in the ballet as though nothing had happened, she couldn't believe what she had just been through. It was like a dream.

But it wasn't a dream, she knew. It was real. Everything her husband and General Figueira said was being recorded right then, and unless someone found the machine she might know in the morning exactly what was being planned for Portugal. She dreaded the moment.

Thirty-One

The phone rang insistently and long. It was green and sat on the kitchen counter, a strident and intrusive voice, unattended. David Farr watched it with a sort of perverse satisfaction. The chances were slim the caller wanted him. It would be someone who wanted Susan. A furious stubbornness, akin to jealousy and punishment, prevented him from answering. His hand remained frozen to his coffee cup.

Susan burst into the kitchen, diving for it. She was in her bathrobe with a towel around her head. She'd washed her hair. He'd come down earlier and made coffee and sat drinking it and listening to the far-off hiss of the shower.

"Why don't you answer it?" She snatched the receiver from its cradle. "Hello? Oh, hi, Barbara. No, go ahead."

Barbara would be half of a young couple they knew. The other half was a chemical engineer. They were two people they enjoyed and saw frequently. A year ago they'd spent a long weekend together exploring Montreal. He glanced at his watch. The husband worked in Baltimore. He would have left for work long ago.

He heard Susan speak to him. "David, Barbara wants to have a drink with me after work. Is that all right? What time do you expect to be home?"

Susan had the afternoon off, he remembered. And a major spinal operation this morning. He shrugged. "As usual."

"But that could mean anything. Six? Seven?"

"Seven."

She spoke to the phone again. "Sure. How about five-thirty? Mass Avenue and Fourth Street? That restaurant-bar with the outdoor tables and the big tree. It's close to your job."

Barbara worked in the New Senate Office Building as an assistant to the Chairman of the Committee on Foreign Relations. She was a white girl, a blonde with a bright curious mind and unlimited enthusiasm which made her exciting and worthwhile to be with. That was her good side. Her bad side was that she'd once made passes at him when she'd had too much to drink and another time he'd seen her openly flirting with another woman. She had beautiful breasts which were very large for someone in her twenties and liked to show them by wearing thin sweaters or half-opened blouses. She also wore provocative perfume and talked openly about the sex she had with her husband who was a black, but shades lighter than himself, a serious, dedicated young man in a constant state of exhaustion from overwork. Like Susan, she also had the energy for endless friendships and knew everybody.

A few days ago he'd found out she knew Valerie Mc-Cullough.

He heard Susan hang up. He was staring into his coffee cup and felt the warmth of her body as she came to stand next to him, one hand on the back of his neck. He didn't look up.

"David, what's the matter?"

"Nothing."

"There is. Something's really bothering you. Why don't you tell me?"

"Nothing's wrong, Susan."

She studied him, then kissed his forehead gently and began to make them breakfast: scrambled eggs and bacon and toast. She poured orange juice first. He glanced up when her back was turned and she was at the refrigerator. Her bathrobe couldn't hide the delicate feminine lines of her slender body.

He wanted her so badly he ached. Wanted to step over and spin her around and flatten her body against his, feel the softness of her breasts and pubis against his half-nakedness, wanted to crush her lips with his mouth and feel the wet flame of her tongue touch his. Wanted to hurl her down on a bed and drive deep into her.

Wanted her and hated her at the same instant. Wanted to lash out and smash his fist across her face. Wanted to cry out how much he loved her in a kind of hurt, desperate, miserable, painful rage that obsessed him day and night. How he hated her in an agony of caring and tenderness.

"You haven't discussed the Volker mess in days. Is that it? What's happening?"

"Nothing. Routine. I told you. Flat-footed police work. Dead ends."

"Do you think anything will surface? Maybe with all this election crisis in Portugal?"

"I doubt it."

He could hardly tell her that Alexis Volker had called yesterday for an urgent meeting with him and Bill Rupert. Not when he'd never again confide in her about his work. Not when he had a special unit shadowing her all the time, watching and reporting her every move, compiling a dossier on all her friends beginning with the orthopedic surgeon who had gone to Paris with Adrian James and another girl.

Nor could he tell her about the tortured hours at dawn when he lay awake listening to the quiet breathing of her deep untroubled sleep and imagined her lying soft and yielding in another woman's arms, perhaps with another man. He could hardly let her know what pain it cost him not to call her at the hospital when she said she was working late for fear she might not be there. Or reveal the relief he felt when the tails he had on her reported she had indeed been working all evening. And how could he ever explain his complete humiliation at the impotency which had crept into their lives or that his failure as a man was now ironically alleviated by his seething emotional turmoil, but that his pride wouldn't let him tell her he was feeling capable of making love again?

The eggs and bacon and toast tasted like sand.

He wanted to cry and lay his head on her bosom and beg her for mercy. Men didn't.

"David, we've got to talk."

"Sure. Tonight maybe."

It was eight-thirty. There was already a report about her yesterday's activities on his desk.

"We love each other too much to go on like this."

He didn't answer.

She waited, then went to get dressed.

He drank his cold coffee.

They were getting close to a break in the case he was building against her. A woman agent had managed to strike up a friendship with Valerie McCullough. He'd interviewed her in his office yesterday. She was willing to go all the way with McCullough or anyone else, male or female, to pull off a successful scam. She was tough as hell. And ambitious. Sealing the leak would get her a major promotion.

He wondered what had happened to innocence and chastity and romance in women. And in men. Making love had become an uninvolved bodily function.

Susan didn't say good-bye to him when she left for work. Her expression as she walked out of the house was hurt and angry.

He drove downtown to the Hoover Building at nine and on the way three times viciously cut off other cars.

Thirty-Two

An hour cassette tape weighs less than four ounces and its measurements are slightly smaller than those of the average wallet. The one in Alexis's shoulder bag also had an overwhelming presence. For her it possessed actual life and she was constantly aware of it. She'd slipped out last night the moment she'd come home and collected it before the security alarm was turned on. In the morning, after breakfast with Harold, she'd played it in the privacy of her office. Since then, it had become the dominating factor in every second, minute, and hour that slipped by.

Waiting for Bill Rupert to finish the inane story he'd picked up from the President, one she'd already heard herself a half-dozen times, she remembered the cold detachment she'd begun to feel from Harold as she'd listened to his recorded voice. As he talked he became not the man she laughed with and drank and ate with and shared good and bad times and bed with, but a stranger.

"The timing is critical, Francisco. If you don't get underway at least twenty-four hours before the President returns to Lisbon, his presence back there could stop it. The Army still wouldn't have sufficient control over the situation."

"But that's just it. Catarino says he needs more time to get his armor positioned. He was emphatic about it."

"Tell him he hasn't got it. There's also my own timing

involved. I've held up a settlement on the hostages for this. I can't any longer and I need national focus on Libya to help persuade the President and Congress to adopt a hands-off policy in Portugal until it's too late to intervene."

She heard David Farr speaking. "What's on the agenda, Mrs. Volker?"

She turned to face him. When she'd come in, she'd thought he looked drawn and tired. He'd given her the silent impression of a man with his back to a wall.

"It obviously isn't something you felt you could say on the phone," he went on, "and we pretty well cleared the decks last time of small talk or minor details."

"You're right," she said. She'd rehearsed what to say a dozen times. She'd worked it out even before she'd finished playing the tape the first time. "I have a proposition to make. You might call it plea bargaining."

Farr studied her. So she knows, he thought. He wondered for how long and how she'd found out. He glanced at Bill Rupert. The Director looked vaguely uneasy. There was premonition in his eyes. He rolled his pencil nervously between thumb and forefinger.

"I take it you're referring to our former talk," Rupert said. "What's come up?"

"What always was there, Bill."

"I'm afraid I don't follow."

Farr wondered at Rupert's complete lack of appreciation for her intelligence. He smiled inwardly at her acid reply.

"I think you do."

And said, himself, "Go ahead, Mrs. Volker."

He waited, ignoring the annoyed glance Rupert shot him. She seemed to hesitate a moment as though mentally bracing herself. She looked very beautiful, he thought, in a skirt and blouse and because the weather was cool, a light cardigan. She had the same Gucci leather shoulder bag

208

she'd carried the first time he'd met her and it was again slung casually from the back of her chair.

But he'd been aware, from the moment she came into the office five minutes ago, of far more than just a well-bred and lovely woman. She was like a suppressed volcano. She knew something and she knew something that was dynamite. He was convinced of it. Sandy had told him she left the ballet to go home and had to be rescued from near trouble with Riker. Sandy didn't know what she'd done there, but it looked bad. Volker had had an apparently secret meeting with General Figueira.

"I'd like to make a deal," she finally said. The look she gave him was very direct. "It's this. I persuade Harold to resign and you drop your investigation of him. I want until Sunday."

Farr saw Rupert glance his way again. The Director was a man who hated facing the truth. Even now he was going to try to save face because she'd discovered he'd lied to her in their first meeting.

"I can't remember our having said we were investigating your husband," Rupert said.

"*We* didn't," she replied. Her voice was firm. "But you are. You know you are. I know you are, so please, don't waste our time. Yours or mine." She shrugged. "You have a leak here at the Bureau. Let's just let it go at that."

It was a complete surprise to Rupert. He swung around sharply in his chair, started to speak, then abruptly shut up. His eyes became furious. Farr hadn't told him about the leak. And he didn't intend to start now. Replying to her remark himself would only focus on it, make things worse. But his silence was just as bad. It told Rupert he knew. The Director would be livid he'd been once more ignored and he'd probably have to threaten to resign to calm him down. But it wasn't that which depressed him. He'd get away with it because the President knew what the score was with Rupert and with his own skin in jeopardy would rather put his money on the Bureau's professionals. What depressed him was all Rupert's unnecessary posturing. And the persuasion he'd have to employ to get the man to understand the obvious and do the only thing that could be done. He was tired. He'd never felt so tired in his life. Ever since Fein had told him about the leak, the job had turned into an albatross. The only reason he could keep his mind on it was the woman who sat waiting for him to say something. He sensed her life, like his own, teetered on the edge of ruin. He was in a way partly responsible. The least he could do was try to help her.

"I take it, Mrs. Volker, that you've come onto something you can use as leverage to persuade your husband to resign?"

She smiled faintly. "Let's put it this way. On Harold's behalf as well as on my own, I plead the Fifth Amendment."

"Could I ask if this leverage could be considered as working against him outside of the context of marriage?"

"I'd have to refuse to answer that, too," she said. She waited. She thanked God for him. She thanked God that in the whole monstrous bureaucracy which was the government, fate had put her in the hands of a man who was human as well as intelligent. She studied his dark, thoughtful face. One of his massive hands rose to rub his chin.

He moved suddenly, turning to Bill Rupert. "I recommend we accept her proposition."

Rupert pushed a further rush of resentment from his eyes and put on the expression of a man taking charge. "I appreciate your gesture, David," he turned to Alexis. There was a certain vindictiveness now in his tone. "And Alexis, I appreciate what you've offered, whatever your motives might be. But I'm afraid neither Mr. Farr nor I have the authority to do what you request. Only the Presi-

210

dent can do that. If you want me to set up a meeting with him, I will."

It was precisely what Farr expected. Rupert was opting to take no responsibility and that could be dangerous. The President would again feel obliged to ask the opinion of his Chief of Staff, "Duke" Chancery and his Security Adviser, Bernard Kornovsky. Both would take a different position than before when with no hard evidence against Volker in sight, only suspicion, they had urged the President to "Watergate" any investigation. Now they would decide, as he had, that if Alexis Volker's leverage was hard evidence, such evidence might surface elsewhere. To protect themselves they would decide to pressure the President to turn down her request and order the investigation continued. Getting rid of Volker would no longer be enough.

Worse, neither man, Farr knew, had sufficient intelligence, experience, or understanding of the ruthlessness of the KGB to appreciate the situation. They would quite likely hound Alexis Volker for what they thought she had and in doing so would surely expose her position and put her in serious jeopardy.

He thought he knew a way out. "There's something," he said abruptly to Rupert, "I think you and I must discuss a moment. Privately."

He fixed Rupert with a hard stare and waited. He was counting on Rupert's smaller and self-serving view of the situation. If it ever turned out Volker were innocent, Rupert wouldn't want to be in a position with Alexis Volker where he had refused to listen to arguments from someone who was clearly on her side. He would have made an enemy for nothing.

It obviously didn't take long for Rupert to decide that listening wouldn't commit him to anything. He wasn't a politician for nothing. He put on a dinner-party smile.

"Sure," he said. "Alexis, would you mind waiting outside for a moment?"

She rose silently. He left his desk and held the door for her. When he closed it, his smile had vanished. "Let's have it," he said to Farr.

Farr explained to him what he thought about Chancery and Kornovsky. "My guess," he added, "is that something's about to happen in Portugal, but they'll never believe it with the Portuguese President here and Volker wining and dining him. They won't understand that Volker might have a lot of pressure on him to pull off one last one because time, for him, might be running out, that the KGB might know we're after him, witness Adrian James. But I think if anything does happen, it will occur while the Portuguese president is still here. That's only a few days. Frankly, I wouldn't want to be in your shoes if anything did. Those two guys at the White House would pass the buck to you and fast. It would be your fault Volker wasn't stopped. Not theirs."

Rupert's eyes were suddenly small and mean again. He said, "Not necessarily. There's an alternative. What makes you think anyone would ever have to know what her proposition is or even that she made it?"

"But she did," Farr said.

"Screw it," Rupert exclaimed. "It's the Bureau's word against hers and if Volker were proved guilty, I don't think anyone would be inclined to listen to what his wife has to say."

Farr felt a wave of fury. It was typical and he should have seen it coming. Bury the fact Alexis had made an offer and if anything went wrong, the ball was in the President's court. Or in his. The President had placed him in charge of the investigation. If Rupert kept quiet, Rupert would be out of it. He hadn't wanted to hold a pistol to Rupert's head, but he knew now he had to.

212

"You might be right about Mrs. Volker," he said quietly, "but I think they'd listen to me."

"What do you mean?" The color slowly drained from Rupert's face.

"I mean I'd blow the whistle on you."

"You wouldn't dare."

"It's your option to take the risk," Farr said. He felt more cheerful. He'd used Rupert's inexperience and lack of Bureau know-how to corner him. Rupert had forgotten something a first-month trainee would probably have remembered. "Of course, you could decide to fire me," he said, "but it would all come out anyway. And it wouldn't be the word of a disgruntled employee who'd broken his oath of confidentiality, someone who could be bullied into keeping his mouth shut with a rigged-up court order. Every meeting you hold in this office is taped. This one is no exception. Are you going out to tell your secretary to erase it and have two potential whistle blowers on your hands?"

When after a few moment's silence Rupert surrendered, the full politician in him emerged. He smiled with sudden amiability. "All right, Mr. Farr. You certainly won that one. What do I do?"

Farr managed to suppress his own smile. He cast himself back in the role of a respectful employee advising an intelligent boss. "Simple, sir. You agree to Mrs. Volker's request, as I recommend. If she's successful and Volker resigns, *then* we'll go to the White House. With a dead-end case. No evidence. No hope of any. The President did the right thing. He ordered a complete investigation. We tried, but got nowhere. Why go on? Volker's out and nobody can be accused of a cover-up."

Rupert thought it over. "I think I rather like that," he said. He buzzed his secretary and asked her to show Alexis back in.

When he'd accepted her proposition, he was unable, however, to resist a last touch of vindictiveness. "You realize, Alexis, that applying your so-called leverage to your husband could be risky for you."

"Why?" she replied. "Harold loves me."

"It might go beyond Harold."

"I've considered that, too, Bill. But what do you think my life is like the way it is?"

This time Rupert let Farr see her out.

Farr walked her down the hall to the elevator. He gave her his personal card with his home number on it in case she needed to reach him urgently. He remembered doing the same thing for Adrian James and felt cold fear in the pit of his stomach. Her call yesterday for this morning's meeting and then Sandy's report had alerted him she had not dropped the matter of her husband. During the night he'd racked his brain for ways to guarantee her protection. Today, anything he could do seemed inadequate.

When he touched the call button, it was as though she read his mind. She said, "Mr. Farr, if anything should happen to me, I want you to have this. If nothing does, I count on you to keep it completely confidential."

She pulled the tape from her shoulder bag, looked at it reflectively, then handed it to him.

Farr put it in his pocket. "The leverage?"

"Yes."

"Portugal?"

"Yes."

"Good luck," he said. It was satisfying to know he'd figured the situation correctly. What was more important was that she had trusted him.

The elevator arrived. They shook hands, and she got in it.

The last glimpse she had of him, he was standing quietly, watching her, his expression somber.

The last he saw of her before the doors closed, she had

her head up, there was a faint conspiratorial smile on her face for him, and he had an impression that she no longer felt completely alone.

He hoped not.

Thirty-Three

The aerial map, which was recent, did not show the road to be as rough as the gray-haired man was finding it. Nor had he expected the rented Avis compact to have bad shock absorbers. He had to hold onto the wheel hard to keep it from being jerked from his hands. Twice his head hit the roof.

The road was dirt, nothing much more than a wagon track. It ran through a narrow strip of woods separating two twenty-acre potato fields which had lain fallow for several years and were heavy with weeds. A garrulous country garage owner had told him the farmer was dead and the place was up for sale. He hadn't worried the man would ever remember him. He was the sort who was always so busy telling everyone how much he knew about other people's business that he soon forgot anyone he'd spoken to.

The road, a private access, had begun several hundred yards back at a little-used county blacktop leaving Maryland State Highway 5 which ran down the long peninsula between the Chesapeake and the Potomac. He'd spent many hours the evening before with his younger colleague pouring over the map and trying to find a field that met all their requirements. They had decided on a field because the digging would be easier. There would be no roots and probably few rocks. That was important because

216

they'd been told to go down at least six feet. There might eventually be a search by dogs.

But not any field would do. It had to be one where they could dig uninterrupted, and where they could dispose of their target unseen and in an area where a strange car would not be noticed. Last night his colleague had cursed the fact they couldn't set up another suicide. It would have been much less work. But their employer had told them, when they'd suggested it, that complete disappearance forever was favorable. The target had been thoroughly researched and there was no believable motive for suicide, and a planned accident could be disastrous if it didn't work out. Their employer, at the same time, had vetoed disposing of the body at sea or in the bay. They were told it involved too many steps where something could go wrong.

They'd eventually found, the gray-haired man thought, the almost perfect place. The nearest house was a half-mile away. At one point woods deeply indented the field. He could see the place now from the car. If they dug on the other side of it, they would be screened from the road. It meant they would have to make the target walk a hundred feet, but they doubted they'd have much trouble. They had also considered the possibility that somebody would buy the property to put up a factory or a housing development. In that case, a decomposed carcass or bones might be discovered and eventually traced, but there'd be no way ever to connect the remains to him and his colleague so they decided it didn't matter. The only person put out would be their employer and the worst that could happen would be no more jobs.

He wasn't worried about the car, either. In the event that some farmer or other local might drive down the road, a young couple looking for privacy for example, they'd taken their usual precautions. The car could not be traced to them. They had showed false identification, and used an American Express card which was credited against a bank account established under a false name. If the car was ever remembered and successfully traced, it would do forensic technicians little good to come up with suit fibers or the odd hair or even blood. There would be no clothing and no person to make a comparison with.

He stopped, turned off the motor, and got out. The ground was even, the brush not inhibiting. He found that walking through the wooded indent was easy. When he reached the edge of the field, he noted with satisfaction that there were areas close to the woods and under tree branches which would screen the grave from an aerial sighting and which were shaded and bare of weeds. That would also help things. The ground would be softer, less baked by the sun. Vegetation would not have to be disturbed. With a little care they could restore the surface to its original appearance. They would only have to carry away a few baskets of leftover dirt displaced by the body. The open grave could be covered with branches between the time it was dug and the time it was filled up and so could the heap of dirt they excavated.

He went back to the car, turned it around, and with no interference rejoined the county blacktop, then the state highway, and headed north for their motel. It was part of a national chain and situated near an interstate exit. That meant it was usually fully occupied which was good. In a less-frequented place, they might have been noticeable. When he let himself into their room, he found his colleague seated before the television with a beer, his balding head incongruous with the children's cartoon he was watching.

It was Saturday morning. They would do their digging tomorrow very early and had allowed two hours for it. If they started at five, they would be through before most people were awake and up. As long as it didn't rain and turn the dirt road into a quagmire, they'd be okay.

The younger man had walked over to a nursery and gardening center not far away and purchased a shovel and a pick. He had also purchased a roll of heavy-duty plastic which they would spread out on the ground next to the grave. This was to keep excavated dirt from being pressed into surrounding weeds, making it difficult to get back into the grave and leaving evidence of digging that would last most of the winter.

Although the younger man seemed calm, the gray-haired man knew he was nervous. He was, himself. For the first time they weren't operating alone. There were other people involved, people they didn't know. Even though they had been guaranteed the others were also professionals, he had at first flatly refused the job. When you started to trust strangers, you were in trouble. It was only the considerable increase in their fee that eventually made him change his mind.

He took off his shoes, then his jacket and tie, and lay down on the bed to rest. He wasn't getting any younger and work was starting to require more and more concentration. He ran over their employer's requirements as well as his own to see if they'd missed anything. He didn't think they had.

Then he forced himself to take his mind off work and think of the vacation he was soon going to enjoy. They were being paid a lot for the job and they had discussed quitting for a year or so when it was finished, then perhaps moving their operation to California. They'd been too long on the East Coast. Certain contacts were beginning to remember them too well. But first he'd spend some time at Miami and enjoy the bright lights and pretty girls. It had been a while since he'd done that. There'd be plenty of money soon, enough to keep some youngster around as long as he wanted. Women didn't care how old you were as long as there was money in it for them.

His colleague had decided to go to Mexico. That was okay. They should split up occasionally. Maybe he'd even do a job by himself down south. It would help keep him from becoming too dependent on a partner. It would be like a refresher course. And maybe his colleague would do the same. Then they'd get back together again. They had a good thing going and when you had that, why try anything else?

Thirty-Four

Missy had cooked a special crab creole. The recipe came from her grandmother who'd been a slave in New Orleans. It was truly delicious and Alexis knew Missy had spent hours in the hot kitchen suffering aching feet and legs to prepare it. She could hardly look her in the face when she wasn't able to finish and Missy took a half-filled plate back to the kitchen. It was tension. She hadn't eaten properly for days.

It was Saturday evening. She and Harold had come down to Brigham Bay Friday for thirty-six hours so he could work on the policy speech the President would give Monday morning. The occasion was the departure of Luis Cabral for New York. The Portuguese President had originally been scheduled to fly direct to Lisbon, but had been persuaded to stay another day in the United States to address the United Nations. Harold had arranged it ostensibly to help project to the Portuguese electorate an image of Cabral as a world statesman. Alexis suspected the real reason was to concede to Colonel Catarino the extra twenty-four hours he'd said he needed to maneuver his tanks.

Tomorrow evening she and Harold were to attend a White House Gala in honor of Cabral and Alexis knew her final chance to confront her husband lay between now and then. Last night and today, she had either lost her nerve or he had been locked in his study and inaccessible. She'd spent her time playing tennis with Sandy.

They ate in a silence broken only by Missy's soft foot-steps and the clink of cutlery against china. Harold finally broke it. "You're very quiet tonight," he said.

Alexis looked at him through the glow from twin candelabras which lit the old mahogany dining room table. His expression was concerned and he looked exceptionally handsome. She felt heartsick. If only the whole nightmare would disappear and leave everything the way it was when they first married with all the happiness, the optimism, and belief. But it wouldn't. He had made that impossible.

"I have a hell of a headache."

"Oh? I'm sorry, darling." He reflected, "Do you think there is something here that you are allergic to? When we came down with the Wildersteins you were sick, remember?"

She tried to keep hostility from her voice. She wanted to scream. She said, "It's not Brigham Bay, Harold."

He pushed his chair away, rose, and came to her end of the table. "Early bed for you, I think." He kissed the top of her head. Missy had begun to clear dessert plates. "I'll have my coffee in the study, Missy."

"Yes, General."

"Don't wait up for me, Alexis."

He could have been talking to a child, she thought. She watched him go out. Presently Missy came through with his coffee.

It was now or never, she knew. Do it.

She heard her own voice. It was shaky. "I'll take the tray in, Missy."

"Mis' Alexis . . ." Missy hesitated. Then she blurted out. "Mis' Alexis, somethin's layin' between you and your husband. Whatever it is, honey, don't hide nothin'. Have it out now, 'fore it gits too late."

222

"Thank you, Missy. I intend to."

She gave the old woman a kiss and took the tray down the hall. Nothing was real. It was like being back in school and almost sick with stage fright before the yearly play. She'd rehearsed a dozen times what she would say to him. She could remember none of it. She knocked at the oak paneled study door and went in. He was seated in a deep chair studying the *Heidelberg Review*. There was an open file of letters on a side table next to him.

Something in his expression told her at once he was not surprised to see her.

"Here's your coffee," she said. She glanced at the file. A number of letters were in his own handwriting.

She tried to speak. She had to. Now. It's why she'd come in. She couldn't. She turned away.

Then she heard him say, "You want to talk to me, don't you? Why don't you sit down?" It was a command.

She turned, surprised. He was smiling pleasantly. She obeyed, a robot. She sank into the chair opposite him, hands in her lap. And realized at the same instant why she was so reluctant. She was terrified of him. It wasn't just the aura of power he carried, there was more. She'd been frightened ever since she'd first started checking up on him. Her guilt made her feel imminent punishment.

"We're due to have a talk," he said. "What better time? We're here alone. Why don't we begin with these?" He picked up the letter file and smiled again, disarmingly. "Everyone wants to know about the dates, don't they? Why the postmark on the envelope is different from the inside date? Well, it's very simple. I'll give you an exclusive."

It was so sudden, it caught her completely off guard. Her mind stopped. She could only think one thing: she'd been discovered. What else did he know? It was hard to breathe. There was a rushing sound in her ears.

"The date is not a date, you see," he explained. "It's a page number and a paragraph on that page. In this." He held up the *Heidelberg Review*. "Consultation across the Atlantic, if you wish. This paragraph on page eighteen, for example. It has to do with a revolt against a Frankish count in Austrasia. In AD 654. The situation is precisely parallel to present events in Portugal. Of course it's made up, most of it, but nobody has ever thought to put twenty learned scholars to work to challenge it. Professor Schaeffer is considered the world expert on that period."

Alexis knew how a small animal felt when cornered by a predator. She found her voice. "Harold . . ." It was a whisper, nothing more.

He held up a silencing hand. "Wait. I've just begun." He pulled a small dark metal object the size of a thick coat button from his pocket and held it up for her to see. "A miracle of modern technology," he said. "There's one of these in your car. And another sewn into the bottom of your favorite shoulder bag. They transmit, so I know about your meeting with Andrew Taylor and Valerie McCullough. I also know, of course, about your seeing the FBI and the deal you made with them. I go to Princeton and teach history, they take their foot off my neck, all that. But, even without this, I probably would have been able to add it all up. You left a pretty clear trail."

Alexis heard herself as though from a great distance, "I suppose you know about me and Jimmy, too."

"Yes. But I don't blame you for that. Or Jimmy. Two old friends, both upset. These things happen. People are only human after all."

"I was drunk, Harold. And I'm desperately sorry." She immediately hated herself for making excuses, especially right now. She said numbly, "I suppose you also know about the memorandum from Germany."

"The one that started it all? Of course. It doesn't concern me. What does is the tape you made of my meeting with General Figueira. You were seen, you must have known that."

She burst out. "Harold, it can't go on. The FBI, the CIA, Valerie McCullough. Someone's bound to find out."

"Someone like yourself?" Anger crept into his voice. And a sneer. "What made you decide to go back to journalism?"

Alexis stared at him. She felt a growing incredulity. He was the one faced with ruin and disgrace, and probably prison. Yet, somehow, he had her on the defensive. She had to pull herself together and turn it around.

She forced a smile. "I decided to go back to journalism," she said, "because it seemed to me the only way to save my marriage."

"Save your marriage?" he echoed. "Save your marriage how? By spying on your husband?"

His laugh was ugly. And it finally changed something in her. She found she wasn't frightened anymore. The ice was broken and she was strangely relieved. All that mattered was to persuade him.

"I'll hardly have a marriage if you're in prison, will I?" she demanded. "Or if you have to pull a Philby and defect to Moscow in order to stay out of one."

"You mean that's all you're expecting to get out of all this? Me in a cardigan and old slippers, smoking a pipe by the fire?"

"Yes. If I'm included."

He laughed again. "Alexis. Please. Do me a favor."

"Harold, it is." She rose impulsively and went to kneel by him. "Harold, darling, listen to me, for God's sake. I'm your wife, I love you. I couldn't live with the suspicion. I had to know. If I didn't, how could I help you? Whatever's going on, it's something I can live with as long as you stop now. I'd have you and it's you I care about. You and me. Our life. It's all that matters."

"It's too late, Alexis."

"It's not. It never is. You know that. Harold, what are you involved in? Why have you done this? We're talking about treason. You've got to tell me."

He laughed harshly. "Why don't we just say it's nasty and let it go at that?"

"Is it blackmail?" she insisted. "Does it have to do with our going to the sex club, or what? It couldn't be the affair you had at school."

He gave her a sharp look. Then he said pointedly, "Couldn't it?"

"The boy?" She wasn't able to believe it. "But nobody gives a damn anymore about homosexuality."

"Homosexuality, no. Whom with, yes. The 'boy' was a rabid Marxist wanted by the German police."

"But it was years ago," she protested. "You were a child."

"How would you like someone to tell that to Immigration when you were applying for citizenship. You start there." He went on bitterly. "One black mark in a school book to get you to do some innocuous little bit of snitching about some relatively unimportant little thing and it all becomes self-perpetuating. So forget it. It doesn't make any difference anymore and you closed the last door when you made a tape of me and Figueira. I've got to have it, Alexis. Where is it?"

She nearly told him, then. But she didn't. He would never understand her trusting Farr and something in her said the tape was the only control she had over the situation. If she were to succeed, she knew she had to keep that control. Harold was perhaps too frightened to think clearly.

"It's in a safe place," she said.

His eyes went dead cold. He smiled thinly. "To be brought out only if little Harold doesn't do what he's told?"

It took a moment to absorb what he meant. She felt a

hot rush of anger. She stood up. "That was rotten of you."

"Was it? I'd say it was realistic. If you're not planning to use the tape against me, what was it for?"

"I could hardly stand outside your window without getting caught by that horror Riker. That's what it was for. It was for me to play to myself without interference." She forced herself to control her anger and lower her voice. "Harold, I am not the KGB or whatever blackmailer you have around your neck. I'm your wife." There was liquor on a tray from before dinner with an ice bucket and setups. She went and made herself a drink, slamming the ice furiously into a glass.

"I want you to call off Portugal," she said. "Your part in it anyway."

He laughed again. "How do you suggest I do that? Fly over and deliver a lecture on democracy to Catarino's tankmen?"

She ignored his sarcasm. "I don't know how. You'll figure it out. I want you to call off Portugal and write a letter of resignation to the White House."

"I see. And the KGB?"

She spun furiously from the drink table to face him. "You tell the KGB to go to hell. Harold, you've obviously become so inured to blackmail you've lost all sight of reality. The Russians are not going to admit publicly they had an inside track to an American Secretary of State. They want detente from us too much for that. They want beginning with grain, technology, and a nuclear disarmament treaty."

"You don't tell the KGB what to do." He was suddenly shouting, his face flushed. "You tell the KGB what to do and you end up on a garbage dump or hanging from a balcony."

"No," she shot back. "You're not Nasciemento. Or Jimmy. They know the FBI is in on this and they know it's in your interest to keep silent. So why risk another murder? Besides, we'd get government protection, both of us. And if you tell Wilderstein the Russians have threatened you, you'll have a private army around you also."

"Bodyguards! Don't make me laugh." He rose to make himself a drink. "Do you know what I've got for a bodyguard?"

"You're talking about the mole," she said.

"Yes, I'm talking about the mole."

"Who is it?"

"I don't know. I wish to God I did."

She was genuinely surprised. "What do you mean? You must know."

"I mean, I—don't—know!" He pounded on a chair back to emphasize his words. "That's their game, goddamnit. Nobody knows the whole picture of anything. Just parts. All I know is this goddamn thing!" He grabbed the *Heidelberg Review* and slung it furiously into a corner. "And phone calls occasionally from some unknown sonofabitch, probably the Russian Ambassador himself. That's about his speed." When she didn't speak, he sat down and said wearily, "I want the tape, Alexis. Now."

She managed to stand firm. "I'm sorry, Harold. No."

She was unprepared for his reaction. He leapt from the chair and seized her by the shoulders. "I want the tape." He began to shake her violently. "Where is it?"

"Harold, stop!" She tried to break loose. He shook harder. "You're hurting me!"

"Idiot, do you actually think you can trust the FBI on anything? What the hell have you done? You've ruined us both."

"Harold, let go of me."

He did suddenly, but his lips remained white with rage. "Sure, let you go. I'll be glad to. Permanently. You talk about a future. You've fixed it so we can't possibly have

228

one. Nobody had anything on me. Nothing. All they had was suspicion and speculation. They didn't have one single thread of evidence. Now there's a damned tape flying around loose."

Something in Alexis turned. His rage did it. All the disappointment she suffered, the Wildersteins, no home of her own and no children, it all choked up at once in an explosion of resentment. She'd had enough. Enough lies, enough bullying, enough disappointment. Farr would return the tape to her. She knew he would. Farr was the only element of reason left in anything.

"You can have it back," she said quietly. "It's in Washington. I'll give it to you Monday or drive in and get it tonight if you want. And then you're on your own. I just hope you have enough decency left to do something quickly about those poor devil hostages you and Khadhafi have been playing with."

She walked out of the study, leaving the door open.

He called after her.

She didn't answer or turn. She went to her car and ripped up the carpet. The bug was under the passenger seat. She threw it and the one from her bag into the grass beneath the trees. Then she went to the kitchen and opened the refrigerator. Missy never threw out anything. She found a bowl of uneaten crab creole and put some on a plate and poured a glass of milk. She came back out and headed for the stairs. She'd go to the guest room, lock the door, eat the creole, and sleep there. In the morning, Missy would see it half-gone from the refrigerator, find the plate when she came to make the bed, and would feel better.

When she passed the study, Harold was seated in his chair, staring at nothing. It was the first time she had ever seen him look old.

He heard her. "Alexis." He sounded dead. "Alexis, I'm

229

sorry. Please forgive me. I didn't mean a word of it. You know that. I love you. Don't walk out on me. Not now. I need you."

She saw tears in his eyes. She put the creole and her milk on the hall table and went to sit again in the chair opposite him.

"You're right," he said. "You and I are what count. Nothing else. I couldn't do it alone, but with you helping I can. I think I could even face prison if it comes to that."

"It won't," she said gently. "They won't want anybody ever to know."

She watched him. Something happened in her again. Her cold anger vanished. He was Harold once more, somebody she knew, and she loved him. And as long as he loved her she could bear anything.

He ran a hand over his forehead. "I'm tired of it all. Really tired. Arnold Wilderstein isn't going to be very happy, but that's his problem. Princeton will arrange housing for us. And pay us enough to live on."

"Of course, they will."

He smiled wanly. "Maybe I'll learn to enjoy being called Professor, or whatever. I never really liked Mr. Secretary."

She went to him, then. She sat on his lap and put her arms around him and kissed him hard. He held her very close. She cried silently and for a long time couldn't speak.

When she finally did and they talked, it wasn't about their trouble. It was about the future. About being suburban and having children, about schools and colleges and young people growing up and new friends.

It was almost dawn before they finally went hand in hand upstairs to bed. Alexis knew it might be the last time she'd sleep at Brigham Bay. She was going to lose it. That was sad, but it didn't matter. She'd have her husband now instead.

Thirty-Five

When she awoke, it was mid-morning. She felt drugged. She hadn't slept so heavily in months.

She found Harold's note on the dresser. He had cancelled their attendance at the White House Gala and had written out a draft of his resignation letter for her to look at. He'd slipped it into the *Heidelberg Review* to avoid the prying eyes of a secretary who had come down from R Street to help him with the President's speech and she'd returned to Washington without seeing it. He also said he'd contacted Figueira and was meeting him along with Arnold Wilderstein who was flying in from New York. Last night, he'd decided that the way to defuse the Portuguese coup d'etat was to persuade Figueira to make a last-minute switch and betray Catarino. Without Figueira's influence, the plot didn't stand a chance and Catarino would be imprisoned or exiled. As a reward, Volker would persuade President Cabral to return Figueira's wife's confiscated estates and meantime would provide him with a million dollars and a guarantee of American residency in case anything went wrong for him in Portugal. There was no question but Arnold Wilderstein would put up the money when he understood Figueira was saving Portugal from Communism.

Alexis was euphoric. She called Farr at his home, but there was no answer. It was Sunday and he'd probably gone out for the day. She'd call him again in the evening. She played tennis with Sandy and for the first time ever won a set. She and Sandy celebrated and cooled off with iced white wine on the terrace, laughed about everything, and then ravenously ate all of a special salad Missy prepared for their lunch.

Late afternoon, when she was doing some gardening, Harold called. At Sandy's suggestion, she'd given Missy and Sam the afternoon and evening off and they'd gone in their old pickup truck to a nearby town to see a movie. She ran to answer the hall telephone before it stopped ringing.

"Where are you?"

"R Street. Arnold's here. I'm expecting Figueira any moment."

"Will Arnold do it?"

"No problem."

"Oh, darling, I can't believe it, it's so wonderful. I love you, I love you."

He laughed. "You're the one responsible."

"Will you be back for dinner?"

"Unless you hear to the contrary, count on it. Meanwhile, could you do something for me?"

"Of course."

"You'll have to go out."

"That's all right."

"Do you remember that little antique store on Route 5 about halfway up to the Interstate? We bought those two horse prints there?"

She remembered easily. On a wonderful autumn afternoon two years ago, they'd gone exploring after a long champagne lunch. Their reward had been the delightful old place and the equally delightful old woman who owned it.

"I reserved a mantelpiece clock," he explained, "a couple of weeks ago. Just until today. Somebody else wants it

232

and I'm afraid we'll lose it. It's something you'll love. I don't think they close until six."

"I'll go right away," she promised.

"I forget how much it was, exactly. A hundred and something. Take a checkbook."

Ten minutes later, she'd stripped off her tennis shorts and blouse, showered, and was presentable in a light summer frock.

Sandy had swum and with Sam and Missy absent and the other agents in Washington with Harold, she was sunbathing in the nude on the beach by the boat house.

"I can go alone, Sandy."

"We've been through that one."

"Isn't there somebody else?"

Sandy laughed, and brushed sand from her hips and thighs. "Do you think I'd be down here like this if there were? Boss lady, I'm afraid you're stuck with me." She glanced at the sun, now not far above the trees across the estuary. Afternoon shadows were lengthening. "Anyway, the sun's all gone."

She wrapped her towel around her and went to put clothes on. Twenty minutes later they drove off down the dirt driveway.

The antique shop was northwest, toward Washington. Traffic was light. They had the roof down, and played cassettes and got whistles from male drivers. About five miles short of their goal, they slowed for an intersection.

Sandy suddenly said, "There's a great house just off the road down here. Can we take a look?"

Alexis glanced at her watch. There was plenty of time. "Sure."

Sandy gave directions and she branched off onto a blacktop county road. They drove about a mile and then Sandy said, "Stop here." It was almost a command and her voice was unexpectedly strident.

Surprised, Alexis automatically slowed and turned to

look at her. There was a strange hard set to Sandy's face. She'd never seen her like that.

"Sandy, what's wrong?"

"Turn down that little dirt road."

Abrupt. Cold. Why?

"Can't we see it from here?"

"No."

Alexis swung into the narrow track between the two potato fields. Sandy's mood frightened her.

"It's just beyond those trees."

The car pitched and bucked. Alexis concentrated on driving. When she stopped at the copse, there was no sign of any house. Halfway there she'd known there wouldn't be. But she hadn't been able to stop. Her hands were locked on the wheel, her foot glued to the accelerator. Premonition engulfed her, a windstorm. Then terror. She moved in a dream.

Before she asked the question, she knew the answer. Missy and Sam off for the afternoon had been Sandy's idea. There was no one else at Brigham Bay. Sandy could go back there and say she'd driven off without telling her and nobody would ever know it wasn't true. Nasciemento, Jimmy, and now herself.

"Sandy, what's this all about?"

It took enormous effort to look at Sandy again. She had no strength at all. The young woman sitting next to her wasn't the same Sandy she'd known and come to love all these months. The face wasn't the same. It was a mask and the laughing keen blue eyes set in it were without expression, even without life. She was a stranger.

Please, don't let it be Sandy. Anybody else, not her. But it was. And the black muzzle of the .25 automatic in her hand was no longer a familiar friend, but a hideous enemy.

234

Thirty-Six

Sandy said coldly, "Don't make this any more difficult, Alexis. It has to be done and that's that. Get out!"

Alexis didn't move. She experienced a kind of sharp clear insight. Everything that had happened during the summer swept through her mind. Words, incidents, moods. Detailed. Jimmy James and M. J. Lindley. The photographs. Nothing left out. And in seconds. Had she always wondered if the mole was Sandy? Even instinctively known and kept it hidden from herself because she couldn't face it? But of course, it had to be. It was so perfect. A female asp, attached to her. The day-to-day check on everything she did and every place she went. Harold had said she'd left behind a trail. He'd said he didn't need the transmitter's evidence to know what she was doing. The only thing he hadn't said was how he'd known. He hadn't said Sandy had told him. But she had. Was his request she go to the antique shop a coincidence or was there an equally obvious answer? She had to force words to her lips.

"Harold is a part of this, isn't he?"

There was no reply. Instead, Sandy's hard voice ordered her out again. The muzzle of the automatic prodded, and that told her everything. She obeyed and stood in the dirt road. Last night was a lie. Why pretend it wasn't? Harold was not a broken blackmailed man and probably never had been. He was a calculated traitor to his adopted country. There wasn't going to be peace in Portugal. Or a home in Princeton and children. Ever. There wasn't going to be love. And there never had been. Instead there was only death.

A young balding man in an inexpensive business suit appeared from behind the trees. Sandy came around the car. She said to him, "Get her moving. Right now."

He acted smoothly, quietly. His hand clamped on Alexis's wrist. She pulled away.

"Sandy, my God! Why?"

"You're very dangerous, Alexis. I'm sorry."

"But we're friends. We've always been. I know you cared."

The man seized her wrist again. This time there was no pulling away. His grip was iron. "Keep your voice down." His own voice was thin, almost effeminate. "If you scream or call out, we'll have to gag you."

Desperation. "Sandy, listen. You've got to. I made a tape of Harold. Harold and Figueira. The FBI has it."

"The FBI has a Mozart concerto. I erased your tape."

Of course. She'd been in the garden and seen. Right before Riker. But cling to any straw, any hope. "It's not true. It isn't. Last night Harold wanted it. He had to have it. I promised to give it to him."

"We don't tell General Volker everything. Only what we want him to know." Sandy pulled a small camera from her handbag and spoke to the young man again.

"It's sealed. A couple of shots will do. You know where to leave it?"

"Yes." He dropped the camera in his pocket.

"All right. And just remember. No pictures. No money. Does anyone know you picked this place?"

"No. Nobody."

She turned and got back into the Lancia.

Alexis struggled to get to her. "Sandy, I'll give you

anything. Wilderstein will. I'll never tell anyone. Anything you want."

For just an instant the cold mask dropped. A look of pain fleeted across the eyes. There was a hoarseness in Sandy's voice. "Maybe if your crowd had offered me that six months ago . . . what you have. But they didn't. Somebody else did."

"Sandy, it's not too late."

But the moment had passed. The Lancia motor came to life. It started backing up.

"Sandy, please. God, please! Sandy!"

The car was twenty feet away. A hundred. Bucking and bouncing. She struggled to follow. The grip on her wrist tightened. The man's body moved against hers, turning her. Her arm wrenched behind and upward. Pain knifed in her shoulder.

"Walk that way."

There was a revolver in his hand now. With a long tube at the end of the muzzle. Through her haze of fear, she knew it was a silencer.

Where were they going to kill her?

They went through the copse of trees and before they came out onto the field she saw a pile of freshly dug earth half-covered with branches and knew that next to it there'd be a grave.

She couldn't move against his hold. She tried to speak and heard her terrified "no" only as a whisper.

Last night Harold had known she was to die today. Had known and had helped plan it. And had made love to her in the night. And she to him.

Another man appeared. A graying man. Much older. His face was soft and unlined.

"Any problems?"

"No. She's gone." The balding man gave him the camera.

Her arm twisted up. "Kneel down, please."

The older man examined the camera. Pictures to prove she was dead.

The voice was sharp now. The pressure on her arm unbearable. "Kneel."

Strength forced her down, right to the edge of the hole. It was deep and long. And the earth smelled dank. Some crickets had fallen in and they struggled to escape. Her knees buckled. She had no more feeling and no thoughts. What she did, what they did, unfolded in slow motion. It was all that counted anymore.

"Head forward. Bend your head."

Something hard came up against the very top of her neck where it joined her skull.

"Are you ready?"

There was no more time. She only wanted another moment. But it was over. It was now.

Her lips formed a dumb protest. The muzzle pressed.

A sharp crack. A violent heavy blow across her shoulder. She pitched forward across the grave, clutching the opposite side. A mass of gray came by her, filling the hole as she slipped down. Clothing. A bald head.

Another crack. Farther away. Her hands broke her fall, struck a face. The body beneath her was soft and twisted and still. There was dirt everywhere and dirt trickling down from the edge of the hole above where the sky showed as a pale blue rectangle. She stood up, feet unfirm on the soft flesh beneath them, stumbling against the cool steep dirt at her side.

Hands grasped her arm.

"Hook your elbow over the edge."

She obeyed and felt herself being pulled up and out. She fell face first onto the weeds of the potato field. She rolled and looked up into the eyes of Steve Riker.

He squatted beside her, a .38 revolver in his hand. It was mounted with a silencer. He was sheet-white and sweating heavily, his lean face beaded with it, his shirt soaked. He gasped for breath and his eyes were terrified.

"Jesus Christ, Mrs. Volker, that was close. Are you all right?"

She sat up. She couldn't speak. She could only stare. The gray-haired older man lay beyond the open grave, the camera in the dirt beside him, his jacket grotesquely twisted around his torso, arms askew. There was red spittle at the corner of his mouth and on his chin. His eyes were open and saw nothing.

"Let's get you out of here," Riker said.

He helped her to her feet. She felt surprisingly light-headed. Seconds ago everything had been heavy and dark and a roar of sound in her ears, now she skipped over the ground.

She went too fast and stumbled. Riker said, "Take it easy, Mrs. Volker. You've had a bad time. Do you think you can drive?"

She nodded. He walked her through the woods and down the dirt road. There were two cars parked just before the county blacktop. One was her Lancia. She stopped, looked at it, and then looked over her shoulder and said suddenly, "Why that back there?" Her voice was harsh. "Why not an accident or another suicide?"

"Because they didn't want to take the chance something might go wrong. It was safer if you just disappeared. Wyndholt could be made to say you were capable of that."

They went on. Presently she said, "How did you know? Why are you here? I don't understand."

"The FBI got to me a few days ago," he answered. "David Farr. He thought I was KGB and wanted to buy me. It was a lot, too. If I'd been KGB, I would have taken it. He said not to leave you alone with anyone for a minute. Not even Sandy. Especially not Sandy, he said. He said the person you trusted the most and the last person you'd ever suspect was always the first person to be suspicious of. He said that was something he'd learned the hard way."

They reached the Lancia. Sandy sat in the front seat behind the wheel, her head against the head rest. There was a dark hole in her left temple and a lot of blood on her clothes and on the seat beside her. Her eyes were shut. She looked very young. And peaceful, as though asleep.

"Sorry," Riker said. "I didn't have time to get her out. I just ran like hell." He studied Sandy. He said, "I should have known way back when I caught her in your office with a bug. She said she'd found it when actually she was just about to plant it. Then, to really cover, she turned it over to our boss." He added, "And when I was slugged. I guess it had to be her. But I still don't know why."

Alexis stood to one side as he pulled Sandy out of the car and slid her on her back in the grass and weeds next to the road. She knew why. Sandy must have been scared she'd lose her head and Riker would find out about the tape and recover it first.

"Okay, Mrs. Volker. Are you sure you can manage?"

She said, yes. She was crying now and couldn't stop. She couldn't understand Sandy. She loved her. In spite of everything. Right now, Sandy hurt more than Harold. She bent and touched the light blond hair.

"Don't ask me why she did it, Mrs. Volker. They get them and never let them go. And they pay them a lot. She had a hard time when she was young. Maybe that was it. She wanted everything you had and she didn't belong to anyone or anything. She wouldn't let herself. We all knew that about her."

Riker knelt and pulled Sandy's skirt off her body and began to wipe the seat with it. It left Sandy rolled over, her face in the dirt and Alexis saw the other side of her head, half-blown away where the bullet had come out. It made her sick.

Riker said, "I want you to go up the road to the diner

and wait for me. Can you do that? I have work to do here. We don't want the KGB to know what's happened. To her. Or to them. It's important. Don't go to Brigham Bay. Go straight to the diner. It's the one on Route 5. And here. Take this." He took Sandy's .25 automatic from her purse and dropped it into Alexis's shoulder bag which was on the far right of the front seat where Sandy had pushed it.

"Mrs. Volker, don't hesitate to use this, even if you're just suspicious. Okay?"

Alexis started to get in the car. And stopped. "Mr. Riker." She hesitated. What do you say to a man who has just stood between you and death?

He seemed to know what she was thinking. He smiled slightly. "Mrs. Volker, you don't like me, I know that. I don't know why. I don't like you that much either, to tell the truth. Let's just call it all in a day's work and thank God Mr. Farr saw what was coming and that I could keep you in sight."

She nodded dumbly.

"Be careful," he said. "If you feel faint, pull over."

She drove slowly away.

Just before she turned onto the county blacktop, she looked in the rearview mirror. She couldn't help herself. Riker had Sandy by the ankles and was dragging her along the road back toward the copse and Sandy's blond and bloodied head was rolling and bumping in the dust.

Alexis didn't look back again.

Thirty-Seven

She didn't go to the diner. She drove straight back to Brigham Bay. The barn and staff quarters were silent. There were no cars parked in the driveway or in the garage.

She went down the old brick walk between the high boxwood hedges. At the front door, she hesitated. Was there a trap of some kind? Why had Riker been so insistent she go to the diner and not home? She opened the door and stepped into the hall.

The house had an eerie silence, emphasized by the resonant ticking of the hall clock. And her own hollow footsteps. It seemed a stranger now. Even its familiar musty smell was alien. The doors to the dining room and study were open. Expecting to see someone at any moment, she cautiously inched by them, passed through the living room, and went out onto the terrace.

Nobody. Nobody on the lawn. Nobody at the boat house or on the beach. The sun was just setting and the estuary was aglow with its last soft light. She went back inside and ran upstairs. She flung her bedroom door open. Empty. She slammed it shut and locked it behind her, caught her breath, and went to her dressing table. Her bedside clock said it was after six. It seemed much later. There was an eternity between now and when she had last been in the room to change from her tennis clothes. There was blood on the side of her skirt. Sandy's.

242

She suddenly felt she was going to pieces. She was trembling, not outwardly but inside, a high fast fluttering she couldn't control. She got up from the dressing table again, tore off the dress, and stuffed it in the laundry basket in the bathroom. Death still clung to her skin. She wanted to take a shower and wash herself forever. There wasn't time. She got Valium from the medicine cabinet and took ten milligrams. What she really wanted, she knew, was a drink. But her locked bedroom door was safety and downstairs was the unknown and frightening. She didn't want to go until she had to.

She returned to her dressing table and forced herself to put on evening makeup. It took a long time. Her mind kept wandering, reliving what had just happened. Instead of her own face in the mirror, she saw Sandy's bloody head. She saw the deep grave yawning before her knees, saw the slate-blue rectangle of sky as she tried to climb up out of the dank earth. She remembered her astonishment at Riker and knowing she wasn't dead, the abrupt reversal of everything.

And she kept remembering her incomprehension when she finally understood who Sandy really was, the shock of Sandy's face, cold and hard and merciless above the dark unrelenting muzzle of her revolver.

Shadows deepened, became twilight. With a start she realized she could no longer see her mirror. She'd been at the table for an hour. It was after seven. She turned on lights. The Valium had taken hold, she felt calmer.

She finished her face. At her closet, she picked out a simple white Dior evening gown presented to her two years ago by the Paris courturier. She brushed out her hair and then went to put whatever she needed in an evening purse. Comb, lipstick, mascara, eye shadow, the keys to R Street in case she had to go there and the staff was in bed.

Then she remembered Sandy's automatic. Riker had

said, "Don't hesitate to use it." Did he think she'd have to? Were they going to try to kill her again? The moment she showed up at the White House, they'd know she was alive. Harold would know, they would know. She would have to contact David Farr immediately; she would need protection now more than ever. She didn't want to die. She had never wanted so badly to live. Now, she had to live.

She'd left her Gucci shoulder bag on the bed. She went to it and took out the automatic. She knew something about handguns. She'd learned back in Detroit when she'd covered the crime beat. Years ago. Before Washington and Andrew Taylor. Before Harold Volker. She checked the clip. It was fully loaded. She turned the automatic over in her hand and she had the strangest feeling it had always belonged to her. A vivid picture filled her mind. The half-crazed gunman in the Detroit bar, the handgun held to her throat. The smell of him, the heat of his body as he walked her out onto the street. The sudden blinding glare of television camera lights, the explosions of flashbulbs, the incessant bullhorn police voice coming in waves through all the light. Her captor's scream, "Move it, open up, I'll blow her cocksuckin' head off!"

Faces parting like watery pale leaves to let them through.

The crash of sound, the sick rush of air from his body as the SWAT sniper's bullet cut through his skull. Bodies in blue piling on him even before he crumpled to the pavement. Herself staring at the weapon he'd dropped, picking it up as though in a dream to study it until a police officer gently took it away.

Where had all the years gone?

She checked the automatic's safety catch and tucked it into her evening purse.

At the door she listened. She didn't hear a sound. She turned off the lights and went out onto the landing. The hall clock ticked and struck once. Seven-thirty. The house was dark. She felt her way down the stairs and along the hall to the front door and opened it.

The darkening sky seemed light after the even darker interior. Cicadas whirred. Summer was over, autumn was in the air. There were stars. The Lancia was a shadow at the end of the brick walk. She walked quietly to it and went around to the driver's side and got in. The seat was dry, but she could still smell the blood. She ought to get water and wash it away, but she was afraid to go back into the house and there wasn't time. The gala had already started. Harold would be there, charming the guests. There had never been any question in her mind that he wouldn't be. She'd been eliminated, the one witness who could expose the coup d'etat. It could now go ahead as planned. What better camouflage as it got underway than for its perpetrator to be seen chatting amiably with its Presidential victim. To be safe and securely cloaked in the aura of world respectability that was the White House and the office of Secretary of State.

She started the Lancia's motor.

Less than five minutes after she drove off, Riker pulled up. It had taken him nearly an hour to fill the grave. He'd wanted to meet her at the diner because it was an anonymous place where nobody would expect her to be in case it was discovered the plan to liquidate her had gone wrong. When he got there and nobody could remember seeing her, he'd waited around fifteen minutes and then it had taken him another twenty to make it down to Brigham Bay. Now, seeing no sign of anyone, he parked his car and went into the house. He turned on lights, quickly checked out rooms, then went directly to the hall telephone and dialed David Farr's home number. Something told him they hadn't seen the end of trouble yet. He was beginning to wish he hadn't given Alexis Volker Sandy Muscioni's service revolver.

Thirty-Eight

She entered Washington by the South Capitol Bridge. Traffic was moderate. It was nearly nine o'clock. She could hardly remember the drive from Brigham Bay. Washington itself, always completely familiar, seemed a maze of confusing streets and lights until, as if by instinct, she found herself going past Union Square at the foot of the Capitol.

When she reached the White House, she could see the blazing lights of the gold East Room through the trees and shrubbery of the lawn. Metropolitan police kept traffic moving and the curious away. She put on her indicator and turned into the North West gate.

The guard recognized her immediately. "Good evening, Mrs. Volker." He barely glanced at the formal invitation she showed.

She pulled into West Executive and found a place to park, then followed the path back past the press booth to the North Entrance. As she went up the Portico steps between its massive supporting columns, photographers waiting idly for the evening to be over, came to life. Flashbulbs popped and video cameras focused. Here and there, a familiar voice from the old days called her name.

She forced a smile. After that and for several minutes, it was just impressions.

A Marine captain usher in full dress, welcoming her, impressed by who she was. The blazing chandeliers of the

North Entrance as she went in. The shining marble columns of the Cross Hall. The great seal of the United States over the door of the Blue Room, the silent white busts of Washington and Barlow in their curved niches. The gold and red armchairs spaced along the wall, the sad and haunting cry of a Portuguese fado singer drifting out through the closed doors of the great East Room.

Uniformed and medaled Armed Forces ushers stood about, waiting for the evening to be over. A familiar Secret Serviceman in a tuxedo checked her invitation and White House pass.

"That's a beautiful dress, Mrs. Volker."

"Thank you."

"Enjoy the entertainment."

The Marine Captain gave her his arm. "We can slip through the Green Room, ma'am. Less obvious."

They were by the foot of the Main Stair leading up to the presidential quarters on the first floor. She stopped. "I won't be going in until later. I'd like you to tell General Volker to join me as soon as he can in the Center Hall."

She made it abrupt and authoritative. Before he could reply, she had unhooked the velvet-covered cord blocking the stair and rehooked it behind her. Two Marine privates on each side of the stair innocently came to attention.

"Mrs. Volker, I don't think that's allowed." The Captain hesitated, indecisive, still awed by her.

She started up the wide red-carpeted stairs. As she passed beneath the portrait of Woodrow Wilson, a White House guard came rapidly to the Captain's assistance, his voice sharp. "One moment, please." He followed her onto the stairs, then stopped short. A graying man in tails and white tie had come rapidly down to greet Alexis effusively. It was the White House Chief-of-Staff, Lanard "Duke" Chancery.

"Alexis, darling."

She offered him her cheek.

"Harold said you were under the weather."

She muttered inanities; she was better, she'd decided she couldn't miss the evening, she so loved everything Portuguese, especially fado.

Chancery nodded and took both her hands in his. "Congratulations are due, aren't they? It looks as if Harold's done it again. He's incredible." She looked blank. He said, "Hasn't he told you? He's just saved Portugal from a red takeover. God, it was close. Twelve hours."

It stunned her. She managed to say, "I'm not surprised. We're meeting upstairs in a few minutes. An usher's just gone to get him."

"Then I'll let him fill you in. See you later. We're all thrilled." He squeezed her arm and continued down.

She saw him stop by the anxious guard and the Marine usher, glance back up at her, and speak to them reassuringly. She went on up.

The lights were on in the Center Hall when she reached it. A maid was straightening cushions on one of the couches and collecting ashtrays. Probably there'd been before-dinner cocktails there for the Portuguese President and a few special guests from the Diplomatic Corps and Congress. The room was less formal, its decor warmer than most in the White House.

"General Volker will be joining me and we'd like to be alone a few minutes, please."

"Yes, ma'am." The maid disappeared silently.

For the first time, Alexis had a sense of reality. Coming up the stairs, she had been in a world of her imagination. She had pictured the East Room, its huge chandeliers, its small stage with a lone fado singer before a microphone, a guitar accompanist in the background. She saw the Marine Captain move quietly down the aisle between the rows of gilt chairs and the silent, glittering array of guests. He reached Harold, then whispered. Harold's expression remained impassive. He nodded, waited until applause signaled the end of the current number, then apologized to the President's wife next to whom he was seated, and as unobtrusively as possible slipped away.

From below and what seemed far away, Alexis heard the faint sound of applause. She began to study a painting by Cezanne, concentrating on its blurred impressionist colors, noticing every minute detail as though it were the last thing she would ever see.

The minutes ticked by. How long? She couldn't keep track. Without hearing him arrive, she was aware of his presence. She let him wait for a moment before she turned from the painting. He was in the wide double doorway to the East Sitting Room and, like "Duke" Chancery, was in formal attire. He looked unusually young and handsome, but his face told her nothing. She knew her being there had to be a real shock to him. Only minutes ago he must have presumed her dead, was perhaps even thinking about the distraught role he would play when she was reported missing and for all the months before she was eventually given up.

She tried to understand her own feeling toward him. It was more contempt than hatred. Yesterday, last night, she had loved him. Deeply, almost consumingly. And had still clung to the belief that he loved her. At the open grave, at the horror of Sandy's bloodied head dragging in the dust, her incomprehension had changed to acceptance. Love had simply ceased to exist; had never existed. He was a complete stranger and she could finally face something she had not been able to face for as long as she had been married to him. She could finally admit to herself why she'd had to go to Wyndholt and what Wyndholt must have known right from the beginning.

Harold Volker had never loved her, but had simply and ruthlessly used her dream of life to his personal advantage.

He walked slowly over to her. "What's happened? What made you come?"

She kept her voice steady and put on a slight smile. "Since you didn't show up for dinner, or call, I thought you had decided to come and that I should join you."

His eyes were cautious. "Did you get the clock?"

She dismissed growing incredulity at his pretense. He had to pretend, of course. Until he knew precisely what had happened. Why give anything away? She decided to keep the charade going. "I was too late," she said.

"That's a shame. I'm sorry not to have called you about dinner, but I've had my hands full at the Department. I've only just got here. Things happened. I had to make an appearance."

She said, "I understand you are to be congratulated for something."

He looked vaguely relieved. She thought he also flushed slightly, but realized it was just normal color returning to his face. He'd been very pale.

"Everybody seems to think so," he said. "They really ought to thank you, not me. All I did, really, was to follow your suggestion. Figueira decided it would indeed be in his best interest to switch sides again. As soon as he did, I had a word with the President. He convened the National Security Council at six this evening. Luis Cabral was notified and telephoned Lisbon. Figueira did the same. Catarino's tank divisions are confined to barracks and Catarino is on his way to prison on the Azores."

How brilliantly simple, she thought. All his schemes always were. She felt a fool for not having foreseen it. Instead of hiding the coup d'etat, he'd exposed it and taken credit fo saving Portugal and NATO. In one sweep he'd thus avoided all risk as well as saving himself for the future. By accepting one loss, he'd destroyed any suspicion he might be setting up countries for later Communist coups and simultaneously proved his unique value as Secretary of State. Who would ever know the true story? Sandy had

250

erased the tape. She herself was the only witness to what he'd almost done and he'd thought her out of the way.

As though half-reading her mind, he said, "If you're thinking of your tape, Alexis, of course I worried a little about it in case it accidentally got into wrong hands. But I decided whatever was on it was only a small part of my meeting with Figueira. Anything incriminating could be explained as the way I trapped him into revealing how the coup would work."

Alexis found it hard to keep sarcasm from her voice. "It was quite a switch," she said. "I suppose you've changed your mind about resigning, too?"

He shrugged. "I see no reason for it now, do you?"

"And the hostages?"

"There will be an announcement tomorrow."

Triumph following triumph.

She said, "I see. What do you expect me to do, Harold?"

"I'm afraid I don't follow."

She'd suddenly had enough. "Harold, let's stop fencing, shall we? Time is short. Sandy and two men tried to kill me a few hours ago. I'm only here by the grace of God and Steve Riker. And Sandy's where I'm supposed to be: in a grave in a potato field."

She watched his eyes harden. "You warned me about the KGB," she said, "but you didn't warn me about my husband setting me up for them."

There was deathly silence. Then he smiled thinly. "I'm sorry. I wouldn't know what you're talking about."

"Why, Harold? I don't mean why you married me. I understand that. I was a glamorous convenience your career badly needed. I mean why have you betrayed your office and the trust put in you? Last night wasn't the whole story, was it? It wasn't just blackmail. There's more. There has to be."

She waited. He didn't speak.

"There's a pattern, Harold. It started with Horst Melkin. You were really in love with him, weren't you? Is Schaeffer actually Horst Melkin brought back from the dead, the way they all suspect? Are you still in love? Is that part of it?"

He laughed. "That's exactly the sort of remark most American women would make. If they can't understand something, there must be sex behind it. The catchall label for their own lack of intellect."

"But I'm right, aren't I?" she insisted. "It did start somehow with Horst, didn't it? With Horst and his Marxism?"

There was unexpected anger in his reply. For an instant he forgot himself. "Horst Melkin is not just a Marxist. He's a German. With a damned sight greater view of history than Moscow or Washington will ever have!"

"A German view?" she cried. "Is that what you mean?" She had a flash of insight. Helping the United States and Russia to so weaken each other as to allow Germany to ultimately dominate. Using Moscow to bring down the United States first because Russia would then eventually collapse from its own economic inertia. It was the kind of thinking that had marked his whole career. She could see no further.

He was silent, under control again.

"You haven't answered my question."

He smiled again. "Go to hell!"

She knew she'd goaded him as far as she could. She opened her purse and took out his letter of resignation. "It doesn't matter," she said. "And you and I don't matter. What does matter is everybody else. The future. I want your signature on this. It's what we agreed to and I'm going to hold you to it."

He glanced at it dismissingly. "I thought I made it clear a moment ago. I don't intend to resign."

252

"I heard you and I'm afraid you have no choice." She met his eyes. "I'm alive, aren't I?"

She waited. It was all she could do.

He laughed. "Yes, you're alive. You are also, as everyone knows, on your way to being a drunk. For the right price, how much would Everett say? A half-bottle of vodka a day? And in the care of a psychiatrist, a doctor, incidentally, with an expensive wife and three children, who sits up nights writing obscure books trying to make ends meet. If you see my point. But all of that aside, what exactly will you say, now that you can't tell people I'm planning to rent berth space to the Russian fleet in Lisbon harbor? That I enticed you to a potato field so the KGB could eliminate you? Do you really think anyone will believe that? They only have to call the antique dealer to know I phoned her to expect you. Do you plan to reveal that I communicate with Gunter Schaeffer via the *Heidelberg Review*? They'll have scholars working for years trying to pin that down to anything but mutual interest in history. Or will you accuse Schaeffer of actually being poor Horst Melkin? I think the East Germans can easily be persuaded to bring Schaeffer's missing Dresden records to light."

He took the letter of resignation from her hands, shook his head as if bewildered by its stupidity, and stuffed it in his pocket.

"You have several choices, my darling," he continued. "You could go back to television, for example, if they'd still have you—you're not young any longer. Or," he paused, amused at the thought, "or, you could find some small town middle-class dentist to marry and breed with. But I don't think you'll do either. I think you'll opt for a third choice. I think you'll choose to continue as the wife of the Secretary of State and work at becoming the most important hostess in Washington. Of course, you don't have to, but if you don't, you understand I will divorce you. I'll have no other choice. Your adultery with Adrian James would be the grounds. I have the negatives of you and him. I wouldn't hesitate to release them to a court. Or to a future husband. I wouldn't want people to think I'd left the famous Alexis Sobieski without damn good reason."

He went to the door, and turned.

"Coming?"

She knew then what she had to do. She'd failed and he'd closed every course open to her. Except one. She realized she'd always known he would and she realized, also, why she'd put Sandy's automatic in her evening purse. Riker had given it to her to protect herself and now she had to. She was cornered. She felt it through the fabric of her purse, a hard, awkward object.

He was still in the doorway, waiting. She saw his expression suddenly change and then saw why. She had the automatic in her hand.

She flicked off the safety catch.

He began to move toward her. "Alexis, give me that!"

His hand reached out. His fingers clenched the barrel.

A split second, an eternity. The wide doorway to the East Sitting Room, the brilliant yellow carpet, the Cezanne painting, a vase of flowers, a couch.

And Volker, arm outstretched, framed in frozen clarity.

She pulled the trigger.

Thirty-Nine

Harold Volker died almost immediately from a bullet in the heart, his fingers still clamped around the barrel of the .25 automatic pistol that killed him. In falling, he'd torn it from his wife's hand.

In the ensuing uproar, Bernard Kornovsky, the President's National Security Adviser, and "Duke" Chancery were quick to realize that the White House was confronted by one clear question: Why had she done it? Was the shooting a personal matter or was it tied in with the FBI investigation of Volker? Before any statement could be issued, the question had to be answered. The press was clamoring.

It took little to persuade the President to leave his guests. An urgent conference was held in the Situation Room. The Vice-President was the only other person asked to attend. It was immediately agreed they had to speak to David Farr, who'd arrived minutes too late to prevent the shooting. He was called in from the second-floor West Wing office where Mrs. Volker was being closely guarded by White House security agents.

What Farr told them was profoundly disturbing, but at the same time it gave them a clear indication of precisely what they had to do. Alexis had revealed to him everything that had occurred during the preceding twenty-four hours. With no tape of Volker's meeting with Figueira, it left her as sole witness to his treason. Farr's dark face darkened even more when he related how he had success-fully closed an Agency leak, leaving the United Broadcasting Company with no further information than they already had of an investigation in progress. It was Farr's opinion that Andrew Taylor, a profound patriot, was one man who would not, whatever the cost, indulge in irresponsible journalistic speculation on such a sensitive issue. The venerable newsman could and would control Valerie McCullough. She was vulnerable through her ambition. Any story she broke about Volker would destroy her future as network anchorwoman. The fact that Taylor often dined at the White House was not overlooked.

After hearing Farr, the President had little difficulty in deciding what should be done. It was one thing to harbor suspicion of Harold Volker while he was still alive and be prepared to accept the political consequences if an investigation proved him guilty. It was quite another to reveal such an investigation and possibly be held accountable for his suspected actions when he was dead and no longer any threat to anyone.

But it depended on Mrs. Volker. She was in a position, especialy if put on trial, to condemn publicly the man who had turned her life into a living hell. Nobody could stop her. She was also now a widow and might have difficulty in resuming her career. As an established journalist, what she had to tell the world could be sold for a fortune.

Farr was able to convince them that Alexis would do whatever he asked. However, it was more than a question of trust. Moscow might still want her liquidated since revelation of Volker's Russian connection could be as embarrassing to the Kremlin as to Washington. Farr planned to offer an immediate trade-off to the Russian Under-Secretary who ran the KGB in the United States. He would guarantee White House silence in exchange for a KGB promise of immunity for Alexis and was certain they would accept.

The President agreed and the Oval Office promptly issued a statement that the shooting of the Secretary of State by his wife was a tragic accident. Mrs. Volker's hand had caught in her evening purse as she was turning the pistol over to her husband. She was carrying the weapon only at the insistence of her security agent, and in the presence of her husband at the White House had felt no need for it.

Alexis, in a state of shock, was taken by ambulance to a specially guarded wing of Bethesda Naval Hospital. The President made a point of openly visiting her bedside, as did Arnold Wilderstein and his wife. Several days later, she was removed to a private sanatorium in Virginia. Except for minor formalities with the Metropolitan police and the FBI, her only contact with officialdom while she recovered from a partial breakdown was a short meeting with the District of Columbia coroner and an interview with three sympathetic Senators representing a token bipartisan commission of inquiry established by the President.

In all her testimony, at which the FBI's David Farr was present, she concurred with the statement issued by the Oval Office.

The Volker matter was effectively buried forever.

Epilogue

On a spring day eight months later, David Farr walked slowly along the north towpath of the old Chesapeake and Ohio Canal bordering the Potomac above Georgetown. It was midmorning and a cool breeze coming down the river rustled dry leaves left from last autumn and sent blossoms from wild cherry, Judas, and dogwood in swirling kaleidoscopes of color onto the canal's quiet surface.

Farr was dressed for the office in a dark suit with a narrow pinstripe. His gabardine topcoat was slung idly over one shoulder and his hands were in his pockets. When he came to a certain wooden bench, he sat down, scuffed the dusty yellow earth at his feet in a kind of fierce delight at the new life bursting out all around him, and then closed his eyes to the fresh warmth of the sun.

He'd been sitting there for several minutes when he sensed someone watching him. He looked across the canal. Alexis Volker stood on the opposite towpath. She was wearing a tweed suit with a cowl-neck cashmere sweater and had about her the same aura of worldly beauty and sophistication he'd seen when he first met her. She smiled and waved.

"You're on the wrong side," he called.

She laughed. "I like to be different." They met halfway across an old lock several hundred yards away. Alexis kissed him briefly on the mouth. "Hi, David."

She seemed well, but the past year had taken its toll. There were signs of gray in her hair and the kind of tired lines around her eyes most women acquired in their late forties. He had a brief memory of a different Alexis; a shocked white-faced woman surrounded by Secret Service men. A woman in whose eyes he'd seen both horror and a desperate plea for help. She'd come through it flying, he thought, but realized he'd always known she would.

He took one of her hands, lacing her slender fingers between his own. Resting their forearms on an iron railing, they looked down at the canal. He said, "I saw your show again last night. You were wonderful. As usual."

"Of course." Her tone was light. "What did you expect?"

The half-hour, once-a-week program was a series of informal talks with world statesmen. Alexis had been offered her old job and had refused. "I've got to move forward, not back," she'd said. "And I want somehow to use the experience of being married to Harold, the people I met, the different way of looking at things."

Farr had seen her waver only once. It was when the show was still in the planning stage. They were having late-evening coffee in her new apartment behind the Capitol on Fifth Street. He'd asked her about marriage and children. She'd looked at him in surprised silence and tears had come to her eyes. She'd turned away quickly to hide them and stood with her back to him by the fireplace, holding her coffee in both hands. When she turned to face him again, the tears were gone.

She'd said, "David, if I've learned anything, it's that most of life you have to settle for something less than what you really want." She shrugged and a faint smile came to her lips. "If the right guy showed up, of course I wouldn't turn him down, although I think I'd go at it a little less quickly this time. Meanwhile, life must go on. I have a duty to the people who believe in me. And to myself. It's to stand on my own feet and make my own way."

"I've heard from my friend at Harvard," Farr told her now. It was what they'd met to talk about. The friend was an historian who had culled through months of correspondence and the *Heidelberg Review* trying to understand what motivated Harold Volker.

Without taking her eyes from the canal, she said, "And?"

"He thinks you were right about it starting with Horst Melkin," he replied. "And about a new German ascendancy. Melkin and your husband saw Russia as a nation of barbarians and they thought America had failed dismally to carry the torch of western civilization. Germany was the last hope. They seemed to have had it planned way back in their gymnasium days. They used to joke about using Moscow while Moscow thought it was using them. Of course Melkin is Schaeffer. But I doubt that now anyone will ever prove it."

Alexis said softly, "There would be no point, would there?"

"No," he agreed, "there wouldn't be."

They talked a few more minutes before Alexis had to leave. She had a taping session and they'd met at the canal because it was on her way. Farr watched her walk back along the towpath. In spite of her brave front, he knew she would be faced for a long time with moments of harsh loneliness and sometimes despairing memories. But life was like that and if you didn't accept it, you spent your years in misery and anger.

He thought about what she'd said, when she'd nearly broken but hadn't, about having to settle for something less than what you really wanted. He thought of himself and Susan. His euphoria at discovering his assistant's wife responsible for the Bureau leak had been short-lived. In ever suspecting Susan in the first place, he had destroyed an innocent trust that could never be restored. It had all surfaced when one explosive raging night his insidious suspicion had been stripped bare and with it a dark secret of Susan's own. On her part she had mistrusted him, too. She couldn't have children and had known it when they married. For fear of losing him she'd kept silent and sometimes had hated him for the guilt that keeping silent made her feel. Now, although they still loved each other, something special they'd always shared was gone. It would have been like that for Alexis Volker, he thought, if her husband had turned out to be guiltless.

A sharp gust of wind swirled across the lock. Farr unexpectedly felt cold. Yesterday had been his birthday and Susan had sprung a surprise party. It was nearly dawn before they'd gone to bed and today he was dog tired. He slipped into his coat.

Suddenly Alexis was a small figure far down the towpath, only a splash of color against the spring green. Farr felt a tug at his heart. Strange fate, he pondered, that had woven the life of an African slave's descendant with the bearer of an ancient Polish name; two strangers who, because of it, had found a kind of love for each other which had nothing to do with the attraction between a man and a woman, but had to do, instead, with trust and faith. That was the good which had come from it all. The thought gave him a sense of peace.

He watched her until she turned a corner. When she was visible no more and her presence only a memory, he headed back to where he had left his car.

9